THE TRAINING OF FALLEN ANGELS

Madam Stone stood grim-faced in front of Lisa and Janet. She held a vicious-looking whip in her hand.

'The students Kelly and Serita must be punished for their impertinence. They must be whipped before the whole class, and I wish you both to administer the punishment.'

Lisa looked at Janet nervously. 'But they are so inexperienced, madam,' Lisa said. 'They may not –' Madam Stone interrupted her by lashing a nearby chair in fury.

'Know this, my young charges,' she barked angrily. 'After they have tasted the joys of sensual pain your pupils will be yours to command!' She handed the lash to Lisa, who smiled broadly. 'Now go. The class awaits you!'

By the same author:

FALLEN ANGELS
DEMONIA
THE CLOAK OF APHRODITE
PYRAMID OF DELIGHTS

THE TRAINING OF FALLEN ANGELS

Kendal Grahame

This book is a work of fiction.
In real life, make sure you practise safe sex.

First published in 1997 by
Nexus
332 Ladbroke Grove
London W10 5AH

Copyright © Kendal Grahame 1997

The right of Kendal Grahame to be identified as the Author of this Work has been asserted by him in accordance with the Copyright, Designs and Patents Act 1988.

Typeset by TW Typesetting, Plymouth, Devon

Printed and bound by
Caledonian Books Ltd, Glasgow

ISBN 0 352 33224 7

All characters in this publication are fictitious and any resemblance to real persons, living or dead, is purely coincidental.

This book is sold subject to the condition that it shall not, by way of trade or otherwise, be lent, resold, hired out or otherwise circulated without the publisher's prior written consent in any form of binding or cover other than that in which it is published and without a similar condition including this condition being imposed on the subsequent purchaser.

One

Lisa lay on her back on the hard, wooden surface. She felt confused. She had no idea where she was, nor how she had got there. All she knew was that she was naked and totally vulnerable. Her thighs were splayed apart and her wrists and ankles had been secured to the legs of the bench by invisible but unyielding bonds. A heavily padded cushion had been placed under her bottom which, whilst affording her a little comfort, had the effect of raising her crotch in blatant display of her most intimate charms to anybody who might choose to look.

And there were many who were looking. She could see them all waiting, standing motionless in eerie silence. They were all anonymous, faceless men with their bodies completely swathed in black. Lisa raised her head to look at the long line of nameless figures. The queue seemed endless as it disappeared into the darkness of the chamber. Only their genitals were visible, each uncommonly large and menacing, protruding from their shadowy clothing like white beacons in the gloom.

The first in line stepped silently forward and positioned himself at the foot of the bench. He held his stiff cock firmly erect by gripping the thick shaft at the root. Lisa lay her head back in abject subservience and waited for the inevitable. She felt the touch of the bulbous head against her wet sex-lips. She couldn't understand why she was so aroused. There had been no foreplay or stimulation and yet her soft pussy was as soaked as if it had been licked by a thousand tongues. She sighed deeply as the delightful pressure of the stranger's flesh against hers caused him to enter her warmth in one slow, smooth movement. Their groins met, and she realised that she could feel him throbbing heavily inside her.

Then he was gone. Lisa hadn't even felt him withdraw. He had vanished, as though he had faded into the darkness along with his sated lust. Then there was another entering her, with equal finesse but a lack of emotion. He, too finished the act before she could respond and his image quickly blurred into nothingness.

Then another, and another. Over and over, Lisa's prone and shackled body was penetrated by an endless procession of well-endowed, unknown lovers. Their actions were identical, and their ejaculations immediate. The more cocks she accommodated, the more her frustrations increased. Her loins craved for release as every nerve-ending in her body seemed to become alive with lust.

She heard music. At first the gentle strains soothed her and helped to take her mind off her agonising need for the ultimate satisfaction. Another stiff erection slid into her soaked pussy. Lisa strained the muscles of her inner thighs in an endeavour to force her orgasm, but to no avail. The immediate, rhythmic thumping of the thick, hard shaft inside her told her that yet more sperm was filling her honeyed depths. She attempted to press her crotch against his and rub her hard little bud against him, but he vanished as if into thin air.

The music was becoming steadily louder. Instead of

the Wagnerian strains which would have suited her predicament, it was the raucous wail of modern rock music. Lisa raised her head and looked at the dark figures before her. They were fading into a swirling, black mist. Her limbs seemed to have become freed of the shackles, and the bench was suddenly softer against her back. She touched herself between the legs. She was very wet, but it was her own juices that soaked her probing fingers.

Lisa looked in the direction of the men. The mist had melted into darkness, and the figures had gone. She was alone. She lay back again and closed her eyes. She allowed her fingers to play around the soft lips of her sex then purposely rubbed them against her erect bud. She moved her hips as if in response to a lover's insistent thrusts and slipped all four fingers inside herself.

Lisa turned and twisted her hand whilst moving her thumb hard against her clitoris. Her loins ached, and her breath came in short, sharp gasps as she rose to the pinnacle of erotic joy. She was close, so very close. But the noise! The music had become deafening. She snapped her eyes open and glared in the direction of the sound. The alarm-radio met her gaze impassively. The rude, illuminated figures declared the hour triumphantly as Lisa allowed reality to goad her into full consciousness.

The sharp crispness of the early morning sunlight quickly replaced the gloom of her nightmare. Lisa blinked against the glare as she gradually focused on the foul machine that had forced her from heavy slumber. The song ended, to be replaced by the inane prattle of some youthful idiot whose job it was to coax reluctant commuters into action. Lisa eased her fingers from between her legs. The moment had gone. She reached out wearily and smacked her hand against the clock to bring instant and welcome silence to the bedroom, then let her arm flop down the side of the bed and pressed her face into the relative coolness of a pillow. Gradually, she began to drift once more into sleep.

The sound of the doorbell snapped her back to reality. Lisa struggled out of the clutches of the dishevelled sheets and blankets and wrapped her naked body in a small dressing-gown that had been thrown casually over a chair. The bell rang again.

'OK, I'm coming,' she groaned, sleepily. She stumbled towards the door and opened it. The postman stood in the hall, a broad grin playing across his handsome features. Lisa clutched the front of her gown tightly. The damn thing was too small; obviously one of Janet's.

'Miss Janet Angel?' the man asked, as his eyes widened in appreciation.

'Yes, er, no,' replied Lisa. She ran the fingers of her free hand self-consciously through her tousled hair. 'I mean yes, Janet lives here, but no, I'm not her.'

The postman thrust a small package towards her. 'Will you sign for this?'

Lisa took the parcel along with his clipboard and pen. She had to release her grip of the gown as she scrawled her name on the pad and the thrust of her large breasts immediately forced the garment open. The man simply stared at her exposed flesh and his mouth fell open. Lisa grabbed the gown and drew it across herself quickly, at the same time handing back the board. For a moment time seemed to stand still. He just stood there, motionless.

Lisa nudged the clipboard against his arm. 'Thank you,' she said crossly. He shook his head as if awakening from a trance and took it from her. She smiled kindly.

'Oh, yes, thank you,' he stumbled. 'Er, are there just the two of you living here?'

'Why?'

He looked nervous. 'Oh, I just wondered if there were a couple of guys here as well, you know.'

Lisa grinned and moved to close the door. 'No guys,' she said, sweetly. 'Just two girls.' She closed the door and wondered if that had been a wise thing to say.

'Can I ring you?' The postman's muffled voice sounded a little more confident, now that he was shielded from her by the heavy door.

'Yes,' Lisa replied.

'What's your number?'

'It's in the book.'

'What's your name?'

'That's in the book as well.' The line was corny, but it served its purpose. She heard him shuffling away to continue with his mundane occupation. He was good looking, that was certainly true, but for the moment she really couldn't be bothered.

Lisa glanced at the small package. There was nothing to indicate its source, save for an indistinct postmark. She tossed it nonchalantly on to a table. Knowing Janet, she mused, it was probably another silly sex-aid to help her get over Phil.

She stopped in her tracks and sat heavily on the edge of the sofa. The memory of their shared lover filled her mind. She missed him too, dreadfully. She missed the laughs and the fun but, like Janet, most of all she missed the sex. The three of them had become totally compatible over the few, short months that they'd been together. So much so that both she and Janet had rarely found the need to take other partners.

Now Phil was gone, a victim of ambition, to

embark on a glittering career in America. The three of them had made the usual promises, of course, to keep in touch, to meet whenever possible, all of that. But, in their hearts, the three of them knew it was over.

Lisa reached into a cabinet and retrieved a large photo-album. Turning to the back, she quickly found the small collection of snaps taken when she, Janet and Phil had spent a couple of days sightseeing in the depths of rural Sussex. These photographs, along with an almost permanent ache of desire between her legs, were all the tangible memories Lisa had of her brief relationship with Phil. They'd had to get a friend to develop the pictures; no reputable company would have touched them. There were snaps of Phil impaling Janet's lithe little body on his huge cock in all manner of positions, and other photos of him and Lisa in similar poses. There was a beautiful close-up picture of Janet attempting to swallow as much of Phil's monstrous weapon as she could in her tiny little mouth. Lisa was very proud of that photograph; she was sure that, in more enlightened times it would be termed artistic, and maybe even win a prize.

But Lisa's favourite was one that Phil had taken of her and Janet. They were lying naked and exhausted on a small, grassy bank beneath an ancient oak. Their hair was tousled, their faces flushed and their bodies were covered in the sheen of fresh sweat as testament to the wonderful fucking that they had both just enjoyed. They were posing with their legs splayed wide apart and the engorged lips of their pussies glistening in the sunlight. It had been a truly blissful moment.

Lisa flicked back the pages to the front of the album to look at some of her earlier photographs. She gasped audibly. She'd almost forgotten how huge she'd been and how bad she'd looked in those days and yet, incredibly, the pictures were less than two years old. And the clothes she wore! Huge, voluminous frocks that had been chosen for the sole purpose of concealing the true shape of her body. She had been fat to the point of being obese, but with virtually non-existent breasts and features that the kindest observer could only have termed as homely.

That was before *he* came into her life, the old man with his devilish and dangerous plans. He'd appeared as if from nowhere one hot, steamy evening and transformed her into a stunning and voluptuous beauty with a rapacious and nearly insatiable desire for sexual gratification. And he'd been the first to satisfy her needs, the first to penetrate her luscious body. Lisa remembered lying with her back to him and watching the reflection in the mirror of her virginity disappearing as he impaled her.

There had been many more lovers after that, of course; far too many to count. Thanks to her stunning new looks and uncanny ability to bend the will of any man, she had been more than able to sate her lusts. But there had very nearly been a price to pay, a price too terrible to contemplate.

Lisa shuddered and closed the book as she remembered how close she had been to causing havoc and misery on a massive scale. The old man and his evil were gone now but Lisa suspected that one day he would return.

She set the album on the coffee table and slipped out of her robe. Walking into the bathroom, she took a huge, white towel from the rail and turned on the shower. She glanced at the large mirror on the wall next to the bath. Even now, Lisa never tired of looking at the image of her new self. Her long, blonde hair cascaded over her slim shoulders and framed her lovely features to accentuate the beauty of her large, blue eyes, her flawless complexion and her thickly pouting lips. She looked down at the reflection of her body in the slowly steaming glass. Her massive breasts jutted forward firmly, defying gravity. The long nipples pointed upwards slightly so that they seemed to be demanding attention. Lisa ran the palms of her hands over the soft mounds and teased her nipples to erection by pinching them between her fingers. She licked her lips, then raised her breasts a little by cupping the huge mounds with her hands. She bent her head forward and licked each nipple in turn then sucked one and then the other. She rasped her front teeth against one of the hard buds as she sucked herself. The sensation made her shiver with pleasure.

Lisa moved her hands from her breasts and smoothed her palms over her narrow waist. She pushed her chest out and stood sideways to look at herself again in the mirror. Perhaps her breasts were too large for her otherwise slim body, but she'd always dreamt of having the kind of figure that made men's legs turn to water, and she was proud of it.

Lisa turned back to face the mirror full on and slipped a hand between her thighs to cup the softness of her shaven pussy. She felt wet, but then she nearly always was, and her strange dream hadn't helped. Lisa badly needed to come.

She stepped into the shower and began to soap herself liberally. Inevitably, her hands moved to caress her aching sex-lips. She slipped the fingers of one hand inside herself and steadily moved them in and out whilst once more gently coaxing her little bud to erection with her thumb. The water cascaded over her lush body and formed soapy rivulets which slipped sensuously down her long legs, like the erotic release of a hundred lovers.

She twisted her hand inside her hot, silky sheath

and pressed her palm hard against her throbbing clitoris. She closed her eyes and rotated her hips as she moved forward slightly so that the water slipped sensuously between her pert buttocks.

Lisa began to shake, and realised that she was actually trembling with lust. She removed her fingers from her delightful warmth and steadied herself by resting her hand against the tiled wall of the shower. Her heart was pounding and her knees felt as if they might give way at any moment.

This was getting ridiculous. Lisa turned off the shower and stepped out on to the softness of the thick bathmat and grabbed her towel angrily. Her pussy throbbed involuntarily. She resisted the temptation to fondle her aching flesh again and instead began to rub her body vigorously with the towel. Three days without sex and she was a quivering wreck!

The doorbell rang again. 'Shit,' she muttered to herself. 'Now what?' She wrapped her nakedness in the towel as best she could and walked back into the sitting room. Fixing the security chain into its clasp she opened the door a couple of inches. The postman's handsome face smiled back at her.

'Yes?' she said, barely concealing her annoyance at being disturbed again.

The man was clearly put off by her sharpness of tone. 'I, I'm sorry,' he began, then paused as if trying to think of something to say.

'What do you want?'

'I forgot to get you to sign, you know, for the package.' His gaze travelled up and down her body quickly. 'I'll . . . I'll come back later, if you like.'

'I've already signed,' replied Lisa abruptly.

'Yes, I know, but I made a mistake. I got you to sign in the wrong place. It's OK. I'll come back when you're dressed.'

Lisa didn't believe his reason for returning for a moment but, she thought, what the hell, she needed some company to coax her out of this ludicrous depression. She pushed the door closed, removed the chain and opened it wide. 'You'd better come in,' she said, stepping back.

'Are you sure?' he said, nevertheless moving quickly into the room.

'Come on,' said Lisa, feigning exasperation. 'It's no problem.'

Her visitor slipped the postbag from his shoulders and dropped it to the floor before sitting down on the sofa. Lisa stood for a moment and regarded the intruder curiously. He was young, and certainly very good looking. He was dressed in regulation summer uniform of a blue shirt and dark shorts, the latter revealing muscular, tanned legs. The shorts seemed unnecessarily tight, and there was a promising bulge at the crotch.

'D'you want a coffee?' she asked, quietly.

'That'd be great, yeah,' he replied as he settled back on the seat and crossed his legs.

'I'll just go and dry my hair, then I'll make you one.' She moved into the bedroom and closed the door. What am I doing? she thought to herself. The postman? Has it come to this? She sat down heavily on the edge of the bed and took up the hairdryer and a brush. The rush of hot air played through her long, golden tresses as she stared into the dressing-table mirror. 'He may only be a postman,' her reflection seemed to be saying, 'but he *is* pretty gorgeous!'

Lisa quickly finished drying her hair and let the towel slip to the floor. She looked round the room for something suitable to wear. Janet's little dressing-gown would still be lying on the floor in the bathroom where she'd left it. She opened the wardrobe and grabbed the first thing that came to hand. It was a long, white shirt that had actually belonged to Phil. She pulled it on and quickly fastened the buttons, leaving only the top one undone, then stood before the mirror.

The shirt came down to a couple of inches above her knees. It was too large for her, of course, except across the chest, and her mountainous globes and erect nipples were clearly defined through the thin cotton. She undid two more buttons to ease the tightness of the material. Her breasts pushed the shirt apart to reveal a deep, tanned cleavage. She smiled proudly to herself and opened the door to the sitting room.

She gasped suddenly. Her visitor was sitting as before on the sofa, but now he was carefully studying the precious photographs in her album. She moved over to him quickly before he could close the book. To her relief she saw that he was looking at some of her older snaps, the ones that had been taken before her metamorphosis. He looked up at her and smiled, glancing appreciatively at her mode of dress.

'Who's this?' he asked, as he pointed to a photograph of her as she had once been.

'Just a friend,' she lied. She took the album from him and pushed it under some magazines that lay on one of the other chairs. In doing so, she bent forward with the expressed intention of giving him a fleeting glimpse of her naked bottom. She turned quickly. He was certainly looking in the right direction. He looked up and smiled innocently.

'Coffee?' he reminded her.

'Oh, yes. How d'you like it?'

'Black, please, no sugar.'

Lisa hurried into the kitchen and switched the kettle on. She glanced back nervously into the sitting room a couple of times as she prepared the coffee. The album remained under the magazines. She wondered for a moment if she would have minded that much if he had looked at the more explicit photographs of her and Janet. But no; the sight of Phil's impressive equipment might have put him off completely.

She carried the two, steaming mugs back into the sitting room and set them on the table before sitting opposite her visitor. She leant forward and picked up her drink, taking her time to ensure that he was able to have a good look down her cleavage. Then she leant back and pushed out her chest blatantly. He licked his lips nervously and reached for his mug. His hand was shaking. Some of the hot liquid spilled over the side and over his fingers. He set the mug down again quickly.

'Careful, you'll burn yourself!' Lisa put her own drink down and moved to kneel at his side on the floor. She took his hand in hers and put his fingers to her lips. She looked up at his handsome face as she delicately licked the coffee from his skin. His expression had suddenly become serious and questioning.

'Oh, sorry,' she said as she dropped his hand self-consciously.

'It's all right. It was nice.'

'I'm sure it was,' she said, standing and moving rapidly to the kitchen to find a cloth, 'but I don't even know your name and here I am, licking your fingers!'

She returned with the cloth and wiped the spill from the surface of the table. Her breasts swung heavily inside the loose shirt as she laboured. She was fully aware of the effect she was likely to be having on her handsome guest and made much of the task. She looked up at him and smiled sweetly. He gulped hard. 'What is your name, then?' she purred.

'It's Pete,' he said, 'just plain Pete.'

'Pete's a nice name,' Lisa said, for want of anything better to say.

'What's yours?' he continued.

'Lisa, Lisa Angel.'

'Lisa Angel? Are you and the other girl sisters, then?'

'No, we just liked the name and decided to adopt it.' She took the cloth back into the kitchen and threw it into the sink, then returned to sit next to Pete on the sofa. There was some truth in what she'd said. During the short time when they had been part of the group the old man called his 'fallen angels' life had been incredibly exciting and the name had stuck. It seemed eminently suitable, in a strange, contradictory way. She and Janet were anything but angels.

'Nice name,' he said, unconvincingly.

'I like it.' The conversation was going nowhere, and Lisa knew it. She leant forward and took another sip of her hot coffee. She felt the shirt fall forward under the weight of her breasts. She knew that he would be able to see most of one of her luscious mounds, and maybe even catch a glimpse of one of her erect nipples. He'd already had a brief eyeful that morning when he'd delivered Janet's package, but this was different, more intimate somehow. She glanced down at his groin. The bulge in his shorts was definitely getting more pronounced. She felt a familiar tingle of anticipation between her legs.

Lisa put the mug down on the table and sat back, crossing her legs and moving herself closer to him. He smiled nervously and looked down at the newly exposed length of her thigh which was almost touching his own bare leg.

'That's a great outfit you're wearing,' he said, hoarsely.

'It's only a shirt.'

'It's nice. You've got a great body.'

'Thanks.' She ran her fingertips along the inside of his thigh. 'You've got great legs,' she cooed.

Pete coughed and stood up quickly. 'I'd better get you to sign my paper,' he said. His voice was shaking and his hands were trembling as he fumbled in his sack. Lisa smiled to herself. It was a nice feeling to be the seductress for once. Usually she would be lying on her back whilst her lover of the moment ripped her knickers off (if she were wearing any) and took her as he pleased. This time it was she who was making all the moves, and it excited her. As he tried clumsily to find whatever he was searching for she took the opportunity to undo another button on the shirt.

Pete handed her his pad and a pencil. She rested the pad on her knees and leant forward to sign her name in exactly the same place as before. Her breasts fell forward and became fully exposed. 'Oh, sorry,' she said, as she sat back and made much of drawing the flimsy material over herself but not attempting to refasten the button. 'This shirt belongs to a friend, and it's a bit too big for me.' She pressed the pencil intentionally hard against the pad and the lead snapped. 'Oh, now I've broken your pencil.'

'It's OK, it doesn't matter.' He made to take the pad from her, but she pulled away and rose from the sofa before turning her back on him and walking over to the cabinet.

'I think I've got one in here,' she said. She bent forward whilst keeping her legs straight and slightly apart and began to rummage in the lowest drawer. She knew that he would be able to see most of her bottom now, and that the shirt would have ridden up sufficiently for him to view the full perfection of her naked charms. The knowledge that this stranger was staring at her naked backside thrilled her. She bent lower, still keeping her long legs straight. Now he'd be able to see her pussy. She wondered if it would be obvious to him that she was soaking wet.

'Oh, look, it really doesn't matter,' he suddenly blurted out. 'I don't need you to sign it again, I only wanted to, to . . .'

Lisa stood up slowly and turned to him. She regarded her nervous visitor coquettishly. 'To what?' she teased.

'To ask you out. I, I'm sorry. Look, I'd better go.' He jumped up and grabbed his sack in near panic then turned to make for the door.

'Pete,' Lisa said, firmly, 'if you wanted to ask me out, why are you running off like this?'

He stopped in his tracks and looked at her, a long, wistful gaze. 'It's just that you're so beautiful. I can't imagine you being interested.'

She walked over to him and rested her hand on his arm. 'I *am* interested, Pete. Can't you tell?' she breathed.

'I, I don't know, I wasn't sure,' he stuttered. The poor man was shaking like a leaf.

'You're not very experienced with girls, are you?' Lisa chided. He said nothing, and let his gaze fall to the floor. Lisa stood back and unfastened the remaining buttons on the shirt, then let it fall from her shoulders so that she was completely naked. 'Pete, look at me,' she whispered. The young man looked up and his eyes widened dramatically.

'You're *gorgeous*!' he sighed. Lisa moved towards him and put her hands on to his slim shoulders. Her nipples brushed against the roughness of his shirt. She tilted her head slightly to one side and gazed into his eyes.

'Kiss me, Pete,' she breathed. She closed her eyes

and felt his hands slip around her narrow waist. Their lips met, hers wet and pouting, his dry and pursed. Lisa parted his lips with her tongue and snaked it between his teeth to force his mouth open as she pressed her lower body against his. She could feel the bulge of his crotch crushed against her groin. He was hard, that was certain, and she wanted him badly.

She let one hand fall from his shoulder and moved it down between them, quickly finding the zip of his shorts. She unfastened it slowly as her tongue probed and searched his mouth with her thick lips remaining clamped firmly against his. She reached up and undid the waist-button of his shorts then stepped back slightly and eased them down over his narrow hips. They fell to his ankles.

Pete breathed hard as Lisa moved from him and began to unbutton his shirt. Then, finally grasping the initiative he unfastened his cuffs and almost tore the garment from his body whilst at the same time stepping out of his shorts. Lisa watched in amusement as he stumbled about trying to drag his shoes and socks from his feet until at last he succeeded.

Now, all he wore was a small pair of briefs which were bulging ludicrously at the front. Lisa knelt in front of him and gazed at the promising mound. She reached out and traced his shape with her fingertips, then smoothed the palm of her hand over the bulge and squeezed him gently. She moved her hand in a circular motion and teased his hardness with her fingertips. His breathing was becoming erratic.

Lisa reached up with both hands and tugged at the waistband of his pants. Slowly, she inched the tight material downwards, gradually revealing the thick, matted hair of his groin. His legs began to shake visibly. She pulled his briefs down further and gazed at his crotch as though she had never seen anything like it in her life before.

Suddenly, his penis sprang from the restraint of the elastic waistband and the angry, purple end pointed directly at her face. It was wet with his excitement, and Lisa saw that it was throbbing. She knew that he wouldn't last long in this state. She tugged his pants down to his ankles and pulled them from his feet, then looked up into his eyes. His hard erection was inches from her succulent mouth.

'Would you like me to suck it for you?' she breathed.

The postman nodded. There were beads of sweat on his brow, and his legs were trembling again. 'D'you want to?' he asked, stupidly.

Lisa didn't answer. Instead, she moved her face closer to him and opened her mouth. She took his thick stalk within her luscious lips and ran her tongue round the end. Pete groaned and rested his hands on her head. Lisa began to suck him heavily. She drew on her experience and her natural gift for pleasing men orally, determined to give him the best blow job he'd ever had in his life. She began to move her head backwards and forwards, slowly at first, then gradually increasing in pace. He responded by moving his hips rhythmically. She gripped his thighs and moved her head faster and faster whilst snaking her tongue around his hard shaft until, with a loud moan, he came and she felt him pulsating within the soft grip of her lips. Lisa allowed him to move his length in and out of her mouth as his cream jetted over her tongue. Pete gripped her head and pushed his groin towards her face and almost choked her as he filled her mouth with his throbbing stalk. She swallowed copiously and sucked voraciously on his cock until she knew that he had no more to give.

Reluctantly, she let the now drooping phallus slip from her wet mouth and wiped her lips with the back of her hand. Pete stepped back and appeared to collapse on to the sofa.

'Nobody's ever done that to me before,' he panted. 'Swallowed it, I mean.'

Lisa smiled proudly. 'Did you like it?'

Pete nodded. 'It was wonderful. I can't believe you swallowed it.'

Lisa grinned. The first time that a man experiences full oral sex can be one of the most unforgettable moments of his life. 'You tasted nice,' she said, simply.

Pete ran his fingers through her long, blonde tresses. 'You are so lovely,' he whispered.

Lisa took his hand in hers and lightly kissed his palm. 'You're going to find out that I taste nice too,' she breathed. 'Would you like to go to bed?'

He sat up and reached for his shorts. 'No, no, I really had better get on with my round.'

Lisa grabbed his shorts and threw them across the room. 'Oh, no you don't,' she said, with mock anger. 'You're not going to cheat me!' She grabbed him by the arm and dragged him to his feet. 'Come on, Mister Postman, you're coming to bed!'

She hauled her reluctant conquest through the door and almost threw him on to the mattress. Pete lay back and regarded her with a mixture of surprise and bemusement. Lisa stood before him with one foot on the floor and the other on the bed. She ran the middle finger of one hand suggestively between the pouting, wet lips of her pussy. She looked at his drooping cock, and saw to her delight that it was already beginning to thicken as he watched her stimulate herself.

'You really are something,' he sighed.

'You're pretty gorgeous yourself,' she responded as she crawled on to the bed and lay next to him. She reached down and circled his rapidly rising erection with her fingers. Slowly, she began to move her hand up and down. She felt him hardening in her soft grip.

'Did you like it when I let you come in my mouth?' she murmured.

'Yeah, you certainly knew what you were doing.'

Lisa smiled and kissed him lightly on the lips, then moved her head down to lick his hairy chest. She felt his hand stroking her bare bottom as she ran her tongue around one of his nipples. She bit it gently, then moved to the other and sucked it like a baby. His fingers began to probe her wet sex-flesh from behind.

She moved her face lower and ran her tongue over his flat stomach. He tasted of fresh sweat and the scent excited her. She licked sensuously around his navel then shifted herself across him so that her groin was close to his face. She continued to steadily pump his cock, which now stood hard and erect within her gently undulating grasp. She thrilled as she felt him trace the line of her cunt with his tongue and responded by pressing her mound hard against his chin. His stubbly skin stimulated her hard little bud as she ground herself against his face whilst he lapped greedily at her hot, wet flesh.

Lisa licked around the end of his prick for a moment, then closed her pouting lips around his stalk and sucked him gently. She was anxious that he should not come in her mouth a second time, and was well aware that her oral skills could easily make that happen. She drew him from the heavenly clasp of her mouth and ran her tongue up and down his stiffness, then moved herself slightly so that she could lick his balls. She traced their shape with the tip of her tongue then took both of them into her mouth.

Pete had started to push his tongue in and out of her pussy. To Lisa, it felt for all the world like a small, soft cock exploring her outer lips as she continued to rub her clitoris against his chin. She let his balls slip from her wet mouth and licked under them, then moved her face again so that she once more engulfed his hardness within her mouth. She felt his stalk throb between her lips and his taste became salty.

She moved from him reluctantly and swallowed hard. He hadn't come, but it had been a near-thing. She sat next to him in silence and gently stroked his chest with her fingertips. Pete lay gazing at her in total adoration. His handsome features were wet with her juices. She bent forward and kissed his forehead, then licked her taste from his face before kissing him passionately on the mouth. She moved her body across his and lay on top of him with her crotch pressed hard against his erection and her large breasts crushed against his chest. She wriggled her hips in order to rub herself against his hardness. Pete's rough hands stroked her back, then moved down to cup her pert buttocks. He squeezed and fondled her perfect arse as he pushed his groin hard against her.

She needed him inside her now. She needed to be fucked.

Lisa raised herself up and sat on his thighs. She took hold of his erection and rubbed it against the softness of her wet, hairless pussy whilst fixing his gaze with hers. 'I want you to fuck me,' she pouted, 'and don't come too quick.'

'I'll do my best,' he breathed. Lisa raised herself on to her haunches and guided his hard cock to her waiting opening. She sat down slowly, and thrilled as her body absorbed his stiffness. Their pubic mounds met and she held him motionless within her tight sheath. The feeling of total fullness delighted her. She stiffened the muscles of her groin to grip him even harder and felt him throbbing heavily inside her.

'Are you OK?' she asked, anxiously.

He nodded. 'Yeah, I am now. I nearly came when you took me inside you, but I'm all right now.'

'Don't come before I do,' she chided, 'or I'll bite it right off!' Pete grinned and ran his hands up to cup her breasts. He bent his head forward and took one of her nipples into his mouth. Lisa shivered as he sucked her and, just for a moment, forgot about the stiff intrusion held within the softness of her cunt.

Pete moved his head back and rested it on the pillow without taking his eyes off her breasts. Lisa rested one hand on his knee behind her and the other on the bed. Gradually, she began to move her body gently up and down. By moving her hips backwards and forwards slightly at the same time she was able to stimulate her clitoris with every movement and, from his benign expression Pete was now clearly enjoying the vision of this beautiful, big-busted blonde fucking herself on his body. He put his hands behind his head and watched, his face a picture of contentment. Lisa grinned and increased the pace of her movements. She leant back further and gripped his ankles in the full knowledge that he would have a perfect view of his engorged shaft moving in and out of her luscious cunt. She began to hump herself up and down rapidly. Her breasts bounced heavily as she thrust herself against him, totally in control. Pete caught hold of her thighs and met her rough movements with thrusts of his own as he dug his fingernails into her flesh.

With a sudden, guttural cry she came. The frustration of three days of abstinence flowed from her along with her copious juices which soaked her lover's lower body. She fell forward and gripped his shoulders, then pounded her groin wildly against his as a second wave of orgasmic joy hit her. She squealed, the sound muffled as she bit into his muscular flesh and he gripped her bottom tightly as he forced his cock as deep inside her as he possibly could. Their lower bodies slapped together loudly and the bed creaked and complained as they pounded faster and faster.

Lisa was coming again. She couldn't believe it; three times in a row. She rammed her body hard down on her lover and absorbed every inch of his stiff rod then tensed her muscles and gripped him tightly within her throbbing depths. She squealed loudly as the sensations tore at her loins and she bit hard into his shoulder. She began to pound up and down again as her every thought and movement was controlled by the power of her third orgasm. For a few seconds she was totally oblivious to his needs; he could have been anybody.

Gradually, the ecstatic sensations subsided and Lisa slowed her movements before slipping from him to lie panting at his side. Their bodies were covered in sweat which formed little rivulets over their skin that slipped down to soak the bed beneath them. She looked down. Pete's glistening shaft was still hard, resting against his stomach. A small blob of white fluid seeped from the end and formed a pool in his navel. Lisa bent over him and pushed her tongue into it and lapped it up like a cat enjoying fresh cream. She lay back, sighing happily and closed her eyes.

'That was wonderful,' she said, after a few moments. Her pussy was still beating, more from the force of her assault on Pete's supine form than the after effects of the three orgasms. He ran his hand over her breasts.

'You have the most amazing tits,' he said. 'So big, and yet so firm.' He cupped one, and then the other. 'It's incredible, the way that they jut upwards, even when you're lying on your back. What do they measure?'

Lisa laughed to herself. If she'd been asked this question once she'd been asked it a thousand times. And she always answered proudly. 'When I wear a bra, I need a 34 triple G. If I put a tape measure round my chest, then it's 43 inches.'

'Wow,' said Pete, simply. 'Wow.'

They heard the sound of the front door to the flat being unlocked. Pete sat up nervously. Lisa rested her hand on his shoulder. 'It's OK,' she said. 'It'll be my friend, Janet.'

'She won't mind, will she? I mean, me being in here, with you?'

Lisa looked at him incredulously. 'Of course not. Why should she mind?'

Before he could answer, the door to the bedroom opened and Janet appeared, smiling broadly. 'Hi, there!' she called, happily. 'Ooh, who's this?' She sat on the edge of the bed as though it was the most natural thing to do. Pete looked at her in astonishment.

'This is Pete, the postman,' said Lisa as she propped herself up against some pillows.

'The postman? Oh, Lisa, honestly!'

'And what's wrong with postmen?' said Pete, somewhat hurt.

'Not a thing,' laughed Janet. 'In fact, you're a very nice postman.' She ran a hand along the inside of his thigh, stopping less than an inch from his genitals. His cock remained firmly erect. 'Am I interrupting something?' she continued as she stared blatantly at his firm length.

'No, we were just having a break,' said Lisa, nonchalantly.

Pete sighed. 'This is unreal,' he said, as though talking to an invisible audience.

'He brought a package for you,' Lisa said to Janet. 'It's in the other room.'

Her friend jumped from the bed like an excited child. 'Oh, I know what that must be! D'you want me to show you? It's really very sexy!'

'Do you think Pete will like it?' Lisa reached down and circled his stiff cock with her fingers as she spoke.

'I hope so. D'you want to see me in something sexy, Mister Postman?'

Pete could only nod as Janet rushed from the room. They heard the sounds of tearing paper followed by the rustling of clothing. He turned to Lisa who by now was rubbing him gently and making it clear that she was ready for more action.

'You and your friend are very uninhibited, aren't you?' he said.

'We're very close friends. We don't really think about it.'

'Have you ever walked in on her, when she's been in bed with someone?'

'It happens. We don't take much notice of it, to be honest.'

'I think that's great,' he said as he slipped the tips of his fingers into her soaking pussy. 'I wish more girls were like you.'

'I think that most girls would like to be,' said Lisa, 'but they're just too scared to admit it, even to themselves. I'm a strong believer in the old saying "if it itches, scratch it".' She opened her legs wider so that he could push more of his fingers into her.

'You certainly had an itch this morning,' he breathed. He kissed her on the side of her face, then licked her ear whilst moving his fingers in and out of her hot, tight sheath.

The door opened again. Pete made to move his hand from between Lisa's legs, then seemed to think better of it. The fact that she was continuing to pump his stiff erection probably had something to do with it.

Janet had returned, and he gasped at the sight of her as she entered the room. She was wearing a tight, basque-like garment made entirely of shining, black rubber. The clinging material moulded itself over her pert, apple-sized breasts and her nipples were clearly defined. The shiny rubber accentuated her shapely form with its narrow waist and flat stomach. Even the outline of her navel could be discerned.

The erotic garment finished slightly above her crotch. Two suspenders were attached to the hem which supported black, fishnet stockings. Apart from a pair of black, high-heeled shoes Janet had chosen not to wear anything else.

Lisa glanced between her friend's legs. The thick, luxuriant bush of dark, pubic hair glistened to signify her arousal. Pete just stared, open mouthed.

Janet stepped forward, and closed the door behind her. 'What d'you think, Mister Postman?' she asked in a sultry tone. 'D'you like it?'

Lisa felt Pete's cock throb and watched as a sliver of his cream slid down the long stalk and on to the back of her hand. She let go of him and held her hand up to Janet for inspection. 'I think that answers your question,' she laughed. She licked the sperm from her skin and lay back on the bed.

Janet giggled girlishly and crawled on to the bed to kneel by Pete's side. She reached out and grasped his erect cock and squeezed it gently. 'Mmm, that's a nice one,' she purred. 'Mind if I join in?'

'Course not,' answered her friend, 'and I'm sure Pete won't mind, will you?'

Their lover merely shook his head as he watched Janet lazily move her hand up and down his hard shaft. Lisa cupped his balls with her palm and bent over to kiss him lightly on the mouth. 'I told you we were close friends,' she said.

Janet turned herself round, still kneeling at his side. In this position Pete was presented with the delightful view of her perfect bottom framed by the black, rubber basque, her suspenders and her stocking-tops. Lisa watched as he ran his fingers lovingly over her friend's pert behind. She knew how much Janet loved to be caressed in this way. Janet took his cock into her mouth and began to suck it slowly, still gripping his shaft tightly by the root. Lisa moved her head down and rested her face against his muscular thighs. At first she simply watched her lovely friend suck on his stiffness, then she started to slide her tongue wetly over his balls and up and down the hard stalk.

Janet took her mouth from him and offered the plum-coloured end to Lisa, who took the prize gladly and engulfed it within her generous lips. She felt him run his fingertips along the cleft between her buttocks, up and down, teasing her sensitive sphincter with their light touch. She heard Janet moan softly. Lisa knew that, if Pete touched her friend's anus, even for a second, it would be enough to drive Janet wild.

The two girls continued to lick and suck him for what seemed like ages. Pete appeared content just to lie back and gently fondle their upturned bottoms as they ministered to his needs. Occasionally, Lisa and Janet would allow their lips to meet and they would kiss passionately whilst still holding his thick cock between their mouths. To Lisa, this was the deepest intimacy that she could share with her friend.

Suddenly, Janet pulled her face away. 'Oh, God,' she sighed to Lisa, 'he's got his finger in my bum.' She closed her eyes in ecstasy. Lisa kissed her mouth. She knew exactly what her friend needed.

Janet moved away from them and knelt on the large bed with her shoulders resting on the mattress and her bottom pushed high. She looked at Pete imploringly. 'Fuck me, Mister Postman,' she begged. 'Fuck me hard!'

Pete was clearly in no mood to refuse her entreaties. He moved quickly to kneel behind her and gripped his cock by the root, ready to impale the lithe, suppliant form so blatantly offered to him. Lisa watched as his cock-head touched her friend's hairy little pussy and he pushed in deep. Janet moved her body backwards immediately to meet his thrust. Despite the slightness of her frame she accommodated him easily in one, slow movement so that his groin pressed hard against her bottom. He began to slide his stiff rod slowly in and out of Janet's succulence. Lisa knelt at his side and stroked his backside gently with her fingertips as if to encourage him. She kissed him tenderly on the mouth and took his hand to put to her breast. He fondled the soft, firm flesh as he thrust harder into the prone form of Janet. Lisa felt him stroke her own bottom with his free hand and sensed her skin turning to goose-flesh.

She looked down at Janet and their eyes met. She knew exactly what her friend wanted. She reached down and gripped Pete's plunging stalk by the root and forced him to slow his movements to a stop. She eased his thick cock from the wetness of Janet's cunt and put the bulbous head to her other, tiny hole. She knew that there would be no need for any lubrication other than her friend's own juices. Janet was well used to this kind of lovemaking.

'This is what she likes best,' Lisa whispered to the astonished man. She pressed her hand against his backside and Pete pushed forward again. Both he and Lisa watched in fascination as he entered the tight, puckered orifice. Janet groaned loudly, so loud that Pete obviously thought that he was hurting her. He pulled from her quickly.

'Are you all right?' he asked as he leant over her trembling body.

'Yes, yes, of course I am,' Janet cried desperately. 'Put it back in, put it back in! Fuck me up the arse!'

'Wow,' said Pete, both shocked and excited by her obscenities. Lisa parted her friend's buttocks and grinned at him.

'Go on,' she coaxed, 'she loves it.'

He moved himself back and pushed the thick, bulbous head of his cock once more against the tiny little hole. Lisa watched entranced as the tight sphincter opened under the pressure and he entered her again. The puckered flesh moulded itself around his shaft and gripped it just under the ridge.

'Christ, she's tight,' he groaned as he grasped her upper thighs and pulled her towards him. 'I've never done this before! I've never fucked a girl in the arse!' He moved gently backwards and forwards, sinking his stalk deeper and deeper each time until, at last, Janet held his full length within her perfect bottom.

'Oh, yes!' she sighed. 'Now give it to me hard, really give it to me!'

Lisa sat back, content for the moment to watch her friend enjoying her ultimate pleasure. Pete raised himself so that he squatted on the balls of his feet and hammered his groin against Janet's backside. The slap of skin against skin resounded around the room.

Janet moaned loudly with every hard thrust and Pete grunted like a wild animal as he fucked the most perfect bottom he was ever likely to see.

Lisa moved herself so that she sat with her legs on either side of the rutting couple with her hairless pussy less than an inch from Janet's face. She mewed softly as her friend's tongue began to lap hungrily at her engorged sex-lips. Pete watched in astonishment.

'I don't believe it,' he panted, barely slowing the pace of his heavy thrusts into Janet's rear. 'You two are amazing!'

Lisa said nothing. Instead, she surrendered all her feelings and emotions to savour the delights of Janet's tongue fluttering rapidly against her clitoris. Her friend was sweating heavily in her excitement and Lisa could smell the rubber of the basque. The scent intoxicated her.

Suddenly, the inevitable tremors of delight began to course through her body. The nerve-endings within her loins seemed to twist and tear at themselves, sending little electric shocks down the insides of her thighs. 'I'm coming!' she breathed, 'I'm coming!' She gripped the mattress tightly with her fingers and threw her head back. Her release was sudden, and tore at her very soul. She cried out involuntarily as her juices seemed to gush from her into her friend's welcoming mouth. Janet licked furiously at her pulsating sex-lips and swallowed all that she could give. A sudden, muffled squeal from Janet told Lisa that she had joined her in her joy.

She looked wildly into Pete's eyes. He was still banging himself hard against Janet's backside. His body was soaked with sweat and his eyes were glazed.

'Come over me!' said Lisa, suddenly. 'Come over my tits!'

Pete pulled his cock immediately from the tight grip of Janet's anus and squatted across her back. Lisa caught hold of his stiffness and rubbed it furiously with both hands. She could smell her friend's exotic scent, and it delighted her.

Pete's expression turned into a grimace and, with a long, low moan he came. His cream jetted from his steel-hard, throbbing cock and soaked Lisa's heaving mounds of flesh. Jet after jet of hot sperm spurted from him and streaked across her skin. Lisa gripped his balls with one hand and squeezed them tightly whilst continuing to pump his erection with the other. Gradually, the force of his ejaculations lessened and the last of his cream slipped over her fingers. She kissed the end of his slowly wilting phallus. Pete fell back suddenly which caused her to release his cock from her grip. More semen trickled from the swollen head of his cock and soaked the black rubber of Janet's basque. Lisa bent forward and licked the cream from the sensuous material voraciously. The taste of the rubber was bitter-sweet, ideally complemented by the flavours of male release.

She moved herself round her friend's kneeling body slowly as she licked every drop of juice from her. Then she slipped behind her and ran her tongue wetly over Janet's anus, as though meaning to soothe her tortured flesh. Janet moaned softly. It was a very precious moment.

Pete sat back against some pillows and watched happily as the two girls continued to lick and caress each other's bodies as they drifted down from their euphoria. They moved to one of their favourite positions, their heads between each other's legs and their tongues savouring the delicate tastes of aroused femininity.

Soon, very soon, their caresses became more and

more earnest. They began to claw and bite, hands roaming over bare flesh and fingers probing.

Neither Lisa nor Janet heard Pete dress and leave the flat.

Two

Janet lay back on the bed and breathed slowly as she watched a fly buzzing lazily over her head. She felt a dull ache between her legs. It was a pleasant sensation, a gentle reminder of the delights which she, Lisa and their handsome visitor had enjoyed together.

She glanced across at the prone form of her lovely friend. As was usual after a frenetic bout of sexual excess, Lisa had fallen into a deep sleep, despite having only woken up a couple of hours previously. Janet gazed lustfully at the gorgeous blonde's superb figure. Even though she was lying on her back her breasts jutted upwards and her nipples remained sharply erect. Janet reached forward and ran her fingertips lightly over the huge mounds of firm flesh. They were certainly big, and yet in no way matronly. Lisa's breasts didn't spread across her chest as happened to many women with what was often politely termed as a fuller figure. Instead they thrust forward arrogantly, as though begging to be touched.

They certainly got the attention. Janet smiled to herself as she thought about the countless times that she'd witnessed men almost fighting to get their trembling hands on her friend's wonderful attributes and, for an instant, sensed a slight pang of envy. But no: she'd had the chance when the old man had worked his magic on her, and she'd opted for the most perfect, pert bottom a girl could possess. Large breasts were fine in their own way but, as Janet well knew, a man could just as easily be enslaved by the sight of her firm buttocks, especially when they were clad in tight denim or leather jeans or when they were sensuously outlined under sheer silk. She never wore panties, and this was usually quite obvious thanks to the normally clinging nature of her choice of clothing. On the few occasions when she wore a fuller skirt, she would always tremble with excitement as a lover fumbled under the loose garment, knowing his delight when his searching fingertips found no barrier between them and her wet pussy.

She was hot, and the rubber corset was beginning to feel decidedly uncomfortable. She unclasped the suspenders and rolled her stockings from her long, shapely legs, then peeled the restraining garment from her body. As she pulled it over her head her breath took in the strong, intoxicating scent of the sensuous material. She touched herself between her legs and breathed deeply. She pulled the garment free and held it to her face. Her tongue tasted the bitterness of the luxuriant material and she slipped the fingers of one hand inside her soft, wet sex-flesh. She lay back, still holding the rubber basque to her face and breathed in hard. The powerful aroma invaded her senses. She moved her fingers in and out of herself as she rubbed her thumb against the hard bud of her clitoris. She sucked the rubber as if it was a lover's cock.

Lisa mumbled something in her sleep and turned herself over on the bed. Janet sat up, allowing the garment to slip from her face into her lap. She took her fingers from within her hot sex and threw the corset on to the floor. No more, she thought to herself, at least not for a little while.

Janet slipped from the bed and pulled on a small

pair of shorts and a T-shirt then padded quietly out to the lounge. The curtains were drawn tightly against the daylight and the room was in near darkness. She stopped in her tracks. She knew that she hadn't drawn the curtains before joining Lisa and Pete in the bedroom. Maybe their exhausted lover had done it before letting himself out. But why should he do such a thing?

Nervously, she tugged at one of the drapes. A shaft of bright sunlight cut through the darkness like a laser.

'I would rather you didn't do that.' The voice was thickly male, deep and with a menacing tone. Janet let the curtain fall back into place and swung round.

'Who's there?' she demanded.

'There's no need to be afraid, Janet Angel. You will not come to any harm.' The voice seemed less forbidding now, but Janet was in no way reassured.

'Who are you? What are you doing in my home?' There was a momentary silence, then a switch clicked and a small table-lamp was turned on. Janet looked in the direction of the light. The man sat nonchalantly in the corner of the room. He was dark, in his late thirties and extremely handsome. He was smartly dressed in an expensive suit and his eyes were shielded by gold-rimmed sunglasses. His appearance gave Janet the impression that she was in the presence of a gangster.

She took a deep breath and moved forward a step. 'I asked you who you were,' she said, courageously. She tried to feign anger but her voice trembled as she spoke. Her eyes darted around the room. The telephone was on the far side; she would have to walk past him to get to it. She looked at the door to the hallway. She might make it, but she knew that she couldn't leave Lisa alone with this menacing stranger.

She was about to cry out to waken her friend when the man leant forward in his seat and removed his sunglasses.

He looked directly into her eyes and she felt that her knees would give way. The expression on his face was benign but the look in his eyes seemed to be penetrating into her very soul, as though reading her thoughts. 'I told you,' he said patiently. 'There is no need to be afraid. We have a mutual friend.'

Try as she might, Janet found that she couldn't tear her gaze from his. She moved slowly and sat opposite him, her hands tucked between her thighs like a schoolgirl who had been caught misbehaving. The stranger's smile broadened, but his dark, piercing eyes remained cold. 'You and your friend Lisa are known in some very high places,' he said. 'Even the President of Europe himself speaks highly of you.'

'You know the President?'

'He is a friend. From what he has told me, you are just the type of girls I am looking for to assist in my new enterprise.'

'What do you mean, enterprise?' Janet was beginning to feel a little more relaxed and sat back in her chair.

'I run a kind of college and therapy centre in the heart of Sussex, attending to the needs of the very wealthy and their precocious offspring. Your friend Lisa and you will make excellent therapists and tutors.'

'I don't understand. We haven't any training or qualifications.'

'You have much experience in matters of the flesh which will prove invaluable, and you will be given suitable instruction.'

'I don't understand,' said Janet, becoming increasingly confused. 'What do you mean?'

'Grantham Manor offers sexual therapy to men and women who suspect that they are going through all manner of personal and intimate crises. Your knowledge and your complete lack of inhibitions will suit you both well to the task. Additionally, the Manor serves as a kind of finishing school for the daughters of the very rich, where they may receive instruction as to the more hedonistic of adult pursuits.'

Janet sat quietly for a moment as she pondered on her strange visitor's words. 'I don't know,' she said, presently. 'Let me wake my friend.' She made to stand up, but the stranger leant forward and stared hard into her eyes. Janet shrank back into the seat. For some reason she felt unable to move.

'There is no need to disturb your friend,' he said, slowly. 'You will make the decision.'

There was a long silence. The stranger's gaze remained fixed on Janet's, unblinking and totally absorbing. She began to sense that her will was deserting her but, more than that, she was starting to feel incredibly aroused. She crossed her legs, but that made the feeling worse. She uncrossed them again and shifted uncomfortably in her seat without, for one moment, taking her eyes off his. An incongruous heat was building up within her loins.

'What are you thinking, Janet Angel?' he said. Janet opened her mouth and tried to speak, but to no avail. The nerve-endings between her legs were becoming more and more alive as his eyes drained her with their unremitting stare. She swallowed hard. 'You are thinking how much you would like to fuck this stranger, sitting in your room,' the man continued as his voice became deeper and faded into a near-whisper. 'You are imagining the taste of his cock, and wondering what it would feel like as it entered your lithe little body.' He leant back and grinned malevolently. Janet began to breathe in short, sharp gasps. 'Imagine it, Janet, long, thick and hard, slipping deep inside you, filling you completely.'

She sensed the lips of her pussy opening within the constraints of the tight shorts. Her hands were still clasped between her thighs. She pressed them hard against her mound and began to tremble, not with fear, but with sheer, unsated lust. The man just stared at her. She knew that she wasn't being hypnotised – that would be too easy an explanation for what was happening to her. No, she was transfixed and completely at the mercy of his all-consuming sexual presence.

There were no more words. None were needed. Her cunt started to throb involuntarily. She moved her hands away from herself and lay back with her legs spread wide apart in blatant subservience. She saw him lick his lips slowly and imagined him slipping his long tongue inside her hot sheath. The heat within her loins grew in intensity and a burning itch clawed at the erect bud of her clitoris. The man's eyes widened into a menacing leer.

Suddenly, almost without warning, she was coming, without the slightest touch or caress. Resisting the temptation to rub herself with her fingers, she opened her legs even wider and thrust forward with her hips so that her tight shorts gripped her pussy like a lover's hand. She threw her head back and grimaced as the sensation took hold of her every emotion. 'Oh, my God!' she moaned. 'Oh, I don't believe it!' The force of the orgasm seemed to be unending. Janet thrust her hips up and down wildly as if she were attempting to drain some unseen lover. The man smiled proudly.

Then it was over. She fell back into her seat

exhausted. Her heart pounded within her chest and her skin seemed to be alive with sensation. She looked at the stranger through glazed eyes. The stare had lost its intensity, though none of its magnetic attraction.

'You will come to Grantham Manor?' he asked, simply. Janet nodded. 'Persuade your friend,' he said as he rose to his feet. 'You will not regret your decision.' He reached into his pocket and retrieved a small card. He handed it to Janet, who took it and tried vainly to focus her eyes on the wording.

'Take the east-bound train to Doleham Halt tomorrow afternoon,' he continued. 'A car will collect you.'

With that, the stranger made for the door and opened it. 'May I know your name?' asked Janet weakly, her voice shaking with emotion.

'I am known as Mr Gee,' he replied as he stepped out into the hallway. 'You would find my full name unpronounceable. Until tomorrow, Janet Angel.'

Then he was gone, and the room seemed incredibly empty. Janet looked again at the card, and this time managed to read the words: GRANTHAM MANOR, INSTITUTE FOR HEDONISTIC RELAXATION AND INSTRUCTION.

As the train wound its way through the sun-baked Sussex countryside, Janet stared out of the window and pondered over the situation in which she and Lisa had found themselves. Yesterday, as she had explained the mysterious Mr Gee's offer to her friend, it had all seemed perfectly reasonable but now, in the light of day, the doubts were beginning to set in. They knew nothing of him, nor his college and therapy centre, and only had his word that the President himself had recommended them to him. But he must have known that they had met the President and, anyway, it would be an adventure. Lately, life had become incredibly dull after the excitement of the previous summer.

And, as Lisa had said when Janet had told her about Mr Gee, you find a strange man in your room, he makes you come without touching you and then offers you a job. What could be better than that?

She looked across the carriage at her friend who, as usual, was sleeping peacefully. Like herself, Lisa had chosen to dress simply for the journey in jeans and skimpy top. She was curled up on the large seat with her knees pushed against her breasts and her face buried against the upholstery, completely immune to the noise of the old diesel as it struggled complainingly up a long rise.

Janet glanced back out of the carriage window and was just in time to catch a glimpse of two horses copulating in a passing field. It seemed to her like a good omen for the immediate future.

'How much further is it?' Lisa's sleepy question broke the spell of the moment.

'It can't be much longer,' replied Janet as she glanced at her watch. 'It's already after three.'

Lisa uncurled her legs and held them rigid in front of her whilst she stretched her arms above her head. Her bra-less breasts jutted firmly upwards and forced the thin material of her T-shirt loose from the waistband of her jeans. Janet smiled and looked out of the window. The train seemed to be slowing down. She glanced at her watch.

'This must be it; Doleham Halt. Come on, get your stuff. I can't imagine that the train will hang about for long at such a tiny station.' They grabbed their bags from the rack and slid the window in the carriage door open. Lisa leant out of the window with her blonde hair billowing in the breeze.

'It's not much of a station,' she said as she pulled

the window closed. 'There's just a platform, nothing else.'

'I suppose that's why they call it a halt.'

The train shuddered to a stop and the girls clambered from the carriage. They were the only passengers to disembark. No sooner had Lisa slammed the door than the train moved away, quickly disappearing around a bend in the track and leaving them in relative silence. They stood for a moment and surveyed the scene.

'It's beautiful here,' said Janet, deliberately keeping her voice quiet so as not to intrude on the peaceful ambience of their situation.

'There's no sign of a car,' said Lisa after a moment. Janet looked down the narrow lane that stretched from the halt and disappeared behind the hedgerows. Somewhere in the distance a dog barked. She glanced at her watch.

'We're early,' she said, setting down her bag on the platform. 'We might as well wait.' She sat down on the edge of a low wall and nonchalantly picked a long stem of grass that was growing out of the crumbling mortar. She chewed thoughtfully on the fleshy blade as she watched Lisa lean against the gate. The young blonde's tight jeans accented the perfect shape of her bottom as she bent forward to rest her elbows on the top of the gate. No panties, of course. It would be a sin to spoil the smooth curves of such delightful buttocks with their tell-tale line. Janet ran her tongue slowly across her upper lip. If the car didn't arrive soon she would be dragging Lisa into the field and tearing those jeans from her lovely body.

She touched herself between the legs and began gently to caress the prominent, fleshy mound covered only by the thin denim. Lisa stepped up on to the lowest spar of the rickety gate and leant further forward so that her weight coaxed it to glide slowly open. Janet rubbed herself harder as she gazed at her friend's beautiful bottom.

The blonde suddenly jumped to the ground. 'There's a car coming! I can hear it!'

Janet slipped from the wall and walked to the gate. She could hear the low murmur of a big, powerful vehicle and the hiss of tyres on the road. 'Let's hope it's for us,' she said.

'It must be,' said Lisa as she picked up her bag.

They walked out into the road. A sleek, American limousine rounded the bend, its windows blacked out and its paintwork glistening brightly in the sunlight. The car glided to a halt and the driver's window purred as it slid open. The large, round face of the chauffeur appeared.

'Janet and Lisa Angel?' a gruff voice enquired.

Janet stepped forward excitedly. 'That's us,' she said. 'Are you from Grantham Manor?'

The big man grunted a positive reply and climbed out of the vehicle. He was wearing a light-coloured uniform, complete with peaked cap. He stood well over six fect in height, towering over the two friends. He held his hand out. Janet looked at him quizzically. 'Your bags,' he demanded.

'Oh, yes, right,' said Janet. She handed over her possessions quickly. Lisa followed suit and the man ambled to the rear of the car to throw the bags unceremoniously into the boot. Lisa shot a concerned glance to Janet, who smiled and shrugged her shoulders. The chauffeur opened the rear door and motioned for them to get inside. They did so quickly and sank into the sumptuous white leather seat. The door was slammed shut immediately.

A heavy, glass partition separated them from the driver's compartment. They watched as the chauffeur climbed into his seat and heard the click as the doors were electronically locked.

'Oh, well,' said Janet, 'there's no going back now.'

'He's a little chatterbox, isn't he?' said Lisa.

Janet grinned. 'I'm sure everything will be fine,' she replied, determined to ignore a feeling of apprehension that was gnawing at her.

The car was turned noiselessly around and they headed down the narrow, winding lane. Janet relaxed back in the seat and watched the countryside drift by outside. 'Everything will be fine', she repeated to herself.

'Oh, my God, look at that!' Lisa was sitting erect and looking in amazement out of the car window. Janet followed her gaze. The vehicle had rounded a sharp bend and they could now see a house, or rather a mansion, nestling within the gentle folds of the lush, green hills.

'There's certainly some money here,' Janet breathed. 'I wonder what fees Mr Gee charges his clients!'

The car crunched its way along the long gravel drive until it pulled up at the front of the manor. The car locks clicked and, after a moment, the door was opened. Lisa and Janet clambered out into the sunlight. Mr Gee stood on the steps leading to the main door, flanked by two young girls dressed in the skimpiest of maid's costumes. He stepped forward as the chauffeur handed Lisa and Janet their baggage.

'Welcome to Grantham Manor,' their host said proudly as he took their bags. 'I trust your journey was not too difficult?'

'No, not at all,' said Janet. 'You have a lovely home.'

'It has been in the family for many generations,'

said Mr Gee as he led the way up the steps, 'and it serves my purpose admirably.' He guided them through a large, oak door and into the hallway. A giant staircase swept grandly ahead of them. It divided beneath a huge, stained-glass window before turning back in both directions to form two ornate galleries that met again above the front doorway. Janet looked upwards. Above her head was the largest and most splendid chandelier that she had ever seen. Its sheer size put even the displays in the presidential palace to shame. The crystals caught the multi-coloured shafts of light streaming in from the decorated window in the most magical way and cast beams around them like a laser light-show at a rock concert.

'Wow,' gasped Lisa, 'that's incredible!'

'The maids will take you to your room,' said Mr Gee. 'Tell me, what do you have in your bags?'

'Just clothes and toiletries,' said Janet, surprised at the question. 'Why?'

'You will have no need of clothing. Everything is provided. Come, you will wish to bathe and freshen up. Be ready by five o'clock. The maids will bring you to the pool, where you will meet your new colleagues.'

Mr Gee turned and strode back out of the house before either of the girls had the chance to ask any more questions. The two maids picked up the bags and moved towards the stairway. Lisa and Janet walked after them slowly, still looking around in wonder at the sheer opulence of the place. They followed the maids up the long staircase. Lisa nudged Janet and grinned, nodding towards the maids. The young girls' uniform skirts were cut remarkably short, the effect being to reveal two pert, naked bottoms.

'I wonder if we'll have to wear things like that?' breathed Lisa excitedly.

'I certainly hope so,' answered Janet in a whisper.

They were led into a long, brightly lit hallway. On either side of them were doors to what must have been the bedrooms, each bearing an elegant, brass number. On the walls hung paintings, mostly Victorian in style and all of a highly explicit and erotic nature. One in particular caught Janet's attention and she stopped to look at it in detail. The picture showed a young girl in the image of a garden-nymph who was squatting over the form of an elf-like creature with an enormous phallus partially embedded inside her ludicrously stretched pussy. Another elf was standing before her with his own, fine stalk in her mouth and a third knelt behind her, clearly about to force his equally superb erection into her bottom. 'Now, that's what I call art!' she laughed.

Lisa and Janet walked slowly down the hallway and savoured each painting in turn. Finally, they reached a door that was being held open for them by one of the maids. They entered the bedroom and stood in wide-eyed amazement.

Everything in the room was white. The carpet, the walls, the furniture, even the curtains shimmered in the reflected sunlight. In the centre of the room was a huge, circular bed, above which, set in the ornately carved ceiling, was a giant mirror.

'Do you like the room?' It was the youngest of the two maids who spoke, a small, delicate girl in her late teens.

'It's beautiful,' sighed Janet.

Lisa walked over to the far side of the room and through another door. 'Hey, Janet, come and look at this!'

Janet followed her into what turned out to be the

bathroom. But this was no ordinary bathroom. The centrepiece was an enormous circular bath, already filled to the brim with hot, perfumed water. The taps and other fittings, and even the frames of the many mirrors fixed to the walls, were all made of gold. The sunlight that streamed in from the small window played against the billowing steam and reflected in the mirrors to create an enchanting, almost magical scene.

'I'd love to fuck in this bath,' said Lisa as she ran her hand enviously over its marble edge.

'I have a feeling that we'll both get the chance,' grinned Janet.

She returned to the bedroom to find that the maids had left. Their bags had been placed on a small table. She unzipped hers and took out her toiletry bag, then returned to the bathroom. Lisa had stripped herself and was already wallowing in the soapy water.

'Come on in, the water's lovely,' she said as she patted the surface playfully. Janet pulled off her top at the same time as kicking off her trainers then peeled off her tight jeans and slipped into the soothing warmth of the bath. Lisa moved to sit next to her and put her arm gently round her waist. They looked into each others' eyes and knew what they both wanted. Their mouths met and their tongues entwined in a long, loving kiss. Janet ran her hand over Lisa's breasts as they bobbed on the surface of the water then ran her fingertips down until she touched the creamy softness of her friend's hairless pussy. She caressed the opening lips gently as she felt Lisa's fingers slip between her legs and fondle her already fully aroused cunt.

Janet knew that she would come very quickly under Lisa's expert touch. Their breathing became heavy as they held each other in a long, passionate embrace. Their fingers worked rapidly and their thighs jerked in happy response.

Suddenly, Lisa pulled her face away and threw her head back. Her expression became a grimace, as though she were in pain. Janet knew that look well. She rubbed her friend's clitoris harder, making the water splash over the sides of the bath. Lisa held her arms in the air and clenched her fists. 'Ow!' she squealed, then gasped loudly as the orgasmic tremors overtook her. Janet pressed her four fingers deep inside the blonde's pussy with her thumb crushed against her throbbing clitoris. Lisa continued to gasp in ecstasy as Janet turned and twisted her fingers inside her until she could take no more.

Janet eased from her and sat back. 'Did you enjoy that?' she asked, already knowing the answer.

Lisa breathed out loudly. 'Wow, it gets better every time,' she sighed, 'but what about you?'

'I'm OK,' Janet lied.

'No you're not,' said Lisa forcefully. 'Come here and stand up!'

Janet moved across to her friend and stood up in the bath. The water came to just above her knees. Lisa leant forward and put her mouth to Janet's hairy bush. Janet sighed happily as she sensed her friend's tongue snaking around her aching sex-lips, and then closed her eyes in delight as Lisa began to flick her tongue rapidly over her erect bud.

'Oh, God, you're so good with your tongue,' she moaned, moving her hips in a gentle, circular motion. Lisa's response was to lick harder and faster. Janet was coming. She could feel the surge of pleasure building rapidly inside her and knew that there was no way of stopping it.

'Yes, oh yes, I'm coming!' she moaned. Lisa clamped her pouting lips tightly over Janet's throbbing pussy and sucked hard, drawing the flesh into her mouth and delving deep inside her with her long tongue. The sharp sensations of ecstatic release tore at Janet's loins. She gripped Lisa's head tightly and pulled her hair as her legs shook with the force of her orgasm. She ground her pubic bone against Lisa's face with considerable force but her friend didn't let off her insistent tongue-fucking until, at last, the feelings began to subside, and Janet slipped slowly back into the water. The two girls sat quietly for a few moments, gazing at each other through glazed eyes. There was nothing to be said.

'God, Janet, look at these!' The girls were spending their time rummaging through the many drawers and the huge wardrobe. Each item of clothing was more exotic or erotic than the last. The items ranged from skimpy outfits made of the most delicate, transparent lace to heavy, leather apparel adorned with clips and chains. They had tried on one after the other and could safely say that there had not been a single garment that they could have worn in public without causing a riot.

This time, Janet had slipped on a white lace catsuit which, whilst it covered her body from her neck to her feet, nevertheless hid nothing. She turned to look at Lisa, who was holding what looked like a very large pair of panties.

'Knickers?' she queried. 'They look a bit big.'

'No, look.' Lisa held the black garment towards her and pulled the waistband open. Janet looked inside. There were two, firm protuberances, each about six inches long and conveniently placed so that their purpose was clear. 'One in the front, and one in the back,' said Lisa with a giggle.

'God, that'd be weird,' laughed Janet. Nevertheless, she examined the rubber panties closely.

'And I found this as well,' continued Lisa. This time she held an implement which was more than familiar to both girls. It was a black dildo, about a foot long and as thick as a man's wrist. It was made out of soft, firm leather with straps attached to the base and was perfectly formed in the shape of an erect penis. Carefully detailed, the phallus was complete with veins and ridges, the detail even extending to a delightfully realistic scrotum.

'I think that this will become a very good friend to both of us,' said Janet coquettishly as she ran her hand over the stiff shaft. She found the idea of strapping on the dildo and impaling Lisa's delightful pussy with its full length most appetising.

There was a knock at the door. 'Come in!' called Lisa. The door opened and a tall man entered, carrying some items of clothing. He was a hugely muscular figure who, from the sharp definition of his superb physique, quite clearly worked out regularly. He was wearing nothing but a black pair of skin-tight cycling shorts and a bow tie around his neck. Janet put her hand over her mouth to suppress a laugh. Lisa wasn't so polite.

'Are you the butler?' she asked before bursting into laughter. The man smiled and waited for her to compose herself. 'I'm sorry,' she said eventually. 'It's the bow tie, it looks so funny.'

'All the staff here are required to wear as little as possible whilst making it clear to guests what their roles are. I am, as you surmised, the butler.' He spoke with an eloquence that seemed at odds with his appearance. He stood solidly in the centre of the room, and apparently seemed oblivious to the fact that Lisa was naked and Janet might just as well have been. Nor did he seem to notice the big, black phallus that she was holding. No doubt he was well used to seeing such sights here at Grantham Manor.

The butler laid the clothing in two separate piles on the bed. 'You are to wear these,' he said in a tone that demanded obedience. 'Please dress quickly and then ring for the maid. The buzzer is by the side of the bed. She will escort you to the pool where the others are gathered.' With that, he bowed and left the room.

'What a beautiful bottom,' said Lisa wistfully as she watched him leave.

'Never mind that,' snapped Janet. 'Come on, let's see what we've got here!' She held up one of the garments. It was a short, white dress made from an elasticated type of material. With it was a pair of white hold-up stockings and a pair of matching, thick-heeled shoes. She looked inside one of the shoes. 'These are my size,' she said, 'so this must be my pile.' She looked at the other garments. The dress was identical in style, but in black, as were the stockings and shoes. She looked inside one of the black shoes. 'Yes, these are your size, though God knows how they knew.'

'Nothing surprises me about this place,' said Lisa. She stepped into the black dress and pulled it up over her nakedness. The silky material moulded itself around her sumptuous body and highlighted every sensuous curve. The hem was less than an inch below her crotch. She turned to face Janet.

'Can you see anything?' she asked as she smoothed the dress over her curves.

'No, you're OK. You'll have to be careful when you sit down, though.'

Lisa rolled on one of the stockings, then the other and finally stepped into the shoes. There was a gap of about three inches between the hem of her dress and the lacy tops of her stockings. She looked into a mirror and smiled appreciatively. 'Neat outfit,' she said. 'Very sixties.'

Janet had donned her dress and was just finishing putting on her shoes. She stood next to Lisa. In her reflection, Janet could see that her white dress was subtly translucent; everything could be seen within a teasing shadow. She stood sideways. The pert curve of her bottom looked very inviting, just as she'd hoped. She turned her back and looked over her shoulder at the mirror. Her buttocks were clearly outlined in the clinging material. 'Very sexy,' she said, 'and so simple.'

Lisa reached over to the side of the bed and pressed the buzzer by the phone. 'Well, it's about time we met the others,' she said.

The maid appeared within moments. 'We're ready,' said Lisa.

'You look lovely, madam,' said the servant. 'You both look beautiful. Come, I will take you to the pool.'

They followed the young girl through the house, down a rear stairway and out into the garden. Although it was getting late it was still exceptionally warm and the air was scented with the delicate perfumes of an English summer's day. They could hear the sound of voices coming from behind a large hedge. The maid led them through a small gap in the greenery and they found themselves standing close to a large swimming pool. On the far side was a group of about thirty young people, happily drinking and chatting like old friends. Mr Gee stood at the centre, as if holding court. He noticed the girls almost immediately and beckoned for them to join him.

Lisa and Janet walked quickly round the edge of the pool towards the group. The others greeted them with smiles and nods, the men leering appreciatively at them despite the fact that all the women wore similarly revealing clothing.

'Welcome again, ladies,' said Mr Gee, warmly. He raised his hand to call the group to order. The silence was immediate. 'My friends, may I introduce Janet and Lisa Angel. Please make them feel welcome in the time-honoured tradition of Grantham Manor.'

Lisa looked across at Janet quizzically. Her friend merely shrugged. A tall young man wearing nothing but a very brief pair of swimming trunks stepped forward. He was in his early twenties with short, blond hair and handsome, tanned features. He smiled and slipped his arms around Janet's waist and pressed his body against hers. She could feel the hard bulge of his sex pressing against her stomach. She shivered with excited anticipation and looked up into his soft, blue eyes. Their mouths met and his tongue snaked sensuously between her lips. Janet pushed her lower body firmly against his and moved her hips slightly from side to side as she felt his strong hands grip her buttocks. His fingertips touched the bare flesh below the hem of her dress.

She wrapped her arms around his neck and returned his kiss with increasing passion. Her dress rode up so that he now caressed her naked bottom. She could feel his erection thickening promisingly. Their lips parted and she gazed into his eyes as though they were lovers. Something told her that they soon would be.

'Welcome to the Manor,' he said. 'My name is Mike.' He ran a fingertip between her buttocks and she pulled away sharply.

'Please, I hardly know you,' she chided. The grin on her face belied her pretence at coyness. He shrugged and walked away. Janet looked across at Lisa. Her friend was in the arms of a dark, muscular young man, their mouths locked together in a passionate embrace. It came as no surprise to Janet to see that Lisa had her hand down the front of his swimming costume. Her friend was not one to waste time.

Janet looked back for Mike. He was sitting on the edge of the pool and was chatting to a lovely young girl of apparent Asian descent. She had obviously just climbed out of the water. Her long, black hair was plastered to her head and her olive skin glistened wetly in the sunlight. Mike had his back to Janet, but she could see the girl's arm moving steadily up and down in front of him. It was clear what she was doing, and Janet felt a pang of envy. Grantham Manor was decidedly not a place for inhibition or shyness.

Mr Gee walked over to her and rested his hand lightly on her shoulder Immediately, she felt a sensation like a surge of electricity run through her body. She turned her face towards his and looked into his eyes. She had never experienced such a powerful, sexual attraction for someone before, and she wanted him badly. She willed him to tear the dress from her body and throw her on the ground. She began to tremble; she couldn't help herself.

He smiled benignly and let his hand slip from her. 'We have these gatherings each week. They serve to ease tensions and help the staff to relax but, most of all, they prepare them for the tasks ahead. There is just one rule, and that is there are no rules. Eat, drink and indulge your every whim; no one will refuse you anything. See – your friend Lisa has got the general idea.'

Janet looked across at Lisa who was now happily sucking the firm erection presented to her by the young man who had welcomed her so passionately. Janet turned back to face her host with the intention of offering him similar delights, but he merely bowed his head politely and walked away. She watched wistfully as he disappeared through the hedge, then swung round with a new determination and faced the others.

Most were chatting casually and sipping on cool drinks. A couple of young men were enjoying Lisa's display avidly, as though waiting their turn. Janet walked over to join Mike at the pool's edge. He was kissing the Asian girl passionately. Janet could see that he had removed the top half of her bikini and his fingers were worming their way down the back of her trunks whilst she continued to rhythmically pump his erection.

Janet could see his cock now, long and incredibly thick – just what she needed. Without a word, she knelt at his side and slipped her own hand around the stiff flesh. She copied the young girl's movements as they expertly massaged Mike's bone-hard erection. The girl looked at her and smiled, then bent her head and took the bulbous head of Mike's prick in her small mouth. He lay back on the marble tiles and cradled his head in his hands so that he could watch the two girls work their magic on him. Janet knelt on her hands and knees and rested her head on his thighs. Slowly, she licked his balls and traced their heavy shape within his hairy sac. She was conscious that in this position her pert little bottom would be completely visible to anybody who chose to look, and the knowledge excited her.

Both she and the other girl continued to pump the long, thick stem of Mike's cock whilst Janet sucked his plum-sized testicles. She drew one, and then the other into her mouth and bit gently into the flesh. She heard him groan with pleasure. She released her grip of his cock and let his balls slip from her wet lips then drew her tongue upwards along the thick, gnarled shaft and over the gently rubbing fingers of the pretty young girl who immediately moved her head back so that she was licking just the tip of his erection. Janet joined her in lapping around the swollen knob. Their tongues touched and Janet moved forward until their lips met with Mike's throbbing, wet flesh inside both of their mouths at the same time.

'Oh, man, this is heaven,' he groaned. The two girls began to rub the long stem again as they kissed each other passionately. Janet sensed that there was someone behind her, and she waited for the familiar touch of a tongue or cock to her wet pussy. None came. Unconcerned for the moment, she carried on sucking the end of Mike's prick whilst kissing the beautiful, olive-skinned girl. She heard Mike groan again and his thighs stiffened. She rubbed him faster and faster until his thick shaft began to throb heavily and she tasted the saltiness of his cream. She pressed her lips harder against the other girl and they lapped hungrily as more and more of his release filled their mouths. It was like an elixir of lust to Janet. Finally, they allowed Mike's cock to slip from their lips and kissed each other deeply as though oblivious to his presence. Their tongues circled each other as they lapped up the silky cream from their mouths and swallowed it heavily.

Janet heard another noise from behind her but there was still no touch to her aching sex. She stopped kissing the beautiful girl reluctantly and looked over her shoulder. One of the male servants was kneeling behind her, resplendent in his uniform of tight cycling shorts and black bow-tie, busily filming their activities with a video camera.

'What the hell are you doing?' she said, angrily as she swung round. The servant said nothing and aimed the lens directly between her legs. She pushed it away indignantly. The servant looked shocked.

'Please, madam, we always do this. It's for the guests.'

Janet stood up in a fury. She'd been filmed and photographed in compromising positions before, but never without her permission. She looked around for Lisa. She spotted her over by the hedge. She was now kneeling naked except for her stockings over the prone form of the dark-haired young man, sucking his stiff erection ravenously whilst he, in turn, was paying oral homage to her clitoris. Another man was kneeling behind her and thrusting a not-inconsiderable length in and out of her glistening pussy. Two servants were crouched by the happy trio carefully filming the scene from every conceivable angle.

Janet watched for a moment in astonishment. Lisa must have known they were there, and yet it didn't seem to bother her. She looked back at the man who had been filming her. He stood sheepishly at the pool's edge.

'It's all right,' said the other girl as she stood next to Janet and slipped her arm around her waist. 'Mr Gee always arranges this each week. We all sit with the guests on the first night and watch the finished video with them. It's a wonderful ice-breaker!'

Janet felt more than a little stupid. This was the second time her inhibitions had let her down. What was the matter with her? She wasn't even twenty, and yet she was beginning to act like a middle-aged woman. She grabbed the hem of her dress with both hands and wrenched the garment over her head in one, swift movement. 'Right, let's give them something to film. I'm going to make that camera melt!'

She knelt in front of the other girl and wrenched her bikini-pants down to her ankles, then buried her face in the hot wetness of her hairy mound. The girl gasped with delight at the suddenness of thc plcasurablc assault. The servant knelt close to them and pointed his camera to Janet's face. She moved her head back and pushed out her tongue so that just the tip fluttered against the other girl's pussy. She licked gently between the pouting lips and turned her face slightly to ensure that he got a clear picture of what she was doing.

Suddenly, being filmed like this became supremely exciting. The knowledge that complete strangers would view her enjoying sex began to thrill her intensely. She coaxed the young girl to lie on her back then turned her body and knelt over her so that she could continue to lick her pussy whilst enjoying the same delights herself. She saw the servant move behind her and heard his camera flick into action as her suppliant lover began to lick her hot sex-lips. She buried her face once more into the moist warmth between the young girl's legs and lapped greedily at her delicious cunt. Another servant appeared and knelt in front of her to aim his camera at her face. She raised her head slightly and pushed her tongue out as far as it would go with the tip delving between the oily labia and stared straight at the lens. She held the pose for a moment, then dived her face down again like an animal devouring its prey and sucked the fleshy juiciness that she had come to love so much.

She sensed one or two fingers slipping inside her own pussy whilst the other girl continued to flutter her tongue against her hard little bud. Then, to her delight she felt the unmistakable pressure of a stiff cock pushing slowly into her hot sheath. She arched her back and looked over her shoulder. He was a stranger, handsome enough, and with a broad grin on his cheeky face. Another of the servants was lying behind him, apparently filming the view of the hard cock impaling Janet from between the legs of her new lover.

Mike moved to kneel in front of Janet between the other girl's legs. His cock was rigid again and his intentions were clear. Janet took hold of his thick shaft and put the purple-coloured head to her lips. She teased the end with the tip of her tongue then engulfed as much of him as she could inside her mouth. A servant shuffled to one side and filmed her as she moved her head backwards and forwards whilst cradling Mike's balls in one hand and rapidly rubbing the girl's soaked sex with the other. The other man was hammering into her now, and she quickly forgot the cameras.

She eased the thick cock from her mouth and aimed it deliberately at the young girl's pussy. Mike slid into her without the slightest difficulty and Janet felt her tongue flicking with increased rapidity against her own clitoris. The sensation of being licked and fucked at the same time was one that she dearly loved and, for a few minutes, she surrendered herself to this delight. The man who was fucking her gripped her buttocks painfully and began to thrust wildly in and out of her soaking sheath until he uttered a long, low groan and pulled from inside her. Janet raised herself slightly and looked under her body to see that the young girl was sucking his throbbing cock voraciously, draining him of every drop of his cream. At the same time, Mike was pumping into her like a madman. Janet looked up at him and pointedly licked her lips. Mike got the message. Suddenly, he pulled his big cock from within the obscenely stretched sheath and gripped it by the root in front of Janet's face. She grabbed hold of the thick shaft with both hands and clamped her lips over the throbbing flesh, just in time to feel his sperm jetting to the back of her throat.

She rubbed him furiously and sucked as though her life depended on it until, eventually, he began to soften and he pulled from her. She swallowed the warm mouthful of cream that he had given her, then clambered awkwardly from on top of the exhausted young girl.

They sat quietly for a while, Mike, Janet and their shared lover. Where the other man had gone was a mystery. Janet couldn't even remember his face. They watched the Bacchanalia with more than passing interest as they recovered from their strenuous exercise. The party had by now developed into a full-scale orgy. Everywhere she looked Janet could see groups of young people engaged in every form of sexual variation imaginable.

She glanced around the melée of heaving nakedness and tried to see Lisa. She eventually spotted her walking arm in arm with her dark, handsome lover towards the house. The pair of them looked for all the world like a couple of love-struck newly-weds. Janet's gaze fell to the man's lower body, and her eyes feasted on the way his taut buttocks moved as he walked.

'Looks like Paul's made a hit with your friend,' said Mike. Janet shrugged. Lisa wasn't going to be allowed to keep that hunk to herself.

She pulled herself awkwardly to her feet after disentangling herself from the limbs of the other two. Carefully stepping over the myriad copulating couples, threesomes and even foursomes she eventually arrived at the house. She took a few moments to pull off her stockings and shoes then, satisfyingly naked, she followed the direction that her friend had taken into the relative coolness of the hallway.

She reached their room quickly and stood by the closed door, listening. The familiar sounds of Lisa's groans of pleasure came from inside. Janet opened the door quietly and peeked in. She was treated to the delightful view of Paul's naked bottom thrusting heavily against the supine form of her friend as she lay in the centre of the huge bed. She crept quietly forward and knelt carefully on the edge of the divan behind them. She lowered herself so that she could see Paul's thick cock plunging in and out of Lisa's swollen pussy. Lisa herself was groaning quite loudly now, and was clearly getting very close to coming. Paul's thrusts were long and deep. and each time he rammed his cock home his buttocks rippled enticingly.

Janet couldn't resist any longer. She leant forward and ran her tongue wetly over one of the firm, muscular globes. Paul stopped pumping immediately and looked over his shoulder. Seeing Janet, he grinned broadly and then returned to his pleasurable task, but this time fucking Lisa with long, slow strokes so as not to dislodge Janet. She knelt closer and put her mouth against the top of the cleft between his buttocks. He slowed his movements almost to a stop and began to circle his hips slightly. Janet slid her tongue slowly down the cleft until the tip was just above his anus. She licked upwards again, then down. This time, she allowed the tip to flick against his tight little sphincter. He groaned loudly and Janet laughed coquettishly.

Lisa, suddenly realising that they were not alone, pulled herself quickly from under her lover and glared at Janet. 'Janet,' she said angrily, 'we came here to get some privacy!'

'Not much chance of that in this place,' laughed Janet as she returned to her task of licking Paul's bottom.

'You can say that again.' The three of them swung

round to see the naked form of Mike standing in the open doorway. His erection was once more as stiff as ever, and it swung heavily as he walked over to the bed. Lisa shrugged and slid over to meet him. She greeted him by taking hold of his cock and quickly engulfing it in her mouth.

In a way, Janet was pleased that he had arrived. Mike would keep Lisa occupied for a while so that she could concentrate on the gorgeous Paul. He had remained kneeling on the bed and was thoroughly enjoying what she was doing to him with her tongue. Janet resumed her oral caress of his bottom. She found the taste of his fresh sweat intoxicating.

She parted his buttocks with her thumbs and pushed the tip of her tongue into the tight little hole. This was something she had learnt from Lisa and she knew that, if Paul was enjoying it half as much as she had done that first, wonderful time that it had happened to her, then he would be in sheer ecstasy. He moaned softly and arched his back so that she could delve deeper. She responded by pursing her tongue and pushing hard. It hurt her a little but the knowledge of the pleasure she was giving made the slight discomfort worthwhile.

The bed began to shake rhythmically. Janet raised her head to see Mike lying on top of Lisa and fucking her steadily. Janet put her mouth back to Paul's bottom and licked again. Lisa managed somehow to wriggle her body over the bed so that her head was under Paul's groin. Janet was able to see that she was now sucking his thick cock whilst Mike continued to plunder her lush pussy with his own considerable stalk.

Janet suddenly had an idea. Paul seemed content to remain in the same position with his steel-hard prick being gently suckled by her friend, and he didn't seem to notice when Janet moved from the bed and walked over to the dressing table. She opened one of the drawers and retrieved a shiny, black vibrator. She returned to the bed and knelt again behind Paul and once more ran her tongue wetly between his buttocks. She put the tapered tip of the vibrator into her mouth and soaked it with her saliva, then gently eased about half its length into his bottom. She twisted the base and the implement buzzed into life. Paul took in a deep gasp of air and threw his head back in abject delight as she continued to push until nearly the full length was held inside him.

Lisa saw what was going on and reached between Paul's legs to grip the root of the vibrator and began to move it in and out whilst continuing to suck his thick cock. Mike seemed oblivious to all this and carried on fucking Lisa with long, measured strokes. Janet crawled to the head of the bed and positioned herself on her knees and elbows so that her own bottom was inches from Paul's face. She sighed with delight as she felt him lapping her pert buttocks, then groaned happily as his tongue slithered up and down along her deep cleft. She stiffened her thigh-muscles and pushed her bottom against his face, thrilling as his tongue began to probe her tiny sphincter.

Then he was moving behind her. Somehow he had managed to extricate his cock from Lisa's luscious mouth and was easing the huge head inside Janet's soaking sex-lips. He slid his full length deep into her and she felt his thick stalk throb within her hot sheath. She came with a suddenness that surprised even her and she bit hard into the pillow. Her entire body trembled as Paul began to fuck her, gently at first then with increasing force and rapidity She sensed him ease a finger into her anus, then something that felt quite different. He was now easing the vibrator into her tight little hole whilst, at the same time, continuing to shag her mercilessly. The buzzing started and it tickled her at first, but then tremors of excitement began to course through her loins. Paul held himself still with his long cock firmly embedded inside her cunt. It was clear that he was enjoying the vibrating sensation as much as she was.

Lisa and Mike moved from the bed and out of her line of vision. 'Oh, my God,' breathed Paul, 'your friend's licking my backside now. I don't think I can hold back much longer.' Janet looked over her shoulder to see Lisa kneeling on the bed and assiduously running her tongue over Paul's bottom. Mike was now standing at the foot of the bed on the floor, once more plundering the succulent depths of Lisa's pussy and completing the chain of sublime over-indulgence.

Paul was the first to surrender to the inevitable. He gave a long, low groan and gripped Janet's thighs tightly with his cock rammed into her as far as it would go. She felt it stretch and seem to become even harder against her oozing flesh. Then she felt it pulse again and again and she heard him gasp. She stiffened her inner muscles to grip him tightly as he filled her with his hot seed. Her actions caused her to rise quickly to the edge of her own orgasm. She felt Paul slowly easing the vibrator from inside her bottom and the combination of the extreme sensations took her over into blissful release.

Paul began to pound heavily into her again and knocked her flat on her stomach. He lay on her lithe, little body and fucked her harder than she could remember being fucked until, gradually, he slowed his pace until he stopped.

They lay still for a few minutes. Paul's slowly wilting cock still beat inside her, albeit with less and less frequency. Janet always loved this time, the few precious moments when lust is sated and lovers caress each other with genuine tenderness. Lisa and Mike disappeared into the bathroom, no doubt to continue their mutual delights in the bath or shower.

Paul eased himself from within her and rolled over on to his back. Janet turned over and raised herself on her elbow, then kissed him lightly on the lips. He gazed adoringly into her soft, brown eyes.

'Welcome to Grantham Manor,' he breathed.

Three

Lisa opened her eyes slowly as the heat of the morning sun eased her back into consciousness. The gentle throbbing between her legs reminded her of the previous night's excesses. She pulled herself up on the pillows, half sitting, half lying, and looked around the room. Janet had gone, as had the two young men; what were their names? Pete? No, Paul, that's it, and Mike. She closed her eyes and dreamily remembered their superb, athletic bodies and some of their shared delights. For such young men they certainly knew what they were doing.

She slipped from the huge bed and walked towards the bathroom. Once inside, she quickly squatted over the toilet and began to pee. The urgent, warm torrent reawakened the nerve-endings of her sex in the most pleasurable of ways and stung her raw flesh slightly. She sighed. It had been quite a night.

The job completed, she washed herself between her legs then smoothed her depilatory cream over and around her sex-lips. The coolness of the balm soothed her. She'd lost count of the number of times that Paul and Mike had slipped their hard cocks into her willing sheath during that wild orgy last night. And when Janet had used that huge dildo on her – no wonder that she ached.

Lisa reached over and turned on the bath taps. As

they gushed into life, she smiled to herself as she remembered some of the things that the four of them had got up to in the same bath just hours previously. She reached for a small, blue bottle and tipped some of the contents into the steaming water. The perfume filled her senses immediately. It was strong but subtle, and clearly very expensive.

A tingling sensation between her legs told her that the cream was already working its magic. She blessed the day when she'd discovered it. No more razors, with their attendant dangers. A quick dip in the warm water and all traces of pubic stubble would be gone.

She clambered into the bath and allowed her body to slide against the smooth marble until just her head was above the scented water. The steam began to cloud the mirrors that covered every wall. Lisa closed her eyes and ran her hands lazily over her body. Not for the first time in just a few hours did she feel that she had found heaven.

She heard the bedroom door close with a bang. 'Janet?' she called, her ears straining to hear a reply. There was none, just the firm padding of footsteps on the thickly piled carpet. 'Janet, is that you?'

The bathroom door opened. 'Where've you been?' continued Lisa, 'I was –'

The intruder wasn't Janet. Instead of her friend, Lisa found herself confronted by an exceptionally tall black woman dressed in a bright red corset which appeared to be made of leather. It was drawn in tightly at the waist, the effect being to accentuate the size of her huge, naked breasts and the broad sweep of her hips. Her only other apparel was a pair of red panties of similar material and black, shiny boots which covered her long legs almost to the crotch.

'Who are you?' Lisa demanded as she sat upright in the bath and instinctively covered her breasts with her hands.

The impressive figure stepped forward. She smiled broadly, flashing a row of dazzlingly white teeth. The smile did nothing to quell Lisa's feelings of apprehension. The expression in the newcomer's eyes was cold and stern. 'Do not conceal such wonderful prizes,' said the woman. She reached out and took hold of Lisa's arms and firmly tugged her hands away from her breasts. Lisa looked down, as though she was ashamed of their nakedness. The newcomer gazed at the heaving mounds hungrily. Lisa shivered uncontrollably, despite the warmth of the water. The woman released her grip of her arms and stepped back.

'My name is Heidi Stone,' she said, proudly, 'but you will call me Madam Stone. I am your guide, your mentor and, above all, your instructor.'

'Instructor? I don't understand. I thought that we –'

'Before you can teach you must learn.'

'I don't mean any disrespect,' said Lisa, her confidence returning, 'but I don't think you could teach us much that we haven't already experienced.'

The woman smirked unkindly. 'I observed your performance last night, and that of your friend. Believe me, young lady, you have much to learn. Now, out of the bath, dry yourself off and join me in the bedroom for your first lesson. Quickly!'

The tone and abruptness of Madam Stone's voice demanded immediate acquiescence. Lisa climbed out of the bath without a second's thought and grabbed a towel. Madam Stone turned sharply and strode out of the bathroom. Lisa watched her go, noting the firm swell of her jutting buttocks and the thin sliver of red leather that disappeared into the dark cleft between the sumptuous globes. Despite her feelings of nervousness and not a little anger, she felt an immediate lust for this powerful woman. Lisa had always felt a strong sexual attraction for black men and women, a magnetism that she found it difficult to control. There had been many times in the past that she had surrendered to these urges, and always with highly satisfying results. She quickly dried herself in excited anticipation, then, wrapping the towel around her body she followed as ordered.

Madam Stone was lying at the centre of the bed with her legs splayed wide apart. The red leather panties had been thrown on to the floor. Her bushy crotch glistened in the sunlight which streamed in through the large window. She grinned coldly as Lisa walked over to her to stand awkwardly at the side of the bed.

'Remove the towel!' commanded the fearsome woman. Lisa obeyed immediately. Madam Stone sat upright on the bed and slowly examined her body. She reached out with both hands and cupped Lisa's breasts and raised them slightly, then let them fall from her grasp. She looked at Lisa and nodded her approval.

'Very little movement for such large breasts,' she said appreciatively. Suddenly, she slipped her hand between Lisa's legs which caused her to gasp. 'So smooth,' she continued as she ran the tip of her tongue across her huge lips, 'and so inviting.' Lisa shivered. She could feel the woman snaking her middle finger into her creamy pussy. She began to breath deeply as Madam Stone circled her long finger inside her. 'You like it, don't you? Don't you?' The second time the question was asked it was with extreme severity, and it shocked Lisa. She nodded quickly.

The beautiful black woman removed her finger and lay back on the bed. 'Kneel between my legs,' she ordered. Lisa obeyed without a second's thought. 'Now, look at me. What do you see?'

Lisa was becoming confused. 'Er, I don't understand,' she began.

'Are you stupid?' said Madam Stone angrily. 'Look, girl, what do you see?'

'I see . . . you,' said Lisa.

'Go on. What exactly do you see?'

'I, I see a beautiful, strong woman with skin as dark as coal and eyes –'

'What do you think of my breasts?'

Lisa stared at the heaving mounds and the long, jet-black nipples. She was terrified that she would say the wrong thing. 'They are big,' she ventured.

'Not as big as yours.'

'No, but I'm a bit unusual,'

'Indeed you are. Now, what do you see between my legs?'

Lisa looked down at the thick bush of curly, black hair. 'I can see your, your sex,' she said quietly.

'No, girl,' said Madam Stone, angrily, 'you can see my *cunt*! What can you see?'

'Your cunt,' replied Lisa, deliberately accentuating the obscenity.

'And I can see yours. Your beautiful, hairless cunt, with thick, pouting lips that I am sure will taste divine.' The big woman parted her long legs even wider and put the fingers of both hands to her crotch. She smoothed back the hair and pushed against the flesh to display her thick sex-lips to Lisa's appreciative gaze. The outer lips were deep ebony in colour, but the long cleft between them appeared almost scarlet. 'Do you like my cunt, Lisa?' she said. Lisa nodded. 'Lick it. Show me how good you are with your tongue.'

Lisa was in no mood to disobey. She knelt on her

knees and forearms and lowered her face towards Madam Stone's blatantly offered prize. She took in a deep breath. Her scent was strong and distinctly feminine. Madam Stone raised her hips from the bed and tugged the lips of her pussy apart. Lisa gazed lustfully at the exposed, deep-red flesh of her inner lips and the prominent bud of her erect clitoris. She planted a gentle kiss on the hard, little button and heard Madam Stone draw in a sharp breath. The thickly matted hair was soaked with her arousal and her juices were gently trickling between her buttocks.

Lisa kissed her clitoris again, then circled it with her tongue. Then she began to flick the end of her tongue rapidly against it in a way that she knew drove women wild. She could hear the woman breathing deeply. She slid her tongue down along the full length of the pouting lips then back up, at the same time sucking the flesh and swallowing the copious juices.

Suddenly, Madam Stone pushed her away and sat up angrily. 'Like I said, you have much to learn!'

'I don't understand,' said Lisa as she felt the tears welling up behind her eyes. 'I thought you were enjoying what I was doing!'

'Lie back, Lisa Angel, and I will teach you how to suck and lick a cunt. But first – look at my face.' With that, she pushed her tongue out from her wide mouth. Lisa watched in astonishment as she curled it and pushed it further until she licked under her own chin. It was easily the longest tongue that she had ever seen. Lisa felt a twinge of anticipation between her legs and lay back expectantly against the pile of pillows with her legs spread wide apart.

Madam Stone knelt between Lisa's legs and gazed pointedly at her pussy, then reached forward and ran all four fingertips of one hand along the soaked cleft between her exquisitely tender sex-lips. Lisa closed her eyes in order to savour the sensation.

'Watch!' demanded her tormentor. 'You must watch everything that I do!'

Lisa snapped her eyes open fearfully to see the beautiful woman smoothing the tips of her wet fingers across her own mouth, as if applying a soothing ointment to the thick lips. She ran her long tongue around her fingers and tasted Lisa's juices. The expression on her face proved that she found the flavour much to her liking.

'The secret of giving good oral sex, whether to a male or female partner can be summed up with the letters ATTS – Arouse, Tease, Torment and Satisfy. You will do well to remember this phrase; it relates to most things of a sexual nature. Say the words, Lisa.'

'Arouse, tease, torment and satisfy,' said Lisa, obediently.

'Good.' Madam Stone moved from the bed and walked over to the window. She peered out for a few moments. Lisa gazed hungrily at her silhouetted form. Her mouth went dry as she surveyed the near-conical shape of her large breasts and exceptionally long nipples, the tightness of the leather basque and the firmly thrusting buttocks that seemed to be defying gravity. She wanted to taste that lovely, hairy pussy again – no, that was the wrong word. Between Madam Stone's legs was a ravenous, succulent *cunt*. Lisa was beginning to understand.

Her tutor turned to face her. 'Now,' she said, firmly, 'for the first stage – arousal.'

'I think I'm already aroused enough,' said Lisa, grinning.

Madam Stone flashed her a severe glare. 'Let us understand something from the outset, Lisa Angel. *I* will decide when you are aroused. From now on, you will not speak unless in answer to my questions. Understand?'

Her powerfully authoritarian tone of voice forced the smile from Lisa's face immediately, and she involuntary brought her legs together and folded her arms across her lap. She felt distinctly vulnerable in her naked state but, at the same time, she had a strange feeling of excitement and anticipation.

'I said, do you understand?' Madam Stone was standing at the bedside, now, her hands on her hips and her legs firmly apart. Lisa nodded meekly and hunched her knees against her breasts with her arms wrapped around her legs. She felt the warm trickle of her juices slip from her pussy to dampen the bed beneath her. Madam Stone sat on the edge of the bed and reached out with both hands. She gripped Lisa's wrists and tugged them from her knees. At first, Lisa showed a little resistance, then allowed her arms to fall to her sides.

'Spread your legs wide apart, Lisa, and don't close them again.' Lisa moved her thighs apart slowly. 'Wider, girl!' commanded her tormentor. She obeyed immediately. The muscles of her inner thighs began to ache slightly as she was forced to display herself blatantly. Madam Stone leant forward and gazed at her pussy. 'Such a beautiful thing,' she purred. 'I wonder how many stiff cocks have sunk into that welcoming little hole.'

'I, I don't know,' said Lisa, truthfully.

'Silence!'

Lisa began to tremble with an incongruous combination of nervousness and intense sexual excitement. The powerful woman moved her head further forward and Lisa raised her hips slightly almost automatically. The expected kiss of the thick lips against her hot, moist sex didn't come. Instead, Madam Stone moved away from her and sat back on the edge of the bed.

'The most effective method of arousal is when neither partner makes any form of physical contact whatsoever. The use of the right words, facial expressions or movements can be far more exciting than even the most expert of caresses. The longer that you can resist the temptation to touch your partner, particularly in a sexual way, the more you will increase the desire and soon have her or him begging you to do just that.

'Why do you think that men and women enjoy striptease shows? If the performers merely walked on to the stage stark naked and cavorted about they would soon lose their audiences. People prefer to see them fully clothed, gradually revealing more and more of their bodies. Will they actually take off that final tiny G-string? Will they reveal a nice, hairy little cunt or an erect cock? So it is with seduction and arousal. For a man, the greatest pleasure in sex is the conquest of an erstwhile impossible dream. The joy a man feels after a long and arduous seduction as he at last enters the tightness of a virgin's wet sheath cannot be bettered. But, if she had been willing from the start, if she had made it clear that she would allow him to fuck her, then the pleasure would not be so intense.

'Men, of course, are happy to sink their cocks into any hole, given the opportunity. Most men are easy to seduce, especially if the seductress is as beautiful as you, dear Lisa. But some can be put off by blatant approaches, and these represent the greatest and most delightful of challenges. Think about the last ten or so men who have made love to you. No doubt you thoroughly enjoyed the sex, but do you remember any of them especially? No? Or perhaps there was one. Think hard, Lisa. Is there one that you can remember with particular fondness?'

'Simon,' replied Lisa, quietly as she recalled the youthful innocence of a virginal conquest a few months previously. She smiled to herself as she pictured Simon's face and remembered his nervous fumblings and his delightful lack of finesse.

'Who was Simon?'

'Just a young man,' replied Lisa softly. 'I was his first lover.'

'Exactly. He was probably the worst lover you have ever had, but you remembered him, not because of his sexual prowess, but because of the sheer eroticism of the moment. Think of your position now, Lisa. You are lying on the bed, naked, with your legs wide open. You are listening to a woman who is a complete stranger talk about sex, a subject dear to your heart. You know that I am going to lick you – at least, you hope I am – because I have already told you that this lesson concerns oral sex. But you assumed that the instruction would merely focus on different ways to run your tongue around a hard clitoris or suppliant sex-lips.

'But, perhaps I don't want to lick you. Maybe I've licked enough female crotches for one day. Do you want me to lick you?'

'Yes,' said Lisa, almost in desperation.

'Why?'

'I don't know. I just do.'

'Is it because you need to feel a tongue against you?'

'No, it's more than that. I can't explain.'

'But you want me desperately, don't you? You want to feel my tongue sliding in and out of your hot little cunt and lapping over your stiff bud until you come, don't you – don't you?'

'Yes, yes!' Lisa was shaking with lust and anticipation by now, and knew that she would be willing to do anything for this dominating woman.

'Well, I might but, then again, I might not.' Madam Stone rose from the bed and walked back to look nonchalantly out of the window.

'Please, Madam Stone, please,' begged Lisa. The tall woman turned towards her and smiled mockingly.

'Now comes the next part. Can you remember?'

'Teasing?'

'Teasing. Your partner is now fully aroused, and yours to command. But if you throw yourself on him or her, if you give way to your own cravings the magic will be lost. You must maintain the doubts for as long as you can. Talk about other things, but keep the conversation firmly centred on sex. Do you still have sexual fantasies, Lisa?'

'Yes, although I think I've fulfilled most of them.'

'That can be a problem when a girl is as uninhibited and promiscuous as you are. Fantasies are usually better than reality.'

'Not always, I –'

'Tell me, what's your favourite fantasy at the moment?'

Lisa thought hard. What she had said was true. In a very short time she had managed to fulfil virtually every dream that it was possible to imagine. Men, women, multiple partners, orgies, hugely endowed men, wild, suppliant girls; there was little that she could think of that she hadn't enjoyed in reality.

'Well?' Madam Stone was becoming impatient.

Lisa suddenly remembered something that she had thought about a few days earlier. 'There is one,' she said, slowly, 'but it's silly, mainly because it's impossible.'

'Go on,' said her tutor, sitting once more on the bed and resting her arm on Lisa's knee.

'Well, I've often fantasised about being a guy, you know, a really handsome man with a body to die for and a huge cock. I wake up one morning and find that I've suddenly changed into this stud, but still with the same thoughts and desires that I have as a woman.'

'It's a very common fantasy.'

'Really?'

'Yes. Most people dream of having a different body, younger, older, fatter, thinner. Men often fantasise about their cocks growing to ludicrous proportions and women dream of larger breasts or thinner waists. But it is quite usual for a man or woman to try to imagine what it would be like to be the opposite sex, and these thoughts often develop into fully grown fantasies. Tell me, what happens in your fantasy?'

'I'm dancing with a beautiful young girl in a night club. There are hundreds of people all around us, and I'm pressing my body hard against her so that she can feel my huge erection. Suddenly, she unzips me and takes it out, and makes me fuck her, there and then, in front of the crowd.'

As she was talking, Madam Stone began to smooth the palm of her hand against Lisa's inner thigh. The trembling, naked blonde watched as she moved her fingertips to within an inch of her crotch, then as they circled the area without touching any of her tenderest flesh. Her mouth felt dry and she swallowed hard.

'Is this torment?' she asked in a whisper.

'You are learning quickly,' replied Madam Stone. She knelt between Lisa's outstretched legs and moved her face forward. She pushed out her tongue and drew a trail of saliva along the inside of Lisa's thigh.

Then she turned her head and did the same to the other leg, this time moving her tongue to lick along the top of her thigh, over her hip-bone and on to her stomach. She quickly found Lisa's navel with the tip of her tongue, then drew her tongue lower, lower, until it was agonisingly close to Lisa's throbbing pussy. Lisa could feel her tormentor's breath against her ragingly sensitive clitoris. She began to breathe heavily and beads of perspiration formed on her forehead. She raised her bottom from the bed in an attempt to force her crotch against her lover's mouth but Madam Stone simply moved her head away and began licking the inside of her thighs again.

Lisa gasped in exasperation. The other woman raised her head and grinned malevolently. Then she moved her face down again, this time grasping Lisa's ankles and raising her legs high into the air. Lisa felt that she would scream as the long tongue slipped and slithered over her smooth skin, down and down, ever closer. Madam Stone licked her buttocks gently and allowed her tongue to flutter from one to the other without delving into the cleft between. Then she was circling her pussy again, moving the tip of her tongue round and round as her hot breath burned against Lisa's tender flesh.

'Lick it, you bitch! Lick it!' Lisa was surprised at the strength of her words, but enough was enough. Madam Stone drew back and regarded her haughtily. Lisa sensed that she had gone too far.

'I'm sorry, I –' she began. A tear of frustration slipped down her cheek.

Madam Stone's expression changed from one of stern anger to one of kindness. 'And now, satisfaction,' she said as she moved her head back between Lisa's legs. When her face was inches from her ultimate goal she stopped and glanced up at Lisa's flushed face. 'Satisfaction, but with a little torment. Watch.'

Lisa looked on as the woman pushed out her long tongue towards her soaking wet cunt. She gasped loudly as the tip touched the engorged lips and watched in fascination as it slid deep inside her like a soft, wet prick. Her lover pressed her mouth hard against her crotch and moved her tongue in and out of her hot sheath with long, slow and deliberate strokes. The sight of the beautiful, black face pressed against her pussy and the feelings deep in her loins as the tongue circled and probed inside her were bringing her rapidly to the point of release. She began to shake noticeably.

'Yes, yes,' she breathed, 'oh, God, yes!'

Suddenly, Madam Stone pulled away from her and sat back on her haunches. She fixed her stare on Lisa's pleading eyes.

'What are you doing?' begged the trembling blonde. 'I was nearly coming!'

'I said that there would be torment as well as satisfaction. Look hard into my eyes.'

Lisa couldn't have torn her gaze away from the deep, brown pools if she'd wanted to. 'Please,' she said tearfully, 'I want to come.'

'You are going to come, Lisa, I promise. Look at me. Force yourself; push! Think of my tongue, deep in your cunt. Think of me licking around inside you. Don't touch yourself. Strain your muscles, force that come out of your body. That's it!'

Lisa's eyes became fixed in a wild, manic stare. Her entire body trembled as the force of her efforts caused every nerve-ending between her legs to seem to be on fire. She dug her fingernails into the palms of her hands and gasped for air.

'Go on!' screamed Madam Stone. 'Try harder,

force it! It'll be the best come you've ever had! That's it! You're coming! You're coming!'

Lisa's scream could have been heard many miles away. She squirmed her body, rolled over and buried her face in the sheets, sobbing loudly. Her cunt burned with the sheer intensity of her orgasm. Her clitoris throbbed tenderly and sharp sensations like electric shocks seemed to emanate from between her legs to shoot throughout her trembling body. She arched her back and raised her bottom and plunged all four fingers of one hand into herself, only to have them quickly removed and replaced by her tutor's long, wet tongue.

Gradually, the sensations subsided as Madam Stone expertly slowed her oral ministrations until she finally eased her tongue from inside Lisa's aching pussy. Lisa rolled over on to her back and breathed heavily.

'Oh, wow,' she muttered. 'Oh, wow.'

Madam Stone leant over and kissed her lightly on the mouth. 'And that,' she whispered, 'that was lesson number one.'

Lisa sat quietly on the sun-baked patio, watching as Janet, Paul and Mike played childish games in the swimming pool. She was still shaken up from her experiences that morning. The sun was hot, too hot, and the water looked inviting, but just for the moment she chose to rest on the soft lounger and watch the others. She lay back and closed her eyes. It was good to sunbathe naked; it gave her a sense of freedom, especially in such a luxurious setting. She reached out and took hold of the glass of iced mineral water that stood on the small table by her side. She sipped the cold liquid slowly.

Janet pulled herself from the pool and padded over

to her. 'Aren't you coming in for a swim, Lisa?' she said.

Lisa opened her eyes and looked at her friend. The water dripped from her long, dark hair and formed sensuous little rivulets than ran over her apple-firm breasts. Her nipples were fully erect, probably as a result of the coolness of the water rather than anything else. She reached out and grabbed Lisa by the arm. 'Come on, Lisa, the water's lovely.'

Lisa pulled her arm away. 'I'm not really in the mood for a swim,' she said.

Janet sat down on the edge of the lounger and rested her hand on her friend's thigh. 'Are you OK, Lisa? You've been very quiet.'

Lisa pulled herself up to a sitting position and adjusted the chair to support her back. 'I'm fine, really I am. I had this amazing session with a woman calling herself Madam Stone this morning.'

'What – sex?' asked Janet excitedly.

Lisa nodded. 'It was supposed to be a lesson,' she began.

'I doubt if anyone could teach you anything!' laughed Janet.

'That's what I thought, until now. It was incredible.'

'What did you do?'

'Well, it wasn't what we did; it was how we did it, or rather how she made me do it.'

'What, did you use vibrators and dildos and that sort of thing?' Janet was clearly warming to the conversation, and her grin was broadening by the second.

'No, just oral sex.'

'Just oral? Nothing else?' Janet regarded her with undisguised disbelief.

'Just oral. But it was incredible.'

'Go on, then,' said Janet, clasping her hands between her knees like an excited child waiting for a story. 'What happened?'

'I can't really explain it. You'd have to experience it yourself to understand.'

Janet shrugged. 'Suit yourself.' She turned to look at the pool and watched as the two young men pulled themselves out of the water. 'They really are a couple of hunks, aren't they?'

Lisa regarded the two approaching men and smiled. Their cocks, which the night before had seemed to be permanently erect, now hung harmlessly from their bushy crotches. They grabbed their towels and came to stand next to the girls.

'Not swimming, Lisa?' said Paul as he rubbed his long, black hair vigorously.

She shook her head.

'Lisa's had sex with this woman called Madam Stone this morning and she won't tell me anything about it.' Janet feigned a pout, then grabbed her shorts from the ground and slipped them on.

'You've met the amazing Madam Stone, have you?' said Paul.

'Who is she?' asked Janet.

'She's the chief instructress,' said Mike. He moved to stand next to Janet and slipped his arm round her shoulders. She responded by circling his limp penis with her fingers and gently rubbing him.

'What she doesn't know about sex doesn't exist,' said Paul. 'She's certainly taught me a thing or two, I can tell you.'

'I can't wait to meet her,' said Janet.

Lisa smiled to herself as she watched her friend coax Mike's cock to full erection. She looked back at Paul, but he'd already pulled on his jeans and T-shirt. Lisa shrugged and took another sip of her drink.

'Did I hear my name mentioned?'

Lisa sat up abruptly and turned round to look back at the house. Madam Stone stood in the open patio doorway.

Lisa pulled herself up from the lounger. 'Madam Stone,' she said, 'I've been telling my friends about you.'

The tall woman was dressed simply in a bright red sarong that hugged her sumptuous curves and did little to conceal her stunning form. She walked over to Janet and held out her hand in greeting. 'You must be Janet Angel,' she said warmly. 'Welcome to Grantham Manor.'

Janet released her grip of Mike's cock and shook her hand politely. 'Pleased to meet you,' she said with a grin. The two of them sat down on a couple of patio chairs by another table.

'I suppose you already know Mike and Paul,' said Lisa. Mike struggled to put on a pair of jeans. His stiff erection made the task difficult but eventually he succeeded and then he and Paul sat next to the others on the remaining chairs.

Madam Stone smiled broadly. 'Oh, yes, I know Mike and Paul,' she said, her dark eyes shining.

A maid appeared, dressed in the ubiquitous brief uniform and carrying a tray of drinks which she set down on the table.

'That skirt is not short enough, Anne,' said Madam Stone angrily.

'I'm sorry, miss,' said the terrified girl.

'You will be. Come and see me in my room at eight o'clock.'

'Yes, miss.' The maid bowed her head, then turned and left.

'What will you do to her?' asked Lisa.

'She will be spanked for her impertinence. She

knows the rules. The buttocks must be clearly in view when a maid bends forward. If Mr Gee had seen her she would have been dismissed.'

'Where is Mr Gee?' asked Janet. 'I haven't seen him since last night.'

'He has gone to Gatwick airport to welcome our guests. They will be here this evening.'

'What type of group have we got this time?' asked Mike.

'Americans. Couples, each with their own special hang-ups. It will be a good introduction for Janet and Lisa.'

'Can I spank the maid?' Paul spoke lazily, as though it was the most natural thing to ask. Madam Stone regarded him haughtily.

'If you wish,' she said after a moment's consideration. She clapped her hands loudly. 'Anne,' she called. 'Come here immediately.'

The hapless maid returned as ordered. The offending skirt had been changed to one which was far shorter, bordering on the obscene. Tantalising wisps of dark, pubic hair could be glimpsed just below the hem as she stood subserviently before the assembled group.

'Mr Paul wishes to thrash you,' said Madam Stone.

'Yes, miss,' said the maid. Paul moved his chair and patted his knees. Lisa felt a little sorry for the girl as she moved slowly over to take her punishment. There was a fresh-faced innocence about her and she seemed terribly nervous.

Madam Stone slipped her arm around Lisa's shoulders and casually rested her hand on her bare breast. 'Watch how he deals with her,' she whispered, 'and remember what I taught you this morning.'

The maid bent over Paul's lap without being asked. There was no need for him to raise her skirt. Virtually the entire area of her bottom was bared as the hem rose almost to her waist. Paul stroked the pert, pink globes lovingly. 'What a beautiful little bottom,' he muttered. He slipped his fingers between her legs and drew then slowly up along the cleft between her buttocks. Lisa noticed that his fingers glistened. Clearly the maid was thoroughly enjoying every moment of her torment. The maid shifted her position so that her legs parted slightly and her bottom became raised. From her vantage point, Lisa could now see everything that Paul was doing to her.

She watched, dry mouthed, as he moved his fingertips back down the cleft of her bottom. He paused momentarily as they brushed lightly against her tiny sphincter. The maid moaned softly. Paul moved his hand again and this time slipped all four fingers into the soaking hole between her legs. The maid arched her back and groaned with pleasure as he plunged deep inside her. 'Arousal,' hissed Madam Stone.

Lisa's own fingertips found her rapidly dampening pussy and she pulled at the soft flesh as she watched the erotic scene unfolding before her. Paul started twisting and turning his hand inside the young woman's loose sex-lips and the maid circled her hips in response to his incessant probing. Her eyes were closed and her teeth were clenched. She was clearly in ecstasy.

'This is hardly a punishment!' Madam Stone said, sternly. Janet giggled girlishly. The dark woman glared at her and Janet fell silent. Paul eased his fingers slowly from inside the maid's wetness. Lisa watched fascinated as the engorged sex-lips seemed to grip him as he withdrew. He smoothed her juices over the soft, white globes of her backside. The sunlight caught the delicate curves so that they glistened.

Mike moved over and knelt behind the girl with his

face inches from her bottom. 'Teasing,' whispered Madam Stone to Lisa. Mike took a deep breath then blew gently over the firm mounds then leant forward and kissed her gently between them. He began to move his head around and Lisa could see that he was licking every inch of her bottom, soaking the smooth skin with his saliva. He moved back, and nodded to his colleague.

Paul raised his hand high. 'You have been very naughty, Anne. You know that skirts and dresses must be extremely short. I am going to sting your little bottom with my hand. Are you ready?'

'Yes,' whimpered the maid.

Paul looked up at the group. 'What do you think? How many strokes shall I give her? Ten? Twenty?' He looked back at the perfection of the maid's bottom again without waiting for an answer. There was a long pause. Lisa noticed that the young girl was beginning to tremble.

'Torment,' said Madam Stone.

Suddenly, Paul brought his arm down quickly and delivered a resounding blow to the young girl's buttocks. The sound of flesh on flesh seemed to echo around the pool. The maid didn't make a sound. He slapped her again, harder this time and she gave out a muted yelp. A third stroke, then a fourth smacked against the quivering flesh. Lisa could see that the maid's skin was beginning to glow bright pink.

Two further stinging blows of Paul's hand to her backside resounded like the cracking of a whip. The maid was clawing at Paul's legs with her fingernails. There were six further slaps delivered in quick succession until, suddenly, the maid's body stiffened and she squealed in orgasmic joy.

'And satisfaction,' breathed Madam Stone. She stood up and grabbed the hapless girl by the arm to drag her to her feet. The tall woman's expression was severe, but Lisa realised that it was all part of the game. The maid, however, appeared to be terrified.

'You may not display pleasure in the company of senior members of staff,' the fearsome instructress snarled. 'You will go to my room and await further punishment! Now, go!' The maid scurried away into the house. Madam Stone turned to the others. 'It is so difficult to get good staff,' she said, nonchalantly.

As the afternoon wore on, it became clear that the American flight must have been delayed. Madam Stone had disappeared into the house, probably to torment the maid some more. The group began to exchange accounts of past sexual experiences, more as a way of passing the time than for any other reason. The conversation, however, became more and more frank, and the stories increasingly bizarre.

The subject finally turned to surprise encounters. Janet recounted the story of their recent experience with the postman and Lisa added to the tale by telling them about the somewhat erotic holiday photos. Mike volunteered to be the next to confess all.

'You mentioning the holiday snaps reminds me of something that happened to me,' he began, 'and it's weird. It was almost a mirror of what you did with the postman. It was actually my first time. I suppose you could say that I was a bit of a late starter. I was nearly eighteen, and more interested in spending time working out in the gym than chasing girls.'

'No change there, then,' joked Paul.

'Oh, very droll,' Mike sneered. 'Anyway, it was a hot afternoon, much like today, and I was walking back from a really good session at the gym. Because of the weather I hadn't bothered to change, and was still wearing my training gear – you know, low-cut

T-shirt and tight, lycra shorts. I was carrying my normal clothes in my kitbag.

'I was walking past this block of flats, not thinking of much really when I saw the curtains move against one of the ground-floor windows. For no other reason than idle curiosity I watched as they were drawn open by a woman. She wasn't young, probably in her mid-forties, and she was quite plump. The main thing I noticed about her was that she had the most incredibly large bust. She was wearing a lacy sort of dressing-gown, buttoned up to her neck but it did nothing to hide the shape of these huge, well – tits – that's the only word to describe them!

'I stopped dead in my tracks to look at her as she straightened the curtains. Suddenly, she was looking directly at me. I was about to move off when she smiled, a big, friendly grin. I smiled back and she made a sign as if to say, "D'you want to come in?" I paused for a moment, then thought, what the hell?

'As I walked down the short path to the main door I began to feel a little nervous, to say the least. I pushed against the outer door, but it was locked. I was about to turn and head for home when I heard a buzz and a click and the door snapped open. I pushed my way in and found myself in a long corridor with a flight of stairs at the far end. There were doors on both sides. I assumed the door to the woman's flat was the first one so I went to knock on it.

'Before I could, however, the door was opened and she stood there. If anything, she looked a little older than I had first imagined, but her dark eyes seemed to be sending out incredibly sexy signals to me. I smiled awkwardly, trying to think of something to say and looked down. She'd unbuttoned the robe. She was wearing a very frilly nightdress under her dressing-gown. I could make out the shape of a huge, white bra under the thin material, and I could just see that she was also wearing a very large pair of black knickers. It's funny the details you remember, isn't it?'

'Get on with it, Mike,' said Paul, feigning exasperation.

'OK, OK. Now where was I? Oh yes. Anyway, she asked me if I wanted to come in for a coffee. I just nodded and stood there like an idiot. My knees were shaking and my heart was thumping. I hadn't got a clue what I was letting myself in for, and I think that I was more nervous than excited.

'She turned and walked back into the flat, then looked over her shoulder as if to say, "Well, come on, you bloody fool". I followed her obediently, like a lamb to the slaughter. We were in her lounge. She turned to me again and gave me a big smile. Although she was over twice my age she seemed to exude sex, and yet she was the opposite of what I had always thought I wanted in a woman. OK, her tits were huge, but the rest of her looked plump as well. Her face was still very attractive, and she had lovely, big, dark eyes that she used on me to great effect. She never seemed to take them off mine for a moment.

'She told me to close the door and turn the light on, then she walked over to the window and drew the curtains across the window. I did as she'd asked, then sat on the edge of the sofa. She seemed to be having a problem drawing the curtains fully so I jumped up to help her. I managed to do the job without difficulty. We were standing very close – almost touching. She turned her head and looked me straight in the eye. Her smile had gone. She was looking at me in a very serious way, as though I'd done something wrong. I could feel my cock stiffening and for some reason I felt embarrassed. I tore my gaze from hers and fiddled a bit more with the curtains before returning to my seat.

'She stood by the window for a moment, just looking at me. I half-smiled, then looked down at her feet. Her legs were bare, no tights or anything, and she was wearing a fluffy pair of slippers. "I'll go and make the coffee," she said. She walked across the room and disappeared through a door behind me.

'I sat waiting for her like someone waiting to see the dentist. She seemed to take ages until at last she returned carrying a tray. As she walked in front of me, the first thing that I noticed was that the awful slippers had gone, to be replaced by a pair of black, high-heeled shoes. Her legs were covered in black nylon as well; I remember wondering if she was wearing stockings or tights. She nodded to a small coffee table in the centre of the room. "Pull that table in front of you," she said. I did so, and she bent forward rather more than was necessary and placed the tray down. I found myself looking down at an incredible depth of cleavage. Her breasts were swinging free; the bra had gone. I leant forward slightly, but I couldn't quite see her nipples.

'She looked up at me suddenly and I quickly looked away from the melon-sized mounds. She grinned. "D'you want sugar?" she asked. I nodded. "How many?" I asked for two spoons and watched in fascination as she slowly put the sugar in my cup and stirred the coffee. She bent forward even more as she did so. I looked down her flimsy nightie again. I could just make out the edge of one of her nipples. As she stirred the coffee her tits shook rhythmically – it was obvious that she was doing it on purpose but I didn't know what to do or say.

'She looked up at me again. "D'you like the view?" she asked in a husky tone. I apologised clumsily and grabbed my coffee. I managed to spill half of it into the saucer. I tried to take a sip but my hands were shaking so much that I had to put it down before I spilt the lot over myself. I know how your postman felt.

'The woman took up her own drink and sat at the opposite edge of the sofa. She took a sip, then leant back against the arm and crossed her legs. The swish of the nylon made me look down at her legs. I could see the dark edge at the top of one of her stockings and the clasp of a suspender. My cock was hardening by the second, but I still didn't know what to say or what to do. I suppose that I was frightened of putting her off by saying something stupid.

'She put her coffee down on the table and then sat back again. This time she drew her gown back to her sides nonchalantly. Her big breasts jutted out, now covered only by her thin nightie. I could see the dark shapes of her nipples. I looked down at her lap and wondered if she'd still got those dreadful, big knickers on. It was hard to tell, although I couldn't see the dark shape of them under the white lace. "Have you been working out at the gym?" she asked. I just said yes. "You don't say much, do you?" she teased. She leant forward and slipped her gown off. Her nightie was so loose that I thought her breasts were going to fall out as she threw the gown over the back of the sofa. I could feel my face colouring up. "Would you like to see my holiday snaps?" she continued. I said that I would – anything to cover up my embarrassment at not being able to think of a single intelligent thing to say.

'She got up and walked over to a sideboard. As she bent forward to get the album from one of the cupboards I could see the shape of her lovely, big bottom through the white lace. The knickers had gone as well!

'She returned with the album and sat next to me so that our thighs were touching. She rested the book on my lap and opened it. "It was in Spain, last year," she said as we leafed through endless pages of photographs of her and another woman. There were pictures of them standing individually in front of castles, bars and donkeys – you know, the usual kind of stuff. I was beginning to get bored when she turned to a page of snaps of her in a bikini.

'It was yellow and far too small for her ample body. I looked with great interest at her sumptuous curves. She was plump, as I've said, but in all the right places. Her waist was surprisingly narrow and, although her stomach was a bit big, it curved in the sexiest way towards the tiny V of yellow material between her legs. "D'you like those?" she said, quietly. I nodded. "What about these, then?" she said, as she turned the page.

'My throat went dry. The bikini top had gone, and there they were, the most beautiful tits that I could ever have imagined. Although they were huge, they jutted out firmly without the slightest trace of sag. "D'you like big breasts?" she asked. I told her that I did; very much. She took hold of the album, closed it and put it on the table. I looked down at my legs. My cock was fully hard, and its shape was clearly visible through the tight, lycra shorts. I looked up at her guiltily. She smiled broadly. "My word," she said, "whatever's happened to you?" She ran her fingers lightly along my thigh but didn't touch me where I wanted her to. I mumbled something about the pictures being very nice and looked down at my cock. I willed it to shrivel but it seemed to be getting harder. Then a damp patch appeared where the end was resting and I wanted to die. She pulled her hand away from my leg and I thought I'd blown my chance.

'She sat back and moved her hands under her breasts and lifted them. "Would you like to see them for real?" she asked. She didn't wait for my answer. She caught up the hem of her nightie and pulled the flimsy lace over her head quickly. She was naked now, apart from her stockings and suspender belt. She just sat there, with her legs crossed, looking at me as if waiting for me to make a move. My arms were frozen to my sides. I gazed at the massive globes of firm flesh and the long, dark nipples and swallowed hard. After a moment she smiled and took hold of one of my wrists. She drew my hand slowly towards her until my fingertips touched the smooth skin of one of her wonderful tits. I cupped the big mound with the nipple pressed against the palm of my hand. At last, I took the initiative and reached up with my other hand to take hold of her other breast.

'She closed her eyes and started to breathe heavily as I kneaded the plump flesh with my inexpert fingers. She uncrossed her legs and I looked down to see her thick bush of dark hair between them. I leant forward. She opened her eyes and pulled her face away from mine. "No, don't kiss me," she said. I was puzzled, and a little hurt, but my thoughts were quickly turning to more basic things.

'I took my hand from one of her breasts and moved it to her thigh. She opened her legs and I inched my hand upwards until my fingertips touched the damp hair. She gasped loudly and I moved my hand back down her thigh, fearing that I'd gone too far. She responded by grabbing hold of my wrist again and dragging my hand back up between her legs. I cupped her hot, little pussy for a moment, then slipped my middle finger between her soaking wet lips. I remember being surprised at how wet she was. Still gripping my wrist, she groaned and moved my hand against her, as if to teach me how to please her. I was a willing pupil!

'She ordered me to suck her nipples. I obeyed immediately and put my mouth to one of her huge, fleshy mounds and drew the hard, thick nipple between my lips. I sucked it hard and, at the same time, traced the shape of her cunt with my fingertips. I had never even seen one before, let alone touched one.

'Suddenly, she began to tremble and breathe loudly. She grasped my wrist tightly and forced me to rub her rapidly between the legs whilst I continued to suckle her nipple. She groaned loudly and pressed her body against me so that her breast almost covered my face. I could hardly breathe.

'After a moment she relaxed and lay back on the sofa. She pulled my hand from her crotch and let it fall on my lap. There was a long silence. I wasn't sure what had happened – in those days I didn't even know a woman could have an orgasm!

'I looked at her lovely, plump body and watched in amazement at the way her big tits moved as she breathed. The hair between her legs glistened and I could see the pink lips of her pussy clearly. They were invitingly open. I wondered if I was going to fuck a woman at last. The trouble was, my cock was achingly hard and I knew that she would only have to touch it and there was a good chance that I would come.

'She looked at the shape of my erection under the lycra shorts. The material was still visibly damp where my cock had leaked a bit during my excitement. "You're very close, aren't you?" she whispered. I nodded. I wanted to fuck her, but I knew it was hopeless. "How long will it take for you to get hard again if I make you come?" she asked. I told her a few minutes; I really didn't know. When a man is in that sort of state he really believes that he can come again and again. It doesn't seem possible that the incredible, driving lust he feels will disappear as soon as he shoots his load.

'The woman moved to kneel in front of me and reached for the waistband of my shorts. I lifted my bottom from the seat and she pulled them down to my ankles. My cock was pressed rigidly against my stomach. "That's a nice big one," she said. I suppose she said that to all the guys, but it made me happy. She circled it with her fingers and raised it vertically, then squeezed it tightly. The end turned purple. She bent forward and pushed out her tongue, then licked around the head slowly. I watched her in total rapture. I couldn't believe it – a woman was actually licking my cock!

'She moved her hand to grip my cock by the root and engulfed the rest of my stalk in her hot mouth. The inevitable happened. I felt the twinges in my groin and my cock stiffened past the point of no return. "I'm coming!" I shouted. I was trying to warn her but she didn't seem concerned. She sucked me all the harder and I came inside her mouth. My cock throbbed heavily and jet after jet of sperm shot to the back of her throat. Still she sucked and swallowed, determined to drain every last drop. I was in heaven.

'At last, she moved her head from me and sat back on her haunches between my knees. She wiped her mouth on the back of her hand. For a long time we just sat in silence, simply looking at each other. Then she took a swig of coffee. "It's gone cold," she said. "I'll make some more." She got to her feet and picked up the tray, then walked off to the kitchen.

'I sat in dumbfounded silence as she busied herself. My shorts were still round my ankles and my cock was resting loosely on my thigh. I couldn't believe my luck. I had actually come in a woman's mouth! She had actually *swallowed my sperm*!

'She came back into the room carrying two more mugs of coffee and set them down on the table. She'd put on a tiny little maid's apron which just covered her crotch. It was the sexiest thing I had ever seen. She looked down at my ankles and laughed. "Why don't you take your shorts off," she said. "You look ridiculous." I did as she asked, then pulled off my T-shirt, trainers and socks. She knelt on the floor beside me and took my cock nonchalantly in one hand and her coffee mug in the other. As she sipped her drink she casually rubbed me until I was as hard as steel. "Ooh," she said. "That didn't take long!"

'I smiled proudly, then took a couple of swigs of the hot drink before returning the mug to the table. For some reason I was feeling much more confident now and I lay back in the seat to await her next move. She didn't seem to be in any hurry. She just carried on rubbing me, gradually speeding up so that her breasts jiggled with the movement of her arm.

'At last she put her mug down and removed the apron, then knelt in front of me between my legs. She leant forward so that her tits pressed against my erection. She looked up at me and grinned. "You like my big tits, don't you?" she said. I told her again that I loved them. She shook her body from side to side so that her nipples brushed against my ragingly hard stalk then took hold of it and sandwiched it between her fleshy mounds. "Fuck my tits," she ordered. I moved my hips up and down. I couldn't even see my cock, but I could certainly feel what was happening to it!

'After a few moments of this delightful torture she moved back and let my cock fall back against my stomach. She bent her head forward and kissed it lightly on the end, then looked directly into my eyes.

"I think it's time that you fucked me properly," she said, in a husky voice. This is it, I thought, I'm really going to get a fuck! "Is it your first time?" she asked, with a gentle smile. I told her it wasn't, but it was quite obvious from her expression that she didn't believe me.

'She pulled herself up and straddled my thighs. I stared hungrily at her pussy and my cock throbbed. She reached down and took hold of my stalk with one hand whilst parting her sex-lips with the other. She moved herself agonisingly slowly towards my stiff prick, and then paused when the tip was less than an inch from her succulent prize. I looked up at her face with pleading eyes. She smiled and lowered herself further. I felt the tip of my cock touch her fleshy wetness and bit my lip to stop myself from coming again. Then I was inside, just a little, but enough to make me realise why men go mad for the pleasures of sex. Her cunt slowly engulfed every inch of me until she sat heavily on my lap. My instinctive urge was to thrust wildly in and out of her luscious body, but the position that we held made it impossible. She was in control, and she knew it.

'She began to move herself up and down in a steady, undulating way. I looked down and watched, fascinated, as my cock appeared and disappeared over and over again. She was absolutely soaked, and her juices were drenching my thighs. I couldn't get over it – I was fucking, I was actually fucking!

'She sat back on my thighs and started to move her body backwards and forwards along my legs. Her big, soft bottom felt delightful against my muscular limbs and the new position meant that I could see every inch of myself as my cock was absorbed and reabsorbed inside her hot, silky sheath. I could have stayed like this for hours, but she had other ideas.

'She stood up and allowed my glistening cock to fall back against my stomach again, then she turned and knelt on the carpet. Her big, pink bottom was presented to me and, in the state I was in, it was the most desirable thing in the universe. I knelt behind her and she reached between her legs and caught hold of my ragingly hard tool. She guided it into her hot cunt, then moved her body back to force it deep into her once more. This time I could make the running. I gripped her plump buttocks and began to ram hard against them. She began to groan loudly as I pounded backwards and forwards. I leant forward and reached under her body to cup one of her swaying breasts. Despite being on her hands and knees her nipples were brushing against the carpet. I squeezed her tit and hammered into her as hard as I could. Her groans and moans of delight became louder, matching the rhythm of my insistent pounding.

'I could feel my orgasm building up inside my loins. I knew that I couldn't hold back much longer. I asked her if I could come inside her and she said, "Yes, go for it, as hard as you can! Fuck me, fuck me like an animal!" Hearing such coarse words from a woman was the final trigger. I came with an incredible, almost painful surge, the kind that a man usually gets if he can manage to come a second time within a few minutes. I dug my fingernails into her backside and my hips must have become a blur as I thundered in and out of her. The moment was made perfect when, with a sudden cry, she came with me. I fell on to her back, panting heavily, and she collapsed forwards on to the floor. I slipped from inside her and rolled over on to my back.

'I stared at the ceiling for ages. My mind was racing; I was no longer a virgin! Some men say that their first sexual experience is a bit of a let-down. In my case, it couldn't have been better.

'I dressed, and picked up my kitbag. I waited for her to say something, or kiss me goodbye. She merely smiled and waved. Looking back, I think that she was one of those women who will do anything with a lover but won't kiss him, as that would mean she was being unfaithful to her husband.

'And the other, strange thing – we never even knew each other's name.'

'Sex can be brilliant with an older woman,' said Paul. 'I remember one time when –'

'The guests are arriving – quick, go to your rooms and prepare to greet them!' It was Madam Stone who spoke, calling from an upstairs window.

'What do we do?' whispered Janet to Mike as they headed towards the house.

'The maids will have laid out your outfits for you. Dress yourselves and come down to the hall. You'll have plenty of time; Mr Gee usually walks new guests around the gardens when they arrive.'

Janet looked at Lisa excitedly. Now their adventure was really about to start.

Four

The dresses that had been laid out for Janet and Lisa were simple, black evening gowns. Despite their simplicity, however, the clinging material did much to highlight the very different shapes of the two girls' lovely bodies. Janet's slim, lithe shape, with her apple-firm breasts and superbly pert bottom, and Lisa's voluptuous form were revealed in all their perfection. The manner in which the dresses were split from their ankles to their waists precluded the wearing of any underwear whatsoever, a fact which, of course, was unlikely to trouble either of them.

Janet watched her friend enviously as Lisa paraded herself in front of her. Her large breasts bounced heavily as she moved and the shapes of her long nipples were clearly visible through the sheer silk. She would certainly be a hit with the visitors. Lisa stood in front of the mirror and smoothed her hands over her breasts, down her body and across her waist. She then slowly moved them over her buttocks and thighs. 'I love the feel of silk against my naked skin,' she murmured. Janet had to agree. She had always felt there was something innately sexual in the feel of silk against her flesh, cool and as smooth as a lover's tongue.

She stood next to Lisa and looked at her own reflection. She was pleased with the cut of her garment, especially the way that her long legs seemed even longer thanks to the high-cut design. She stood sideways and posed proudly. There was a tantalising glimpse of the curve of her bottom as she moved. She turned her back to the mirror and looked over her shoulder. The dress clung to her buttocks, accentuating their high roundness and highlighting every curve and every inviting detail.

'If we don't get fucked tonight, we never will again,' she murmured.

Lisa laughed. 'Don't you ever think of anything else?' she asked.

'No, do you?'

'We'd better get moving. Come on.'

The girls made final checks on their make-up then, slipping on the stiletto-heeled shoes that had arrived with the dresses, they headed out of their room. They arrived at the poolside within moments and split up, intending to mingle with the guests. Most of the other staff were already there, chatting amiably to the group of newcomers. There were about a dozen couples, most of them in their thirties or early forties. They spoke with loud voices in barely comprehensible drawls which betrayed their middle-class American backgrounds.

There was one of the visitors, however, who captured Janet's immediate attention. He was exceptionally tall, very black and, from the way his expensive jacket hung awkwardly on his massive shoulders, very muscular. He was standing with an elegantly dressed woman of about thirty-five who had long, bright-red hair and breasts that could comfortably vie with Lisa's for sheer size. They thrust arrogantly from within the inadequate cocoon of her jacket, a thin, white blouse straining to contain them. They were certainly an attractive and sexy couple, and Janet found herself wondering what on earth their hang-up could be.

They were engaged in avid conversation with Mr Gee. Janet decided not to interrupt the flow of their apparently heated discourse. Hopefully she would have the chance to get to know the handsome American another time. She looked around for her friend and found that Lisa was already talking to a middle-aged couple close to the buffet table. She was laughing needlessly as she nibbled the end of a cheese straw. The man was large, both in height and girth, with thinning hair and a very loud voice. His wife was a tiny woman, as thin as a pencil, with short, bobbed hair. She was standing meekly at her husband's side and appeared to be totally uninterested in the conversation. Even to Janet's inexperienced eyes the problem here was pretty obvious. A domineering man who no doubt took great pleasure in forcing himself on his unwilling and subservient partner.

'Hello, my name's Kenrick, and this is my wife Page.' Janet swung round to be faced by possibly the youngest couple at the reception party. He was about thirty, tall and not at all bad looking with dark hair and haunting, brown eyes. She bore the appearance of a mid-West farm girl with a fresh-faced, freckled complexion and bright, blue eyes that seemed to be full of laughter. She was much shorter than her husband and was wearing a simple tracksuit, quite the most sensible thing for a long journey. Despite the baggy nature of her attire, Janet could see that she was buxom, if a little on the plump side.

'My name is Janet, Janet Angel,' she said as she held out her hand in greeting.

Kenrick took her hand and shook it vigorously. 'Pleased to meet you, Miss Angel,' he said. 'Pretty name for a pretty girl!'

Janet smiled sweetly at his inane compliment. There was a protracted silence. The woman giggled for no reason. 'It's nice here, isn't it?' she said finally as she feigned interest in her surroundings.

Janet looked around the pool area. 'Yes,' she said, weakly, 'very nice.'

'It's nice anywhere, if you can get it!' bawled the man. Janet cringed inwardly. Page giggled again like a little girl and hugged her husband round the waist.

'Oh, Kennie, you're so horny!' she howled as her giggles became more and more raucous. Her husband joined her in her admiration for his pathetic joke with a loud guffaw. Janet smiled and excused herself, and headed towards the tall, black man who had taken her interest earlier, and who was now standing alone. Their eyes met and he smiled. Janet's heart skipped a beat. The man was positively gorgeous. She made her mind up there and then that whatever his problem was she would help him overcome it. She continued to walk towards him, trying not to look too eager. She was within a few feet of him when Mr Gee held up his hands for silence.

'Ladies and gentlemen,' he called, 'I am sure that our guests are all tired from their journey. The servants will escort them to their rooms, and we will meet for dinner at eight. Afterwards there will be drinks and, I promise, some very special entertainment.'

Janet's immediate thought was that the beautiful black guy was going to see the video, and see her being well and truly fucked. The idea delighted her. Then she realised that Kenrick and Page would see the same scenes and her heart sank.

Dinner was a strangely normal affair, if such a thing was possible under the circumstances. The guests and staff chatted amiably like old friends. Janet found it difficult to imagine that the visitors were here for plainly sexual purposes, and that soon, very soon, it was likely that she would be satisfying her own salacious needs with one or more of them.

The meal finished, three of the couples rose and took their drinks into another room. Janet looked around lazily at the remaining guests. To one side of her sat Kenrick who, for all his inane chatter, seemed quite appealing, at least in looks. Page, his wife, had dressed herself in a clinging, satin catsuit that appeared to be two sizes too small and merely served to accentuate her plumpness. She hung on to her husband's every word and giggled stupidly at the most inappropriate times. Janet found it difficult to suppress the desire to give the silly girl a good spanking.

The tall, black man, whom she had learnt was called Peter, sat with his beautiful wife at the end of the table. He had chosen to wear a smart tuxedo with red bow tie and looked simply stunning to Janet's hungry eyes. His wife had been introduced as Jeannie. She too had chosen evening attire and was wearing a long, black gown trimmed with silver. It was cut low at the front to reveal much of her large breasts. The ample display of pink flesh served as a sumptuous cushion for a clearly expensive pearl necklace. To Janet's profound irritation the couple were once more engaged in deep conversation with Mr Gee.

She looked at the other end of the table. The heavily built, brash American who had cornered Lisa by the pool was continuing to dominate the conversation with his constant boasts of business successes. She found his broad accent irritating in the extreme. His small wife was sitting silently at his side, her eyes fixed on nothing at all. Janet felt sorry for her. She was quite attractive for her age, her complexion bearing few traces of the ravages of time and her mouth full and sensuous. She must have been very lovely when she was younger, Janet thought. How she had ended up with such a bombastic, arrogant braggart was a mystery.

The small woman suddenly looked directly at Janet and smiled gently. Janet returned her smile and the woman looked down at her plate self-consciously. 'Have you been here before?' asked Janet in an attempt to ease the shy woman into conversation. The woman looked up from the table and her expression gave Janet the distinct impression that she was delighted to have been spoken to.

'No, this is our first time. I'm very nervous; it was my husband's idea.'

Janet smiled warmly and reached over to grip the thin woman's tiny wrist. 'There's no need to feel nervous,' she said. 'I'm sure you'll have lots of fun.'

'Oh, I intend to. It may have been Harman's idea, but I fully intend to make the most of it.' She had suddenly seemed to gain in confidence. Janet squeezed her wrist again, then released it and sat back. She took a slow sip of her wine.

'My name's Emily,' said the woman in the acutely American way of making her statement appear to be a question.

'I'm Janet.'

'You're very pretty, Janet. You have lovely eyes, and such long legs. You make me very envious.'

'You're very kind,' replied Janet. The conversation was bordering on the tedious, but at least she had managed to get Emily talking.

'Harman likes the blonde girl, the one with the big chest.' They both looked across at Lisa, who was standing by the window and looking absently into the garden.

'That's Lisa – she's my friend.' Janet thought it wise to establish her relationship with Lisa before Emily said something derogatory.

'Oh, she's very beautiful, don't get me wrong. Harman always goes for tall girls with long, blonde hair and big breasts. It's to get at me, I suppose.' She looked down glumly.

'Men are like that,' said Janet sympathetically. She looked across at Harman. He had managed to corner Paul and Mike and was still droning on loudly, totally oblivious to anything that his wife might be doing. Another one who needs a spanking, Janet thought to herself.

'What does your husband do for a living?' she asked, although she was barely interested.

'He's an area sales manager for a building supplier.'

'Is he doing well?'

'I suppose. He never stops going on about how successful the firm has become thanks to him. Typical salesman – you know, big mouth, big car and little dick.'

Janet laughed out loud, so loud that for a second Emily's husband stopped his discourse and looked across at her. She put her hand over her mouth and avoided his eyes. 'You don't like him very much, do you?' she whispered.

'Not really. Like I said, he's a typical salesman. Sticks that pathetic little cock of his anywhere and everywhere without giving a shit about who he hurts.'

'Why do you stay with him?'

Emily shrugged and took a sip of her wine. 'Usual reasons, money, the kids, you know how it is. He's a good provider, even if he is a total bastard.'

'Have you ever been unfaithful to him?'

'No.' Emily set her glass down on the table and regarded it glumly. Suddenly, her face brightened up. 'But I intend to,' she declared.

Janet leant over and patted her hand. 'Good,' she said, 'and you'll get plenty of opportunities here. Look around; is there anyone here you fancy?'

Emily leant forward and looked earnestly into Janet's eyes. 'I like you,' she said in a hushed voice. The manner in which she accented the word 'you' made it clear to Janet that there was more to her meaning than mere friendship. She took another sip of her wine as she desperately tried to think of an adequate response. The need was taken from her by their host.

'Let's go into the main lounge,' said Mr Gee loudly as he rose from his chair. 'We have a special treat in store for you.'

Janet took a sharp swig of her drink as she realised that he meant the video of the staff's cavorting by the pool. She took a deep breath, then rose and followed the others, feeling like a prisoner being led to the scaffold.

Inside the lounge, Janet found the others grouped around a huge television set. She sat quietly at the back and waited with feelings that were an incongruous mixture of apprehension and excitement. Mr Gee stood in front of the giant, flickering screen.

'Honoured guests,' he began, 'this short presentation is to give you some idea of the delights to come during your stay at Grantham Manor. You will see the staff preparing themselves to please you. Afterwards, they will return to their rooms where they will be given details of their assignments tonight. Should any of them fail to fulfil your every desire you must report the matter to me, and I will see that punishments are administered.'

He turned and nodded to one of the servants, who pressed the appropriate button on the recorder.

* * *

Without a shadow of doubt Lisa was the star of the video. Lingering shots of her large, bouncing breasts or thrusting buttocks seemed to feature in every scene. Janet wasn't sure whether to feel slighted or relieved. Only once did she appear in the short film, and that was a brief close-up of her sucking someone's cock. Janet couldn't remember who the owner was.

Emily moved over to her as soon as the lights went up. 'There wasn't enough of you in it,' she whispered as she sat next to her.

Janet smiled. 'I'm glad,' she said. 'I didn't much like the idea of being filmed.'

'I would have liked to have seen your naked body, I expect you look really gorgeous in the nude.'

Janet looked down at her knees shyly and said nothing. She had had sex with other women on many occasions, of course, but this was the first time that she had been brazenly chatted up by a member of her own sex. She felt a little awkward, but also realised that she was becoming very aroused.

'You don't mind me talking to you in this way, do you?' Emily rested her hand on Janet's thigh as she spoke.

'No, of course not,' she replied. She looked directly into the other woman's eyes. Emily smiled and squeezed Janet's leg gently before moving her hand to stroke the bare flesh of her thigh which had become revealed by the split in the dress. Janet breathed deeply. The fingers moved slowly to the top of her leg and then slipped under her dress until they tickled her bushy curls.

'Emily, it's time we went to our room!' It was Harman's voice that boomed out from the opposite side of the lounge. Emily pulled her hand away from Janet quickly and stood up.

'Perhaps we'll meet some other time,' she said in a conspiratorial tone of voice. Janet nodded and watched Emily as she followed her husband obediently out of the room. She crossed her legs and felt a familiar wetness between her thighs.

Janet eyed the outfit that was being laid out for her with some trepidation. For one thing, there wasn't much of it, and what there was appeared to be very complicated. Strips of leather and lace which were fastened together by large, silver buckles together with the obligatory pair of black, fishnet stockings seemed to be all there was to it apart from a small, black dildo which was tantalisingly attached to one of the straps.

The maid smoothed the sensuous material of the stockings with her fingertips. 'Madam will look beautiful in this,' she said, wistfully. Janet shrugged off her robe and picked up the flimsy garment. She held it to her naked body and tried to work out how to put it on. The maid took it from her. 'Here, Miss, let me help you,' she said. The young girl detached a couple of the buckles with practised fingers and looped a strip of leather between Janet's legs. She drew it up tightly between her buttocks and attached it to a second strip which was then drawn around Janet's waist. She then took hold of a third piece of leather, the strap with the black phallus cleverly attached to it.

The young girl looked directly into Janet's eyes and ran her tongue wetly across her upper lip. Then she bent forward and took the dildo into her mouth and soaked it with her saliva. Standing up again, she deftly eased the hard length of rubber between Janet's soft, wet sex-lips. Janet groaned involuntarily. The maid fixed the remainder of the thin strand to the strip drawn about Janet's waist. Janet shuddered with excitement as the dildo sank into her welcoming flesh. The young girl grinned and took hold of the end of the implement where it protruded from Janet's thick bush. She rested her other hand on Janet's bare bottom and eased the phallus in and out whilst again holding Janet's gaze with her own.

After a few moments of this delightful torment the maid returned to the task of completing the outfit. Janet could only stand and watch as she busied herself until the garment took some semblance of form about her lithe body. Clearly, the young girl had performed this operation many times before.

Eventually the job was done. Janet smoothed the black stockings over her long legs and fixed them to the leather suspenders. A pair of tight, knee-length boots completed the ensemble. She walked slowly over to the large mirror facing the bed. As she moved, she found that the design of the straps which were tightly drawn around her waist and between her legs caused the stiff intruder within her body to move slightly in and out of her hot little sheath. She walked in a circle around the bedroom, thoroughly enjoying the experience. 'God, who needs a man when you've got one of these!' she laughed. The maid giggled coyly.

Janet returned to the mirror and regarded the image of her erotically displayed form with more than a little delight. The narrow, leather straps criss-crossed her body and accentuated her curves. Her breasts were raised high, the flesh covered by black, translucent lace which did nothing to conceal her long, dark nipples. More lace disguised the gentle sweep of her firm, flat stomach and ended just above her crotch. The flat, splayed end of the dildo concealed her pussy, seemingly designed in this way so that the rubber phallus wouldn't slip completely inside her. The leather suspenders were long, which ensured that the stocking-tops were only halfway up her smooth thighs.

Janet turned her back to the mirror. Her round bottom was naked, save for a thin strip of leather between the arrogantly thrusting curves of her buttocks. The image of her perfect bum, framed as it was by the stocking-tops, suspenders and a thick, heavily buckled strap drawn across her lower back that appeared to secure the complete outfit was erotic in the extreme.

She turned to the maid. 'Is this it?' she asked. 'Is this all?'

'Yes Miss,' replied the girl. 'Madam Stone has instructed that this is the costume that you must wear to meet your first clients.'

'Clients?' queried Janet. 'How many are there?'

'Just two. Mr and Mrs Rose. You must remember them from the reception party. She was the small, thin woman.'

'Emily?'

'Yes miss.'

Janet smiled inwardly as she remembered the way Emily had come on to her earlier that evening. Although the woman was over twice her age there was something intensely sexual about her. In a strange way, Janet knew that she could even put up with the attentions of her bombastic husband, Harman, if it meant that she could make love with the shy, enigmatic Mrs Rose.

'Do I wait for them here?' she asked as the maid made to leave the bedroom.

'No miss. I'm sorry – I should have told you. You are to report to their room, number seven.' The maid left the room and carefully closed the door behind her.

'Good thing that I asked,' Janet mumbled to herself. She had watched the young girl receive a good spanking the previous day and had felt a little sympathy for her. Now she sensed that she would quite enjoy administering such a punishment to the stupid girl herself.

She checked her appearance once more in the mirror then pulled on her robe. Wrapping the silk garment around her exotic form she opened the door and nervously headed along the corridor towards room number seven.

Janet reached the door quickly and knocked nervously on the heavy, wooden panel. The door was opened almost immediately. To her surprise, instead of being greeted by Mr or Mrs Rose, she was faced with the Amazonian form of Madam Stone. The woman grinned broadly, flashing her dazzlingly white teeth, and beckoned for her to enter. Janet moved into the room and looked around. They were alone.

'I thought –,' she began.

Madam Stone silenced her by putting a finger to her lips. 'Mr Rose is waiting for you in the bedroom,' she whispered, 'and his wife is preparing herself. I am here to ensure that our clients are satisfied with the service we provide. There has not been sufficient time to give you separate instruction, so this will be your first lesson.'

Janet regarded Madam Stone questioningly whilst she admired the exquisite form of the tall, black woman dressed in tight, PVC jeans and a see-through, net top. She recalled Lisa's enigmatic description of her 'first lesson' and her excitement and curiosity mounted. Before she could speak, however, Madam Stone put her hand to Janet's crotch and eased the black dildo from inside her hot little sheath. 'It's reversible,' her instructress whispered with a grin.

She twisted the implement around until the flat base pressed against Janet's moist sex-lips. The phallus jutted forwards ingeniously like a small but perfectly formed penis. Janet tried to suppress a giggle, but without success.

Madam Stone squeezed Janet's breast and kissed her lightly on the forehead. 'I am here merely to observe your performance,' she said as she led her across the room towards a partly open door. 'Afterwards, we will appraise the situation and decide what further instruction you may require.'

Madam Stone opened the door and Janet followed her into what turned out to be a large bedroom. She gasped at the sight that met her eyes. Harman, the brash and powerful executive, lay naked on the bed on his back. His wrists and ankles had been secured by thick, leather bonds to the four corners of the bed so that his body was splayed out in abject vulnerability. His small cock jutted firmly upwards. He was clearly delighted with his acquiescent vulnerability. He stared open mouthed at Janet and she saw his penis throb, sending a small jet of clear fluid over his hairy chest. She moved over to him and smoothed the cream into his skin.

'What are you going to do to me?' he said, his voice trembling with excitement.

'Anything that I want,' replied Janet. Madam Stone smiled broadly to indicate her approval and sat down on a nearby chair to observe the proceedings. Janet ran her hand over his paunch and circled his hard stalk with her fingers. His body was hardly the most appealing that she'd ever seen, but there was something strangely arousing about being in control of such a self-important and domineering individual.

She released her grip of his cock and let it fall to his stomach then walked slowly around the bed.

Harman's eyes followed her as she moved. His expression was of both fear and lust. Janet clambered on to the bed and squatted over his chest. She felt his hairs tickling against her bottom as she moved herself so that the jutting dildo was inches from his face. 'Suck it,' she commanded, 'and taste me.'

Harman raised his head from the pillow as best he could and took the black phallus between his thin lips. Janet eased herself forwards and forced the full length into his mouth. He suckled it voraciously. She undulated her hips and fucked his face steadily whilst reaching back with one hand and gripping his steel-hard erection. His stalk throbbed again and his cream soaked her fingers.

'That's the most beautiful sight that I have ever seen.' Janet recognised the voice as that of Emily, Harman's petite and quiet spouse. She swung round to see her standing at the foot of the bed. She was naked, save for a pair of black stockings and matching suspender-belt. To Janet's surprise and delight, she saw that Emily's pussy was completely shaven, and the engorged lips were pierced by about half a dozen small, silver rings. Her waist was very slim and her breasts were tiny, but her nipples were long and fiercely erect. These, too, had been pierced, this time with larger rings that glinted with the reflected light.

Janet eased the dildo from her husband's mouth and slipped from the bed to stand face to face with Emily. Madam Stone said nothing. Instead, she simply sat back in her chair and crossed her legs as though she was awaiting a demonstration of some kind. Emily took hold of the phallus protruding from Janet's crotch and moved it upwards, then slipped the fingers of her other hand into Janet's soaked cunt.

'Oh, we are going to have such a lovely time,' Emily breathed. She eased all four fingers into Janet's welcoming warmth, which made Janet shudder with desire. She returned the compliment and fondled Emily's succulent flesh, thrilling to the feel of the rings playing against her fingertips. Their mouths met and their tongues entwined in a deep, passionate kiss.

'What about me?' Harman complained. Emily pulled away from Janet and stood looking at her husband contemptuously.

'What *about* you?' she queried as though addressing a stupid child. 'Look at you; fat, balding, and with an apology for a dick. I expect Janet's had cocks twice that size.'

Harman turned his head to look at Janet. 'Have you?' he asked.

She realised that this was all part of the game. 'Yes,' she replied after a moment. 'Three times as big, sometimes.'

'See?' said Emily triumphantly, 'and you lie there expecting her to be turned on by that pathetic specimen? You need to be taught a lesson!'

Harman struggled vainly against his restraints. 'This wasn't what was supposed to happen!' he bellowed. 'What the hell's got into you, Emily?'

'Not you, that's for sure,' she replied triumphantly. She walked over to a cabinet and opened one of the drawers from which she withdrew a vicious-looking multi-thonged whip. Janet felt her heart jump in excited anticipation. Emily handed the whip to her.

'Thrash him,' she said venomously. 'Make him suffer for all the years that he has treated me like dirt!'

Janet ran the thick strands of leather through her fingers, then raised the whip above her head. Harman's expression was one of total terror, but his cock remained firmly erect. She brought the flail down swiftly across his upper legs and he yelped loudly. She repeated the action, this time across his paunchy stomach, then lashed him a third time, again over his reddening thighs.

'Harder!' barked Emily. Janet whipped her hapless victim with greater force. The leather strands stung the flesh of his crotch and narrowly missed his fearsomely hard stalk. Almost immediately, Harman threw his head back and groaned as sperm gushed from his throbbing cock to soak his stomach. Emily jumped forward and grabbed hold of his prick and stuffed it into her mouth. Janet watched bemused as Emily sated her husband's lust, and wondered what was going to happen next.

She didn't have long to wait. Emily licked the cream from her husband's stomach then stood erect and took Janet in her arms. They kissed again, and Emily pushed her tongue purposely into her mouth. Janet savoured the taste and texture of Harman's release as they shared this most erotic embrace and she knew that she would do anything that was asked of her.

'Jesus, Emily, you kissed her! You kissed another woman!' Harman had plainly not witnessed such an event before. Janet felt a warm feeling of satisfaction inside herself as Emily led her away from the bed and lay on a nearby sofa. She opened her legs wide and pulled at the rings which pierced her sex-lips. 'I want you to lick me,' she purred, 'and then I want you to fuck me with that.' She indicated the jutting phallus between Janet's legs. Janet knelt on the floor and moved her head between Emily's thighs. She breathed in the strong, womanly scent. She ran her tongue along the inside of her thigh and then circled the tip around the pouting lips of her pussy. Emily pulled harder at the rings, opening herself in readiness for Janet's searching mouth. Janet licked tenderly around the lips, then took one of the rings between her teeth. Emily moaned as Janet tugged at the ring, then mewed happily as she dipped her tongue into her hot, wet cunt. Covering her pussy with her mouth, Janet sucked the lips hard and drew the flesh between her teeth whilst her tongue probed ever deeper. Emily began to move her hips against her rhythmically, and her breathing became sharp and laboured. Janet moved her mouth upwards and flicked the tip of her tongue over Emily's hard bud. She heard her lover gasp with delight and allowed her tongue to flutter rapidly over her clitoris.

Suddenly, Emily grabbed her by the hair and forced her head upwards. 'Fuck me, fuck me now!' she implored. Janet was in no mood to disobey. She moved between Emily's legs and knelt on the sofa. She looked down at herself. The black dildo seemed to be part of her body, inches away from Emily's luscious target. This was a new experience for her, and she couldn't wait.

She inched forwards until the head of the implement pressed against the soft, receptive lips of her lover's pussy. She moved in slowly, until their groins met. They kissed, and Janet began rubbing her pubic bone against Emily's and felt the other woman's hands stroking and fondling her bottom. She would have been content to continue with these movements, but Emily had other ideas.

'I said fuck me!' she ordered. Janet immediately began to move the dildo in and out rapidly. Emily closed her eyes and groaned happily. As she thrust her hips, Janet found that the pressure of the flat base of the phallus rubbed against her perfectly, probably giving her as much pleasure as she was giving to the writhing woman beneath her. She moved faster and faster. Emily eased a finger into Janet's anus which caused her to come with a shout of surprise and delight. It was so unexpected. The suddenness of her release made it all the more pleasurable. She rammed the dildo as hard as she could in and out of Emily's cunt until, to her joy, her lover orgasmed too, filling the room with squeals of passion.

Janet allowed the hard rubber to slip from inside her friend and sat back on the sofa. Harman was watching them wide eyed from his prone position on the bed. His cock was once again firmly erect and Janet knew that they were not finished with her yet.

She looked across at Madam Stone. Her mentor sat impassively, as though making mental notes of things to be discussed at a later time. Janet considered it strange that anybody could sit so close to a scene of extreme debauchery and not yearn to become part of the delightful excesses that she was witnessing.

After a few moments, Emily rose from the sofa and took Janet's hand. She led her to the bed and they stood regarding the prostrate form of her husband in silence. His cock was as stiff as before and his eyes were pleading. Emily unhooked the dildo from Janet's costume and threw it on to the floor. Harman's gaze fell immediately to Janet's naked crotch and he licked his lips hungrily.

'Fuck him,' Emily hissed. 'He's not much, but he shouldn't come too quickly.'

As Janet straddled the prone, shackled form, Emily left the room. Janet squatted directly over Harman's groin and took hold of his small, but extremely hard cock and guided it into her soaked opening. She sat down on him and absorbed him completely in one movement. She could hardly feel his tiny cock inside her, so aroused had she become. She leant forward and gripped his shoulders, then began to move herself up and down. To her annoyance, he fell from inside her a couple of times but, with perseverance, she managed to build up a steady rhythm. She moved in such a way that she could hold his erection firmly inside her hot sheath whilst rubbing her clitoris against his rough pubic hair and soon started to enjoy the experience.

A door opened and Emily returned. This time it was she who was wearing a dildo which jutted from her crotch with startling realism. It was pink, heavily veined and at least twice a large as the one Janet had been using. She knelt on the bed behind Janet and kissed her bottom lightly. 'Don't stop,' she whispered.

Janet resumed her grinding movements against the man beneath her. Suddenly she gasped as she felt the wet touch of Emily's tongue to her anus. She held herself still as the other woman probed her tight orifice deeply with her tongue. Harman raised his head and took her nipple into his mouth and rasped his teeth gently against her tender flesh whilst his wife continued to tongue-fuck Janet's arse. She seemed to be deliberately soaking the area with her saliva.

Janet felt Emily push two, or possibly three fingers into her anus and knew that she was being prepared. Emily turned and twisted her fingers, opening her in readiness for pleasures to come. Then, slowly, she eased her fingers out of Janet's bottom. Janet waited with mounting excitement. At last, she sensed the pressure of the rubber phallus against the tightness of her bottom. She felt the perfectly formed head slip into her until her sphincter gripped it firmly under the ridge. Then it was inched steadily in and out, ever deeper until Emily's groin at last crushed against her buttocks.

Janet bit her lip as Emily began to fuck her bottom with all the finesse of the most experienced male lover. Harman, meanwhile seemed content to allow her to use him as she pleased. As far as Janet was concerned, he might have just as well not existed, and she realised that this, of course, was exactly what Emily wanted.

Determined not to mention him or even acknowledge his presence, Janet began to respond to Emily's incessant thrusts with groans of pleasure and backward movements of her own. 'Oh, Emily,' she moaned, 'that feels so good! I love to be fucked there! Do it, do it harder!'

Emily gripped Janet's hips and hammered the dildo hard and fast into her tight sheath. She fucked her with such ferocity that Janet was forced along Harman's body and his little cock slipped from inside her. She moved slowly but deliberately upwards until her pussy was inches from his mouth. He didn't need telling what she wanted. He raised his head and licked her furiously whilst Emily continued to fuck her bottom mercilessly. Janet camc with a squeal and her juices gushed from her cunt to soak Harman's face. 'Oh, Emily,' she gasped, 'that was wonderful! You're the best, the very best!'

'What about me?' Harman said, for a second time that evening.

Janet merely smiled patronisingly.

Emily slowly slid the stiff phallus from Janet's bottom and clambered stiffly from on top of her husband. Still sporting the huge appendage, Emily moved round the bed and unshackled Harman's arms and legs. He sat up and rubbed his wrists.

'I think we'll let Harman have his reward, now,' said Emily, sweetly. 'Lie on the bed, Janet.'

She did as ordered, and the couple moved rapidly to secure her ankles, leaving her arms free. Now it was her turn to feel vulnerable. The married couple stood by the bed looking at her for a moment and she began to tremble with anticipation. Emily moved to kneel between her outstretched legs. At first she simply gazed at Janet's obscenely displayed genitals. 'You have a beautiful little cunt,' she purred. Janet said nothing.

Harman moved to kneel at her side and offered his hard erection to her face. Janet opened her mouth and took it between her lips. She circled it with her tongue and sucked the stiff flesh wetly. Meanwhile, Emily began to lick her between the legs with all the expertise of one well versed in such practices. Janet bobbed her head back and forth, easily able to take Harman's full length within her wet mouth. He hardly moved, seemingly quite content to leave it all to her. He shifted himself across her and she gripped his plump buttocks tightly as she sucked him.

To her dismay Emily stopped licking her pussy but, as she had half expected, her lover's tongue was quickly replaced by the touch of the monstrous dildo against her suppliant sex-lips. She gave a muffled moan as the thick, hard stalk was eased inside her cunt and she was quickly made to absorb the full length. Emily fucked her steadily whilst rubbing her clitoris rapidly with her fingertips. Janet responded by snaking her arm between Harman's legs until her fingertips found Emily's hard little bud. She rubbed it gently as the older woman thrust in and out of her whilst continuing to suck voraciously on Harman's throbbing cock.

After a few delightful minutes Emily eased the hard implement from inside her and Harman moved his heavy body downwards. He slipped into Janet's suppliant warmth easily. He held himself still, then groaned loudly. Janet tried to see what was happening but his bulk prevented it. His hips were moving against her but his stalk was barely moving inside her pussy. Then, as the movements became more rapid and forceful, she realised what was going on. Emily was behind him, fucking him with the massive dildo as he lay with his cock embedded inside her. He was clearly enjoying the experience and came almost immediately, sending jet after jet of hot cream into Janet's soaking sheath. A groan from behind him told her that Emily had shared his release. Janet stiffened the muscles of her groin in an effort to join them in their pleasure but they moved away from her too quickly.

The couple unclasped the bonds from Janet's ankles and she moved from the bed to sit on the sofa. Emily and Harman lay together on the bed with their arms entwined about each other. They were quite obviously oblivious to Janet's or Madam Stone's presence.

The assignment was complete.

Janet towelled herself quickly, her body fresh and glowing from the effects of the hot shower. Her pussy and anus still ached pleasurably, despite the fact that it had been over an hour since she and her instructress had left Emily and Harman to indulge in their continued mutual delights together.

Madam Stone had ordered Janet to wait for her in her room, where she intended to discuss her performance with the American couple. Janet smiled to herself as she donned a short, silk robe. Madam Stone couldn't possibly have any criticisms to offer, only praise. She sat by the open window and gazed out over the fields. The moon glowed brightly in a cloudless sky and the distant trees seemed to shimmer in the silvery light. Janet felt good, very good. She closed her eyes and relaxed, bathed by the soothing ambience of an English summer's evening.

There was a loud rap at the door and it was immediately opened. Madam Stone entered, closing the door heavily behind her. Janet rose to her feet confidently but her feelings of self-esteem faded quickly when she saw the expression on Madam's face. She was clearly displeased.

'What is it? What's the matter?' said Janet, with genuine concern.

Madam Stone walked briskly forward and stood less than a couple of feet in front of her. She had changed her clothing, and was now wearing a pair of leather jeans and a tight-fitting leather waistcoat which was straining to contain her bulging breasts. At any other time, Janet would have been immediately aroused by the sight of the statuesque figure before her.

'Sit down, Janet,' said Madam Stone brusquely. Janet obeyed immediately. Madam remained standing with her legs apart and her hands resting squarely on her broad hips.

'Have I done something wrong?' Janet felt a coldness in the pit of her stomach. Her instructress said nothing for a few, agonising moments, then shook her head in exasperation.

'You disappointed me, Janet,' she said coldly. 'I had expected better, much better.'

'I don't understand,' Janet protested. 'Mr and Mrs Rose seemed perfectly satisfied. Have they complained?'

'A man or a woman can achieve satisfaction with simple masturbation. That is not what we're here for.'

'But they enjoyed themselves, didn't they? I did everything that they wanted, especially for Emily.'

'Exactly!' said Madam Stone, sitting down on a chair opposite Janet, 'and they could have achieved the same result with a common prostitute! We have to deliver more, much more!'

'I don't understand. What else could I have done?' Janet was trembling, more with anger than fear. Her pride was severely dented, and she didn't like it.

'There was no finesse, no imagination. You threw yourself on them without a thought. You must learn the secrets of true arousal, something you will know as ATTS.'

'ATTS?'

'Your friend, Lisa learnt the meaning of the term quickly. Arousal, Teasing, Torment and Satisfaction. Simple to remember, but not so easy to perfect. The Roses were both fully aroused, but you moved immediately to satisfaction, thereby causing them to miss the important stages in between.'

'But they both came, didn't they?'

'Indeed they did, just as they do whenever they make love together. Your task was to make it different, memorable.'

'But how,' said Janet, sadly. 'I really don't understand what I did wrong.'

'My task is to instruct you, which I will do, after you have been punished.'

'Punished? Why?' Janet began to tremble again, this time with trepidation.

'Grantham Manor has a proud tradition of always giving satisfaction to its clients. You have compromised that guarantee with your shoddy performance. I have taken into account the fact that you were untrained, and that I had mistakenly thought you capable of delivering the service which our clients had every right to expect. I, too, will be punished for my error, at the hands of Mr Gee himself. Your correction will be less severe but, nevertheless, you need to be taught a lesson!'

Madam Stone stood and clapped her hands loudly. The door to the bedroom opened and two male servants entered wearing nothing but black, leather pouches which just covered their bulging genitals. They stood by the open door in silence. A third figure appeared. Janet gasped and rose to her feet.

'Lisa!' Her friend entered the room and moved quickly to stand at Madam Stone's side with her hands clasped behind her back. She was dressed in a tight, leather basque of the deepest red. Her massive breasts were bared and thrust forward arrogantly, her nipples hard and erect. The garment ended just below Lisa's waist, long, leather suspenders stretching to support bright-red stockings which were encased almost completely by shiny PVC thigh-boots. The picture was erotic in the extreme, and Janet felt her throat become dry as she stared, open mouthed, at her friend.

Lisa brought her hands from behind her back and Janet shivered with excitement. Her friend was holding the handle of a wicked-looking tawse in one hand whilst playing the leather strands casually across the fingers of the other. There was an almost manic grin on the beautiful blonde's face. Janet looked down between her friend's legs. Her shaven sex-lips were red and engorged, and her inner thighs glistened damply. Janet felt her own pussy throb with expectation.

'Prepare her!' Madam Stone barked the order and the two servants moved quickly to take Janet firmly by the arms. The silk robe was ripped unceremoniously from her shoulders and she stood shivering and naked, her head bowed in silent acquiescence.

'Turn her!' The men obeyed the order immediately and forced Janet to bend almost double with her legs splayed apart. The servants sat on two conveniently placed chairs and gripped her wrists tightly. Janet couldn't have moved if she had wanted to – but she didn't want to. Holding this submissive position and knowing that she was completely at Lisa and Madam Stone's mercy thrilled her in a way that she wouldn't have thought possible until now. She felt the lips of her pussy opening and a trickle of her juice began to slip down her inner thigh like a warm raindrop on a pane of glass.

'Now Lisa, teach her. Teach your friend what you have learnt so that she, too may know the meaning of ATTS.' Madam Stone mouthed the mnemonic with loving sensuality, and Janet shivered. She heard Lisa move forward to stand behind her. There was a long pause. Janet's heart was thumping loudly inside her chest, and her inner thighs were becoming soaked. Suddenly, she gasped as she felt the leather strands drawn gently across her bottom. She stiffened her buttocks as she awaited the first kiss of the lash, but it didn't come. Instead, the full length of the whip-handle was drawn firmly against the pouting lips of her pussy then moved upwards so that the strands slipped slowly between her pert globes of flesh and the leather became soaked with her juices.

'You have the most perfect bottom,' breathed Lisa as she playfully caressed Janet's taut flesh with the tawse. 'It will be such a shame to mark it.'

Janet felt the whip being moved from her. Now, she was sure she would feel the first stroke. She closed her eyes. There was another long pause. Janet's knees trembled with her eager expectation. 'Do it, please!' she begged. She sensed Lisa moving behind her, then felt her friend's warm breath against her bottom. 'Lisa, what are you doing to me?' she said desperately. The blonde said nothing, but kissed Janet's bottom lightly before drawing her tongue wetly between her buttocks. 'Oh, God, I can't stand it!' she pleaded. She opened her eyes to be met with the sight of the two servants' pouches bulging ludicrously as their erections strained for release from the leather. She wanted both of them in her mouth whilst Lisa licked her bottom. She looked up at the men's faces and ran her tongue suggestively across her lips but the servants sat impassively and ignored her.

Lisa was probing her anus with her long tongue now, at the same time slipping the thick handle of the whip between her soaking pussy-lips. Then she moved from her, and trailed the strands of leather once more over her bottom. Suddenly, Janet felt a sharp, stinging pain as the whip at last lashed across her trembling flesh. She gasped loudly and her knees started to buckle. Despite the shock and the severity of the stroke she knew she wanted more – much more. She wasn't to be disappointed. Lisa whipped her again, the strands spreading uniformly across Janet's quivering buttocks and she yelped with pleasure and pain.

It took just one more stroke, one more kiss of the flail and Janet came with a squeal. The men gripped her tightly but she sank to her knees and sobbed with joyous release. Her pussy was alive with throbbing sensation and her bottom stung hotly. Lisa moved behind her again and, once more, began to run her tongue wetly over her tortured flesh as if to soothe the pain. The servants relaxed their grip of her wrists and one of them tugged the leather pouch from his groin to reveal a superbly stiff cock. He shuffled forwards and Janet took him greedily into her mouth, at the same time reaching out and extricating the other man's stalk from within his pouch. She rubbed the second shaft furiously as she continued to suck the first whilst Lisa lapped hungrily against her bottom.

Janet moved her head back and allowed the thick cock to fall from her lips. She looked up at the first servant through wild eyes. 'Fuck me,' she commanded. 'That's an order!'

The man didn't need telling twice. He moved quickly behind her and immediately rammed his fearsome weapon into her. She gasped audibly as the head of his long, thick cock pounded against her cervix. The second man moved forward and she took his smaller, but not insubstantial length into her mouth. Lisa, meanwhile had somehow managed to wriggle her head under Janet's crotch, and she was now flicking the tip of her tongue rapidly over her friend's clitoris. Janet took the cock from her mouth and looked round at Madam Stone. She nodded her approval, and a trace of a smile appeared across her lips. If this was punishment, Janet thought to herself, then she must be disobedient many more times.

Janet sat alone by the pool-side and watched lazily as the slight breeze caught the surface of the water, causing it to shimmer in the moonlight. She had learnt much from her chastisement. She now understood what Madam Stone meant; that the build-up to a magnificent sexual encounter could be, no, should be as exciting as the act itself. When Lisa had produced the whip she had felt both frightened and aroused but, nevertheless, had trusted her friend not to inflict any unreasonable pain. But Lisa had teased her for what seemed like an age by playing the strands of leather across her bottom, tickling and teasing her unmercifully until she felt like crying out for the kiss of the lash. Even the wet caress of Lisa's tongue against her bottom, a sensation that would normally have been enough to send her into the delightful oblivion of orgasm, had failed to satisfy her carnal needs. She had literally craved for the whip, and she had yearned for it to sting her flesh. When, at last it came, that first stroke had caused her cunt to burn with an alarming need for release. The second, delivered so expertly when she was least expecting it had increased her desire to fever pitch, and the third – *the third*!

Janet automatically slipped her hand between her denim-clad legs and caressed herself firmly as she remembered the power of the orgasm that had torn through her body as the leather strands stung her buttocks for the third and last time. Arousal, teasing, torment and satisfaction. These would be her by-words from now on.

She heard a noise coming from behind her, like the sound of a chair being moved. She turned her head in the direction of the sound and peered into the semi-darkness. 'Who's there?' she said sharply. Her words were carried away by the breeze and became lost in the night. Janet held her breath and strained to hear. Another noise, this time the unmistakable sound of footsteps moving towards her. She leapt to her feet. 'I said, who's there?' she cried, angrily. Somebody, or something moved in the shadows, then she heard the patio door slide open. Janet walked to the house and entered, just in time to see the unmistakable figure of Mr Gee disappearing through a small door set under the staircase. She followed, feeling a little confused. This was his house; why should he be creeping about in the darkness? And why wouldn't he answer her?

She opened the door cautiously. A single, dim light bulb illuminated a steep, narrow stairway which descended into the shadows. She moved slowly down, her hand gripping the rail tightly. Suddenly she heard voices. She stopped, her heart thumping madly. She recognised one of the voices as that of her host, but the other was unknown to her. It was cracked and monotone, seemingly that of a much older man. She listened hard, endeavouring to pick up snatches of the conversation but too scared to move nearer.

'They will arrive tomorrow,' she heard Mr Gee say, 'and this time we will not fail.'

Janet couldn't make out the old man's mumbled response and inched forwards a little to the edge of the step on which she was standing. 'They are the daughters of the rich and powerful, just as you ordered.'

'And they will be suitably prepared?' This time, the old man's voice seemed much clearer now, and the tone was tinged with cruel excitement. Janet shivered. There was something wrong here, and she knew that she must not be caught eavesdropping. She turned and moved quickly but silently back up the steps and through the door. She closed the door quietly, painfully easing the catch soundlessly.

'What are you doing?' Janet swung round to face Madam Stone standing at the foot of the staircase, her expression one of fury.

'I, I heard a noise,' said Janet, lamely.

'What noise?' said Madam Stone as she strode over to confront her. She gripped Janet's arm roughly.

'I don't know, just a noise.' Janet was beginning to tremble visibly.

Madam Stone gripped her even more tightly and Janet winced with pain. 'You must never, never enter that door again. It leads to Mr Gee's private apartment. No one must enter at any time. Do you understand?'

Janet looked at the other woman's dark features in terror. The large, brown eyes were blazing with anger and her full lips were drawn back to bare her blindingly white teeth.

'I said, do you understand?' repeated Madam Stone as she gripped Janet with both hands and shook her. Janet nodded.

'I, I'm sorry,' she sobbed. 'I didn't mean any harm.'

Madam Stone relaxed her grip of Janet's arms and her expression softened. She seemed to force a smile. 'Mr Gee is very strict about his privacy. Now, off to bed. You have a busy day ahead of you. Tomorrow the students arrive, young girls who are here to learn all that you can teach. You must wake fully refreshed.'

Janet hurried up the stairs, glad to be away from the woman with whom, only hours before, she had been happy to indulge her most carnal desires.

Five

'There's something very definitely wrong here.'

Lisa sipped thoughtfully on her iced drink as she listened to Janet's story of the previous evening's encounter. Her friend was clearly worried, but Lisa couldn't bring herself to feel the same way, preferring instead to dismiss any doubts from her mind. 'You're imagining things,' she said, eventually.

'No, no, I'm certain that something's going on,' continued Janet emphatically. 'The way that Madam Stone acted – she seemed really frightened and very angry with me.'

'We've been told not to go into Mr Gee's private rooms. She was right to tell you off. I'm only surprised that she didn't punish you severely.'

Janet leant forward in her chair as if to emphasise her concern. 'I wouldn't have minded that,' she breathed. 'In fact, I was disappointed that she didn't beat me. That makes it all the more strange.'

Lisa shrugged and looked across the pool towards the garden. Although it was barely ten in the morning the sun was already hot. It promised to be another beautiful day.

'What about the voice I heard? It sounded like, like ...' Janet stood up and walked to the edge of the pool.

'Like the old man?'

Janet swung round and stood squarely facing her friend with her hands resting on her hips. 'Yes, the old man. I'm sure it was him.'

'Now I know that you're imagining things,' said Lisa dismissively. 'He's gone; he won't bother us again.'

'How do you know? He was so powerful. I'm frightened, Lisa.'

'And I'm fed up with you going on like this,' said Lisa, banging her glass down on the table. 'We've got everything we could possibly want here – luxurious surroundings, nice people and as much sex as we could ever need. Forget about it.'

Janet looked at her friend in exasperation. She opened her mouth to speak, then clearly thought better of it and walked back into the house. Lisa watched her go as she took up her drink once more and put the glass to her lips. She understood her friend's concern, of course, but they had already beaten the old man at his own game, and that was that.

She put down her drink and adjusted the sun-lounger to a near horizontal position then removed her skimpy T-shirt. She lay back to soak in the sun, naked now save for a tiny, black G-string. This is all so perfect, she thought. Nothing could possibly be wrong.

'Can I fetch Madam some more ice?' The voice made Lisa jump and she swung round to see one of the male servants standing behind her. He was tall and powerfully built, with handsome, Mediterranean features and short, black hair. He was wearing the normal servants' uniform of tight, lycra shorts and bow tie and his tanned, muscular body looked most appealing in the bright sunlight.

Lisa sat up slowly, and noticed that his gaze fell to

her breasts. Her nipples hardened immediately. 'Not just now, thank you,' she said as she rose to her feet. 'I feel like a swim. Care to join me?'

'It is not permitted, Madam,' he said in a stiff monotone.

Lisa wasn't having any of it. She walked over to stand in front of him and rested her hand on his firm chest. The servant looked down nervously. Lisa could see that his eyes were still firmly fixed on her heaving breasts.

'Oh, come on,' she breathed as she stroked the muscles of his torso gently. 'You're sweating. The water will cool you down.'

'If Madam insists,' he answered.

'Madam does insist.' Lisa quickly slipped her G-string down to her ankles and stepped out of it. The man stared at her hairless pussy and she saw him swallow hard. 'Well?' she said, tilting her head to one side and running her tongue over her lips. The servant suddenly seemed to make a decision and kicked off his sandals. He stood for a moment as if unsure again, then wrenched down his shorts. Lisa saw that his cock was already thickening up nicely. She turned her back to him and walked slowly to the edge of the pool. She sat on the marble tiles and dipped her feet into the water. She turned her head to look back at her prospective conquest. He still appeared reluctant to join her.

Lisa leant back on her hands so that her breasts jutted forward hugely. That was all that was needed. As the servant walked towards her his cock thickened and hardened more and more with every step until, by the time he reached her and sat by her side, he had a full, and quite magnificent erection. She circled his stiffness with her fingers and then squeezed it firmly. 'Let's get into the pool,' she breathed. Letting go of his cock, she slipped into the cool water and swam lazily away from him on her back. He followed immediately, and was soon swimming by her side.

They reached the other side of the pool and Lisa clung on to the edge with her breasts pressed against the tiles. The coolness of the marble merely served to coax her nipples to full erection. She allowed her legs to drift in the water, kicking them gently. She felt the servant catch hold of one of her ankles and then the other. Suddenly, he tugged hard at her legs and she was pulled away from the edge and under the water. She surfaced laughing and flung her arms around his neck. His serious, subservient expression had gone; he was grinning like a schoolboy. Lisa pressed her body against his and kissed him passionately on the lips. She could feel his hardness digging into the firm flesh of her stomach as she moved against him. The pool was just shallow enough for them to stand with the water up to their necks. They kissed deeply with their tongues lapping against each other in a frenzy of passion. Lisa reached down and gripped his cock tightly, then suddenly broke away from him and swam rapidly to the far end of the swimming pool.

He caught her as she reached the edge. She gripped the chrome bars of a ladder just as he grabbed hold of her ankles once more. This time, he didn't try to pull her away but, instead spread her legs wide apart and moved his body to stand between them. This was the shallowest part of the pool, and the water barely reached his waist. Lisa looked over her shoulder and saw the end of his cock protruding from the surface. His intention was clear.

She turned her face away and waited for the inevitable. She felt the tip of his erection touch her bottom. She reached under herself and gripped the thick stalk, then guided it to her sex-lips. He pushed deep into her with one, long movement and she groaned with pleasure. The servant let go of her ankles and she curved her legs around his thighs with her heels digging into the taut flesh of his backside. He began to fuck her in earnest. The water churned as he humped rapidly backwards and forwards. With each forward thrust he rammed the head of his substantial length hard against her cervix, making her gasp with delight.

'That's it, fuck me hard!' she panted. 'That's it, give it to me good. Ram that fabulous cock up my cunt!' Her obscene words had the desired effect. He was going at her like a madman now, thrusting his fat prick in and out of her at an incredible rate. He bent over her and gripped the ladder-bars and fucked her even harder. This was just how she liked it. No finesse, no foreplay, just a good, hard fuck.

The servant slowed his movements a little and Lisa turned herself, raising one of her legs until she was able to rest it on his shoulder whilst standing in the pool on the other. She looked down. She could see his magnificent cock moving in and out of her quite clearly just under the surface of the water. She gripped his neck and rammed her body against his so that she absorbed the full length of his superb rod, then ground her pubic bone against him. His expression suddenly became a grimace. He was coming, and she had to join him in the ultimate pleasure. She began to thrust rapidly against him and he matched her movements. The burning ache was building up inside her loins. There was no stopping it now. She raised her other leg and circled it around his waist. The water churned and splashed as she hammered her body against him.

'I'm coming, I'm coming!' she wailed. He gripped her bottom with both hands and slammed his cock deep into her hot cunt. She threw back her head and winced with the agony of impending release. 'Yes! Yes!' she cried. 'Come with me!'

He needed no telling. No sooner had the words left her lips than she felt his big cock throbbing inside her and knew that he was filling her with his cream. The sensations of orgasm tore through her lower body and she tensed her vaginal muscles to grip him tightly inside her. Slowly, the pumping of his rigid tool abated. Lisa kissed him lovingly on the mouth and felt him slip from inside her. They drifted slowly apart in the water, their eyes fixed on each other's in a loving, post-coital trance.

'I'll have that ice, now,' cooed Lisa.

The large coach which had brought the students from the airport drove noisily into the driveway. Lisa jumped up at the sound and quickly pulled on a pair of tight shorts and her T-shirt. The vehicle pulled up at the front of the house as she made her way through the gap in the hedge. Mr Gee and Madam Stone were standing on the steps to the front door, preparing to greet the new arrivals, along with a dozen or so members of the manor staff. Lisa quickly zipped up her shorts and smoothed down the T-shirt and joined them just as the coach door swung open with a loud hiss. Through the windows she could see the faces of about twenty young girls peering excitedly out, looking for all the world like a party of schoolgirls on an outing.

Mr Gee moved forward as the first of the girls stepped down on to the gravel drive. He held out his hand and smiled broadly. He shook the small hand of his first guest warmly and spoke a few words of welcome, then indicated that she should enter the house. He repeated the action with each of the girls.

They filed slowly past Lisa, who eyed them with more than passing interest. They appeared to represent every point on the globe, and were all lovely in their very different ways. They were tired and casually dressed yet, to Lisa, they all possessed an appealing and youthful innocence. She couldn't help but wonder if they knew what they were letting themselves in for.

One of the last of the students to descend from the coach almost caused Lisa to gasp audibly. She had never seen a more beautiful or innocent-looking girl in all her life. She appeared to be of Malaysian origin or perhaps from the Philippines. Her flawless complexion was the colour of the sun and her eyes were of the deepest brown. She was tiny, certainly much less than five feet tall and very slim. She was wearing tight jeans and a plain T-shirt which accentuated her waif-like frame. Her small breasts and button-sized nipples could be clearly seen through the thin material of her top and her jeans moulded themselves around her boyish hips and pert little bottom. Lisa felt her mouth go dry as she gazed at this vision of abject sexuality. The girl caught her stare and looked away shyly as she moved quickly up the steps to the manor. Lisa watched her closely and tried to imagine Paul or Mike impaling her lithe body on their thick erections. That was something that she could barely wait to see.

As the staff busied themselves unloading the suitcases and trunks from the coach, Lisa followed Mr Gee and Madam Stone into the house. The students were all gathered in the hallway as students always do, as if waiting for instructions. Mr Gee stood before them and held out his arms. 'Welcome to Grantham Manor,' he said, proudly, 'and to seven days of pleasure and education. We promise to entertain you, and to instruct you in the delights of womanhood. There are few rules here, except that you are to enjoy yourself and that you must never refuse anything. The staff will indulge your every whim, and will do *anything* that you ask of them.'

A number of the girls giggled excitedly at the way he accentuated the word 'anything'. Lisa smiled. Despite her first impressions it was clear that these students were far more worldly than their innocent appearances suggested. They knew why they were here; they knew that there would be sex, and lots of it. She looked for the beautiful girl who had so captivated her. She spotted her at the back of the group and saw, to her delight, that she had the broadest grin of them all.

Madam Stone stood haughtily before Lisa and Janet, her hands planted firmly on her broad hips. The two girls had been summoned to see her in the library and had been quick to obey. It was a large, airy room towards the rear of the sprawling manor. Rows of desks and chairs had been arranged in the form of an old-fashioned classroom. Lisa and Janet were seated at two of these desks, facing their mentor.

'Today will be your final lesson,' said Madam Stone, her voice booming with confident authority. She was dressed in a severe outfit consisting of tailored trousers and a smart jacket which, for once, concealed her voluptuous figure. Following instructions, the two friends had dressed themselves in similar garments. 'I will take this class,' continued their instructress. 'It will be a general lesson, to outline the rest of the week's goals and to discover the knowledge that our students may already possess. Afterwards, they will split into four groups. You will each take one of these groups, the others will be instructed by your colleagues, Paul and Mike.'

‘Instructed?’ queried Lisa. ‘What are we going to teach?’

Madam Stone smiled and moved over to her. She rested a hand gently on her shoulder. ‘You have both shown the areas where you have the most expertise,’ she said, ‘and you have learnt the art of teasing and torment. You will combine these talents and instruct the students accordingly. You, Lisa, will teach the girls the techniques of giving good oral sex, both to men and to women. You will be ably assisted by two male members of staff, as will you, Janet.’

‘And what will I be teaching?’ said Janet excitedly.

Madam Stone smiled broadly. Lisa had a very good idea what she was going to say. ‘You, my dear, will explain and demonstrate the delights of anal love, a subject which, I am told, is near to your heart.’

Janet looked across at Lisa, who quickly glanced at the floor, blushing noticeably. ‘Bitch!’ hissed Janet as she realised her friend’s indiscretion although, in truth, she was quite pleased.

They heard noises from outside the room. It was the sound of many footsteps echoing in the hallway.

‘Right,’ said Madam Stone as she moved two high-backed chairs to the centre of the room and turned them to face the desks, ‘sit here. Do not speak unless asked to.’

The door opened and the students began to troop in silently. They were dressed uniformly, which gave even more credence to the classroom effect. The outfits had obviously been provided by Mr Gee for just this purpose. They consisted of short, black mini-kilts, crisp, white shirts and striped ties. The uniforms were completed by light blue blazers which sported a badge proclaiming the legend ‘Grantham Manor’ on the breast pocket.

Once they had all entered the library the door was closed behind them and they stood in a group at the back of the room. Madam Stone clapped her hands loudly. 'Right, ladies,' she barked. 'Sit at the desks.' The students obeyed, filling the room with the sounds of sliding chairs as they took their places.

Madam Stone stood in silence as they made themselves comfortable. Lisa surveyed the sea of faces with admiration. Although they were all at least seventeen or eighteen years of age, the uniforms made them appear much younger. They were all lovely, and some were positively beautiful.

The oriental girl who had so captivated Lisa when the group had arrived that morning had sat at the front of the rows of desks. From her vantage point, Lisa could glance under the desk. She had to bite her lip as she noticed that the gorgeous student's legs were slightly parted to offer a tantalising glimpse of the tops of her black stockings and the tiny 'V' of her white panties. Lisa enjoyed sex with other women, of course, but she had never felt such a powerful desire for one of her own sex before. She looked back at the girl, and their eyes met. This time, the student didn't look away but held her gaze and smiled coyly. Her legs opened a little further then she closed them quickly, as if realising her indiscretion. Lisa felt a familiar dampness between her own thighs and took a deep breath.

At last, Madam Stone broke the uncomfortable silence. 'Ladies, you know why you are here. Your host, Mr Gee, has explained everything. Today we wish to learn about you. You must speak openly, always tell the complete truth and, above all, speak frankly. Grantham Manor is no place for shyness. Is that understood?'

A few of the girls nodded.

'I said, is that understood?' repeated their tutor. Her face was stern and her eyes glared angrily.

'Yes,' chorused a number of voices.

'Yes madam!' demanded the tall woman as she paced the floor. 'My name is Heidi Stone, but you will always address me as madam, especially when I am having sex with you.'

Lisa noticed that a couple of the girls looked at each other apprehensively at these last words. Others seemed not in the least surprised, and a few looked positively excited at the prospect. She looked at the small, oriental student. Her legs were open again and her eyes were firmly fixed on Madam Stone's dark features. The young girl allowed the tip of her tongue to play across her upper lip. Lisa's immediate thought was how lovely it would be to have that same tongue fluttering over the hard bud of her clitoris. She looked at Janet. Her friend was sitting impassively, but Lisa knew that similar thoughts were probably going through her mind.

'Hands up those of you who are virgins.' There was some giggling at Madam Stone's sudden command, but no arms were raised. 'Come, now,' she said in a softer tone, 'don't be shy. It is important that we know.' Three hands were nervously raised, including that of the girl who had become the object of Lisa's desire. 'Good. Now perhaps we are getting somewhere. In future, if any of you do not answer mine or your other tutors' questions immediately and truthfully you will be severely punished.'

'May I ask a question, miss, er, madam?' It was the oriental girl who spoke, her voice a lilting song to Lisa's ears.

'Ask,' replied Madam Stone abruptly.

'When you say virgins, do you mean with men?'

'That is correct. I take it that you have had experiences with members of your own sex?'

'Yes, madam.'

'Do you like men?'

The young girl's face was becoming flushed. 'Oh yes, madam. It's just that I've never had the opportunity to, to make love with a man.' Her voice trailed off into a whisper and she looked down at the floor in embarrassment.

'The opportunity to do what?' Madam Stone's tone was mocking. 'Stand up, girl!' she barked. 'Now, repeat yourself, loudly, so that all the class can hear.'

The terrified girl stood at her desk. Lisa could plainly see that her tiny frame was shaking. 'I said that I've never had the chance to make love with a man,' she said in a slightly louder voice.

Madam Stone paced over to stand directly in front of the hapless girl. She towered over her and the young student was forced to bend her head right back just to look at her face. Her eyes were staring in terror but Madam Stone merely held her severe glare. Lisa couldn't help feeling sorry for the student. She wanted to wrap her arms around her and protect her from this fearsome woman. 'You mean that you have never had the opportunity to be *fucked* by a man! Isn't that what you mean?' The girl nodded self-consciously. 'Speak up, girl!' commanded Madam Stone.

'Yes, madam,' she said quietly.

'Now say it – what haven't you had the chance to do?'

The girl spoke her reply slowly, in nervous monosyllables. 'Not had the chance to, to –'

'Say it!' commanded Madam Stone.

'Say it,' echoed Lisa to herself, willing the girl to end her torment.

'To be fucked.' As soon as the words left her mouth, the young girl buried her chin into her chest in shame, as though she had committed the most cardinal sin.

Madam Stone reached out with her hand and raised her face until she was looking directly into her eyes. 'That's right,' she said, her tone unusually tender. 'To be fucked by a big cock going into your virgin cunt.' She stressed each of the obscenities as she stroked the softness of her student's face. 'They are just words, nice words, and you must use them. What's your name?'

'Sammy-Lynn,' replied the girl, her voice a little more confident.

'Well, Sammy-Lynn, by the end of this first day you will no longer be a virgin – none of you will. Grantham Manor is no place for virgins.'

Suddenly the tension that had been building up in the classroom was swallowed up by the sound of laughter. Madam Stone smiled broadly and walked over to rest her hand on Lisa's shoulder. 'Oh, and Sammy-Lynn,' she continued, 'from the way this young lady has been looking at you I feel that you may have plenty of chances to enjoy other diversions.'

It was Lisa's turn to blush. She looked at Sammy-Lynn who grinned back at her, her large, brown eyes sparkling with delight.

'Now,' said Madam Stone as her voice once again took on an air of authority, 'everybody stand.' The students obeyed immediately, as did Lisa and Janet. 'now, sit down if you have had fewer than five lovers.' The three virgins sat down, as well as about six others. Madam Stone looked at them for a moment, obviously making mental notes. 'Fewer than ten?' Most of the others sat down, leaving just two standing, apart from Lisa and Janet. Madam Stone walked over to one of them, a tall, statuesque blonde with a slim figure which could have graced any catwalk. 'Your name?' she demanded.

'Kelly.'

'Kelly what?' snapped Madam Stone.

The girl looked visibly shaken by her sudden change in tone. 'Kelly, madam,' she replied in a meek voice. She spoke with a cultured American accent.

'That's better. You will stay behind after the class, Kelly, and be punished for your impertinence. Now, how many lovers have savoured this delightful body of yours?'

'Eighteen, madam,' said the girl gently. Madam Stone nodded and walked over to the other standing figure. She, too, was tall but very buxom and of apparent Mediterranean origins.

'And what is your name?'

'Serita, madam,' replied the girl, stressing the last word firmly. 'I've had twenty-six male lovers.'

'And females?'

'Probably about the same.'

Madam Stone grinned with satisfaction as she walked back to stand before the class. Lisa and Janet resumed their seats. 'Kelly, you may sit down. Serita, come to the front of the class.' The dark-haired student moved nervously through the rows of desks to stand next to her tutor. Her face was strong, her nose slightly too large, but her mouth was full. Her large, bra-free breasts forced her blazer apart and the striped tie lay suggestively between them. Her pleated skirt was a little too short and revealed the darkness of her stocking-tops and, despite her flat shoes, she was almost as tall as Madam Stone herself.

Madam Stone walked slowly around the standing figure, examining her as though she was a slave in an ancient marketplace. 'You clearly enjoy sex,' she said, presently. 'I wonder if we'll be able to teach you much.'

'My father, the Ambassador, thinks I am still a

virgin, madam. It was he who suggested that I come here. I truly believe that it will be a waste of my time.'

'Really? Well, let us see what you can do, Serita.' Madam Stone picked up a small handbell from a nearby table and rang it briskly. Almost immediately, the door opened and Mike walked in, wearing nothing but a tiny, leather pouch which was already bulging in a ludicrous manner. The students gasped audibly at the sight of his slim but muscular body as he walked up to face the class. He stood still for a moment as though posing, with a grin that seemed to stretch from ear to ear. Serita eyed him cautiously, then her mouth opened slightly and she wet her lips with her tongue. He looked back at her, and Lisa could see that his bulge was growing by the second. For a moment she felt a little envious.

'Now, Serita,' said Madam Stone as she took a seat next to Lisa and Janet, 'show the class how you would satisfy a man like Mike.'

Serita looked across at her incredulously. 'You mean you want me to fuck him, here, in front of everybody?'

'Is there a problem with that?' said Madam Stone, as if it was the most natural thing in the world to have full sex before a group of goggle-eyed teenagers.

Serita shook her head. 'I can't, I can't,' she wailed. 'Sex is a private thing.'

Madam Stone stood up again. 'Go back to your seat, young lady,' she said in a clearly exasperated tone. 'You too will be punished after the class.' Mike watched with genuine disappointment showing on his face as the beautiful, uniform-clad girl returned to her desk through a gauntlet of chuckling colleagues. 'You have upset our handsome friend,' continued the tutor. 'You have been told already that you must never refuse anything. By the end of this week you will all have become proud of your sexuality and will delight in exhibiting your new-found prowess. But now we have a small problem. Mike is frustrated. He fully expected sex when he heard my bell. Whatever shall we do?'

She looked slowly round the class. Lisa smiled to herself at the thought of Mike being frustrated. She knew full well that he had spent most of the previous night in the company of one of the American couples.

'We could masturbate him, madam,' said a small voice from the back.

Madam Stone grinned. 'You mean to say we could give him a nice wank? No, I think Mike deserves more than that. What do you think, Lisa?'

She looked directly at Lisa, her eyes wide and taunting. Her meaning was clear. Lisa stood up and removed her jacket, then unbuttoned the front of her blouse. She quickly shook the garment from her shoulders to reveal her massive breasts and hard, erect nipples. She smiled proudly at the gasps of admiration from the group. She then unbuttoned the top of her trousers and eased the zip down, at the same time kicking off her shoes. She let the slacks fall to the floor and she was naked, save for a pair of black, hold-up stockings.

Determined to practise what she had learnt recently, she walked slowly around Mike and stared into his eyes. He looked down at her heaving breasts. 'God, I love your tits,' he whispered under his breath. She grinned and took hold of one of them and raised the nipple to his mouth. He sucked it greedily and took hold of her other heavy mound and gripped it tightly in his large hand. His other hand went to touch her bald pussy but she pushed it away and moved from him. She turned her back to him and faced the class, then moved backwards until she felt the bulge of his leather-covered crotch pressing against her bottom. He gripped her by the waist and forced himself even harder against her. She heard his heavy breathing and could feel the stiffness of his erection between her buttocks. Her pussy throbbed, and she could feel the lips opening in anticipation of the joys to come.

She took hold of his wrists and pulled his hands from her waist and then moved from him again. She turned her back to the class and looked at him mockingly. His cock was jutting forward and was pushing the leather pouch clear of his groin. She could see his hairy balls and a good few inches of his erection. 'Christ, Lisa,' he hissed through clenched teeth, 'I want you.'

'You'll have to wait,' she replied as she moved to stand behind him.

'I'm gonna come.'

'Don't you dare,' she growled. 'You're not going to deny the girls a good show.'

'Then let me fuck you! What's the matter with you?'

'All in good time.' She held on to his shoulders from behind and licked his back wetly. He shuddered. She pressed herself against him so that he could feel the wetness between her legs against his firm buttocks. She slipped her hands down and circled his waist, then caressed his groin lightly, taking care not to touch his ragingly hard erection. The entire class sat in total silence, scarcely daring to breath. Lisa ran her tongue slowly down his backbone until she was crouching behind him with her face less than an inch from his bottom. She gripped the strands of leather that circled his waist and gradually eased the pouch down until his cock sprang free from its constraint and slapped against his belly. A chorus of girlish cheers echoed around the room.

She kissed each of his taut buttocks in turn, then ran her tongue over them to trace their shape. At the same time, she ran her hands up and down his strong thighs. Occasionally, she would allow her hand to lightly touch his heavy sac, then quickly move it away, teasing him mercilessly.

She noticed Madam Stone watching her every move closely. She was desperate to take him inside her, but she knew that she had something to prove, to show her tutor that she had learnt well. She stopped caressing Mike's thigh with one of her hands and put it to her own soaking pussy. She wet her fingers with her copious juices and put one to his anus, then eased it in gently. Mike groaned. She removed her finger and licked him between his buttocks. She savoured his scent and the taste of her own arousal.

'She's licking his bottom!' she heard a voice say.

'I wouldn't mind some of that,' someone else said. Lisa made much of her actions in response, and rasped her tongue firmly up and down the hairy cleft.

'Oh, God, Lisa, you're gonna make me come, for pity's sake.'

She realised that she had teased him enough. She stood up and walked round to face him. She wiped her mouth on the back of her hand suggestively. He gazed at her, his eyes filled with overpowering lust. She looked down at his fierce erection. She wanted to engulf the monster in her mouth, but knew that he would stand no chance if she did. Instead, she walked over to where Sammy-Lynn was sitting and leant her elbows on her desk with her legs spread apart and her back arched so that her bottom was presented to Mike. Her breasts rested heavily on the coolness of the desk. She looked at him over her shoulder. 'Fuck me,' she breathed.

Mike moved over to her quickly, as though he was afraid that she might change her mind. Lisa turned her head to look directly into Sammy-Lynn's eyes as she waited for the inevitable. To her surprise, instead of the expected sensation of his cock touching her engorged pussy-lips she felt his tongue drawing wetly over her own bottom. Now he was teasing her! She couldn't believe it; he'd looked as though his cock was about to burst!

'Can you see what he's doing?' she whispered to Sammy-Lynn. The pretty little student nodded.

'He's licking your bum,' she said. She leant forward and whispered into Lisa's ear. 'I'd like to do that to you,' she said.

'You will, my darling.' We'll have lots of fun together, I promise.' She felt Mike's tongue licking at the top of her cleft, then he eased it slowly down. He slipped it wetly over her anus and then began to lap against her soaked cunt. Then he moved away from her. She closed her eyes. 'For God's sake,' she said to herself, 'don't tease me any more.'

Her silent prayer was answered almost immediately. She felt the plum-shaped end of his cock slip easily into her oiled sheath. She groaned as the thickness of his long rod filled her completely and he held himself still for a moment with his groin pressed hard against her bottom. She could feel him throbbing inside her. He was clearly having trouble holding back.

She opened her eyes and gazed at Sammy-Lynn. The young girl moved her face closer and their lips met. Lisa pushed her tongue forward between Sammy-Lynn's pouting lips and wrapped her arms around her neck. They kissed passionately as Mike began to move in and out of Lisa's hot pussy. Lisa knew that she would come quickly; she was almost there already. She felt Sammy-Lynn circling her tongue around hers just as Mike started to pound furiously against her. She was so aroused that she could barely feel his big cock inside her. She tensed her upper thigh muscles and he fucked her even more rapidly. The sound of his groin slapping against her bottom filled her ears. She was coming, she was coming now, and it was going to be a good one. She felt the nerve-endings between her legs tingling and the build-up became unstoppable.

She heard Mike groan loudly and knew that, for the second time that day, her hot little pussy was being filled with a man's delicious cream. She stiffened her muscles and gripped his plunging rod tightly and held it deep inside her body. She could feel him throbbing as the sperm gushed from him. Suddenly, the sensation of final release tore at her loins, causing her to gasp into Sammy-Lynn's sucking mouth. Mike reached under her and rubbed her hard bud rapidly as her climax ripped through her lower body, until she could stand it no more.

She pushed his hand away and he eased his still substantial length from inside her. He leant his body against her, and she could feel the wetness of his wilting prick between her buttocks. She kissed Sammy-Lynn lightly on the lips. 'You wait until it's your turn,' she breathed.

'I want you to be there,' replied the bright-eyed virgin.

'I will be, I promise.'

After a few minutes Lisa was dressed and sitting on her chair as if nothing had happened. The atmosphere in the room, however, was electric. She noticed Serita looking at her coldly. She was obviously envious, no doubt wishing that she'd had the courage to perform before the entire class. The girl had learnt a salutary lesson already.

Sammy-Lynn was also gazing at her, but hers was a look of sheer desire. Lisa glanced under her desk. Her legs were wide open this time, and she was gently fingering herself through her tiny, white panties. The flimsy cotton was almost transparent with her wetness and the shape of her engorged sex-lips was clearly visible. Lisa looked around the room at the sea of flushed, excited faces. All eyes seemed to be fixed on her. She took a deep breath. Instead of detecting the musty aroma of old books, she was sure that the library was filled with the scent of sex. She tried to imagine the sight of more than twenty wet, excited pussies, and revelled in the knowledge that their arousal was down to her. And Mike, of course.

Her handsome lover had left the room, his duty done. Madam Stone sat in silence for some time, as if to allow the students to dwell on what they had just witnessed. Presently, however, she rose to her feet.

'Ladies,' she began, 'already you have learnt two important lessons. One, that the joy of having sex can be doubly pleasurable if witnessed by others and two, that the total lack of inhibitions can lead to the most delightful excesses. You saw Sammy-Lynn kiss Lisa passionately. I am certain that she wouldn't have dreamt of doing that before but, the fact that Lisa was, at the same time, being well and truly fucked made it seem the most natural thing to do.

'Mr Gee said that there are few rules here. There is one, however, that you must obey from now on. You must surrender yourself to your innermost desires and indulge in your every sexual fantasy. You must also share in the fantasies of others, and learn to experiment. As the old saying goes, you don't know if you like something until you've tried it.

'Never lock the doors to your rooms, especially when you are having sex. You will come to no harm,

I promise, and you may occasionally get a nice surprise. It is a lovely feeling to be kneeling on a bed, sucking a lover's hard cock and suddenly finding yourself impaled from behind by someone you've never met before!'

The class erupted into laughter at this. Lisa looked across at Janet and grinned. They both knew from experience that this was something that was more than likely to happen.

Madam Stone held up her hands for silence. 'After lunch you will split up into four groups for your first lessons. Lisa and Janet here will each take a group. You have already met another of our tutors, Mike. He will take the third group and Paul, who I know you ladies will find equally attractive, will take the fourth.

'Before lunch, however, there is the matter of our three virgins. The loss of virginity is an extremely poignant event in a person's life so, for this time only, you will be allowed privacy if you so choose. In a moment I will summon a number of male staff. You may select the one that you wish to relieve you of the burden of innocence and take him to your room. Now, I want the three of you to come to the front of the class.'

Lisa watched as the three students moved to stand next to their instructress. Sammy-Lynn stood confidently, with a broad grin on her face. The other two girls seemed more nervous. One of them, a chubby but attractive girl with short, brown hair and remarkably large breasts looked positively terrified. The other, a tall and willowy Asian girl simply stared into space.

Madam Stone moved to face them. 'Another rule of Grantham Manor is that nobody will be forced to do anything that they do not wish to.' She rested her hand on the tall girl's shoulder. 'Do you wish to lose your virginity?'

'Yes, madam,' the girl replied in a hushed voice.

Madam Stone stepped to one side. 'Tell the class,' she said. 'Tell them what you want to happen to you.'

The girl gulped visibly, then took a deep breath. 'I want to lose my virginity,' she said in a trembling voice. Madam Stone looked directly at her, the expression on her face indicating that she wanted to hear more. 'I want to be fucked, madam.' said the girl suddenly, blurting the words out.

'Excellent! You are learning quickly. And you?' She touched the chubby girl on the shoulder.

'I want to be fucked as well, madam,' she said, quickly. Her face was ashen, and Lisa formed the impression that she might faint at any moment.

'Are you sure?' said Madam Stone tenderly.

'Oh, yes, madam. I'm nearly eighteen. It's about time!'

The class laughed loudly, but it was clear from the expression on the girl's face that she had meant every word. Madam Stone moved to stand beside Sammy-Lynn. 'And what about you,' she said as she stroked the lovely student's flawless cheek. 'Are you ready to give yourself to a man?'

'Oh, yes, madam,' said Sammy-Lynn excitedly. 'I want to be fucked and fucked and fucked!' She hugged herself tightly as she said the words, clearly revelling in their sound. Even Madam Stone laughed at her display of obvious enthusiasm. She picked up the bell again and rang it. All eyes turned to the door as the class fell into silence. After what must have seemed like an age to the three girls the door opened and six male staff members entered. They marched over to stand in a line before the virgin students. Each was very different, but all were handsome in their own way. They wore nothing apart from a pair of skin-tight, lycra shorts which did little to conceal the impressive shapes of their genitals. Lisa smiled to herself as she watched the young girls looking from one to the other as though they were selecting dresses in a clothes shop.

'You choose first,' said Madam Stone to the chubby girl. 'Touch the one you want.' The girl reached out and nervously touched the bare chest of the man standing directly in front of her. The man took hold of her hand and immediately led her from the room. As she went through the door she turned to look back with a terrified expression at her colleagues, then shrugged her shoulders and was gone.

'Now, you.' It was the Asian girl's turn to choose. She took her time, moving slowly along the line and looking carefully into each handsome face. Then she walked back, this time blatantly examining the fronts of their shorts and beginning to smile. Finally, she stopped in front of one of the men and stared at his crotch. Lisa could see the attraction. He was a tall, muscular black man with a superbly defined erection that was threatening to burst through the thin lycra.

The student touched his massive chest and he took her hand in his. She turned to look at Madam Stone and mouthed the words 'thank you', then followed her prospective lover out of the room.

Now it was time for Sammy-Lynn to decide. As she stood in front of the four remaining men Lisa could see from their faces that they all desperately wanted to be chosen. She looked so tiny beside them, so vulnerable, and so beautiful. She looked from one to the other, clearly having great difficulty in making her selection.

'Hurry, Sammy-Lynn,' said Madam Stone. 'I wish to continue the class.'

'I have made my choice, madam.' Sammy-Lynn reached out and quickly touched the chests of all four men in turn. There were gasps from the other students as she turned to face Madam Stone. 'That is my choice,' she said, proudly, 'and I want Lisa to be there as well.'

Lisa looked across at Madam Stone, who nodded. Gleefully, Sammy-Lynn took the arms of two of the men and walked towards the door. Lisa and the other men followed, to rapturous applause from the rest of the class.

As Lisa followed Sammy-Lynn and the four, near-naked studs into the young girl's bedroom she realised that she would have to take control of the situation. After all, she was supposed to be the instructress.

The room was larger than the one she shared with Janet, and even more opulently furnished. It was dominated by a huge, circular bed, strewn with expensive cushions. Above the bed, angled to give the occupants a perfect view was a giant mirror. Other wall mirrors had been strategically placed around the room for the same purpose. Sleeping would be the last thing a girl would do in a bed like this.

Sammy-Lynn stood in the centre of the room, close to the foot of the bed. Lisa noticed that for the first time she was looking a little apprehensive. Perhaps she was beginning to regret choosing four men to initiate her into the joys of sexual fulfilment. Each of them looked to be quite capable of satisfying any woman on his own. She stood with her hands clasped in front of her and her head bowed slightly to one side. Her eyes were nervously fixed on Lisa's.

Lisa walked over to her and slipped her arms around her waist. She kissed her lightly on the forehead. 'You are going to learn much in the next couple of hours, my sweet virgin,' she breathed.

The small girl gulped visibly, then forced a brave smile. 'Two hours? I thought –'

'That it would be all over in a matter of minutes? Even with one man, sex should last much, much longer than a few moments if a woman is to achieve complete satisfaction. And there is more to sex than merely fucking. The delights of arousal are just as important and enjoyable, if not more so.' She turned to look at the men. They were lined up like slaves in a medieval marketplace with their manly attributes displayed obscenely within the confines of their skin-tight shorts.

'Take those off,' she commanded, indicating the shorts with a brisk wave of her arm. The men obeyed immediately. Now they stood before the two excited girls naked. Lisa surveyed the row of bronzed, athletically built young men and licked her lips hungrily. Sammy-Lynn had chosen well, she thought to herself. Each of them sported a firm, rampant erection capable of pleasing the most discerning of women. She looked down at Sammy-Lynn. The young girl was staring, wide eyed, at the erotic display.

'Perhaps I should have only chosen one of them,' she said, her voice trembling.

'It's too late now,' whispered Lisa as she ran her hand lovingly through her student's long, black hair. 'You cannot tease a man to such a state of arousal and then let him down. That would be unforgivable.'

'Will you do it with them as well?'

'Of course,' answered Lisa, 'but first, let me prepare you.'

Without waiting for permission, Lisa removed Sammy-Lynn's blazer. Then she unfastened the striped tie and slipped it from around her neck before letting it drop to the floor. She glanced at the men. Two of them were gently caressing their hard cocks as they watched. She was going to give them a show that they would never forget. She couldn't help but wonder if they would manage to hold back.

Sammy-Lynn stood impassively as Lisa slowly unbuttoned her crisp, white blouse and revealed the naked, olive-toned skin beneath. Unfastening the sleeves, she slipped the shirt from the girl's shoulders and gazed at her small, firm breasts and the buttons of her dark nipples. Lisa bent her head and took one of the nipples between her teeth and nipped it lightly. Sammy-Lynn gasped. Lisa did the same to the other, then drew most of the small breast into her mouth whilst circling the warm flesh with her wet tongue. Her pupil groaned with pleasure.

Still sucking her nipple, Lisa unhooked the short skirt and pushed it over Sammy-Lynn's narrow hips until it drifted down to the floor. She moved back and watched as the virgin stepped out of the skirt and kicked it to one side. Now, all she wore was black stockings and a suspender belt, small, flat shoes and a tiny pair of white panties which were still visibly soaked at the front. She stood in silence, compliantly awaiting her tutor's next move.

Lisa turned to the men. 'You,' she ordered as she pointed to one of them, 'take off her panties.' The man stepped forward immediately and crouched in front of Sammy-Lynn, his cock stretching enormously from his hairy groin. He hooked his thumbs under her panties and eased them slowly down to her ankles. Lisa saw him lick his lips as he gazed at her exposed crotch. He moved his head forward.

'Enough!' she barked. The man moved away quickly and resumed his place in line. Now it was Lisa's turn to reveal her charms. She removed her jacket and carefully folded it before placing it on a nearby chair. Then she took off her shirt and smiled as the men gasped in unison at the sight of her bared breasts.

'Oh, they are so beautiful,' breathed Sammy-Lynn. Lisa grinned proudly as she unzipped her trousers. She took them off quickly with her stockings and put them neatly on the chair with her jacket. There were no panties, of course. She was now as naked as the others, and equally aroused.

She took hold of Sammy-Lynn's hand and coaxed her to lie in the centre of the huge bed. She lay next to her and gently smoothed her hand over the waif-like form of her pupil, all the time gazing with genuine fondness into her watery, almond eyes. She bent her head and kissed her on the cheek, then put her lips to the tiny mouth. Sammy-Lynn responded immediately. She wrapped her arms around Lisa's body and pressed herself firmly against her as their tongues circled each other. She mewed softly as Lisa's probing fingers found the luscious wetness of her virgin pussy. She was soaking, and her juices were flowing from her to dampen the satin sheet beneath her writhing body. Lisa reluctantly resisted the temptation to worm her fingers deep inside the succulence of Sammy-Lynn's hot cunt; her virginity had to be taken by a nice, stiff cock. Instead, she moved herself downwards until her face was inches from the engorged sex-lips and her bottom was presented to the eager gaze of the four young men. She kissed the tops of Sammy-Lynn's thighs over and over again whilst savouring the delicate scent of her arousal. The young girl was trembling, not with fear but with sheer lust.

Lisa moved her mouth closer to the glistening flesh. She blew gently, knowing the effect her hot breath would have. Sammy-Lynn moaned and opened her legs wide. 'Lick me, please lick me,' she pleaded. Lisa put her forefinger to her mouth and wet it with her saliva, then traced the line of Sammy-Lynn's small opening. She blew again gently. 'Please, please,' begged her charge, opening her legs even wider.

Lisa moved her face forward and pushed out her tongue until the tip touched the fleshy sex-lips. Sammy-Lynn gasped loudly. Lisa circled her hot little pussy with her wet tongue, then drew the tip slowly up between the lips and traced the line of her opening until she touched the hard bud of her clitoris. Sammy-Lynn groaned as Lisa lapped the stiff little button. 'Oh, God,' she moaned, 'I love it, I love it!'

She gripped the hair on Lisa's head and pushed her face harder against her suppliant mound. Her juices soaked Lisa's face as she all-but devoured the succulent, puffy flesh. Her taste was exquisite. Lisa pushed her tongue deep inside her and touched the barrier of her virginity. She was nearly ready.

She licked her hard clitoris again, this time allowing the tip of her tongue to flutter over it rapidly. Suddenly, without warning her pupil came with a loud squeal of delight. She raised her bottom from the bed and pressed her pussy hard against Lisa's jaw as the orgasm took hold of her. Lisa licked and sucked her cunt expertly, knowing exactly how to draw every emotion, every sensation from her release. Sammy-Lynn gasped over and over again as wave after wave of pleasure tore through her thrusting crotch until, at last, her movements subsided and she fell back on the bed exhausted.

Lisa moved from the prone figure and stood by the side of the big bed. She wiped her mouth on the back of her hand. Sammy-Lynn simply gazed at her as she lay there with her legs still widely splayed. Her pussy-lips were parted in blatant invitation. She was ready.

Lisa turned to face the line of handsome men. Their erections were uniformly fierce, the gnarled flesh purple with lust. She moved over to stand before the first. He was a blond-haired man with Nordic features, and little more than Sammy-Lynn's age. He was also the best endowed of the group. Lisa took hold of his long, thick erection and lead him to the bed. Sammy-Lynn looked nervously at his cock.

Still gripping his thickness tightly by the root, Lisa made him kneel between Sammy-Lynn's legs and guided the heavily veined shaft to its target. The wet sex-lips opened involuntarily like a tiny mouth. The time for teasing was past. Sammy-Lynn needed to be fucked.

Lisa put her free hand on the young man's firm bottom and pushed him forwards. She watched enviously as the huge, bulbous head of his cock parted the soft, virgin flesh. Sammy-Lynn suddenly jerked her body and gave out a little cry of pain. Her virginity was gone. Lisa bent over and kissed her pupil on the mouth, then released her grip of the thick stalk. She watched in fascination as the young man eased more of his length inside her, then withdrew until just the head was held within her tight grasp. He moved slowly forward again, this time sliding over six inches of hard cock into her succulent sheath, then eased back once more. Lisa looked at his face. He was grimacing, clearly having trouble holding back. He moved his hips forward again and eased the full length of his big cock into Sammy-Lynn's welcoming warmth. The young girl groaned with pleasure.

'Oh, shit!' the man hissed between clenched teeth. He pulled himself quickly from inside her and gripped his cock tightly, but it was too late for him. A spray of warm, creamy fluid jetted from the angry knob to soak Sammy-Lynn's body. The young man rubbed himself furiously as more and more semen streaked across her flawless, olive skin. Lisa ran her hands over Sammy-Lynn's breasts and stomach to massage the oily substance into her flesh. Clearly, Sammy-Lynn had been right to choose more than one lover.

The young man who had been lucky enough to take her virginity moved reluctantly away to resume his place in the line. The expression on his face was a picture of self-annoyance. Lisa glared at him. 'You will be punished,' she said, tersely. Her words seemed to have the right effect. Although his head was bowed in shame, he was now grinning broadly.

She signalled to the next man to come forward. He was on the bed in an instant, and immediately plunged his stiff rod deep into Sammy-Lynn's pussy. She groaned with joy and wrapped her arms and legs around his rutting body. He plunged in and out of her rapidly, fucking her for all he was worth. 'Oh yes, oh yes!' she cried as her fingernails scraped the flesh of his buttocks, 'this is what it's all about!' His hips became a blur as he shagged her mercilessly and drove her small body across the bed until her head pressed into the pillows. Lisa saw her bite into his shoulder fiercely, then look up at the ceiling. 'Oh, God,' Sammy-Lynn wailed, 'look at that!'

Lisa looked up at the mirror to enjoy the reflected sight of the young man's bottom bouncing up and down on the barely visible form of her young charge. His groin slapped noisily against her thighs as he hammered in and out of her, clearly determined to make her come. He wasn't to be disappointed. With a loud yell, Sammy-Lynn threw back her head, then shook it from side to side as the tremors of release once again took hold of her senses. Her lover groaned and rammed his cock fully into her and clenched his buttocks tightly. He held himself still and gasped rhythmically, which told Lisa that he was filling Sammy-Lynn's cunt with his hot cream. 'I can feel it throbbing! I can feel it throbbing inside me!' she shouted happily. Her lover began moving again, albeit with less urgency, until he was done. He slipped from inside her and staggered from the bed to join his colleagues.

Lisa nodded to the remaining two men. They moved to the bed and Lisa made one of them lie on his back. She gripped his cock and then bent over him and put it into her mouth. She took his full length to the back of her throat. She felt it throb between her sucking lips and tasted his saltiness.

Moving quickly from him in case her expert mouth should take him over the edge she held his erection upright and motioned for Sammy-Lynn to squat across his groin. Her student lowered her body and greedily absorbed the thick stalk inside her ravaged pussy. Lisa had no need to tell the other man what to do. He moved to kneel with his hard rod inches from Sammy-Lynn's face. She reached up and took hold of it, her tiny hand barely circling his girth, then put it to her mouth. She sucked him cautiously at first then, having got the taste for it, took as much in her mouth as she could manage. At the same time, she moved her bottom up and down, fucking herself on her supine lover.

Lisa moved behind them and kissed her pupil's bottom. She watched for a moment, and thrilled to the sight of Sammy-Lynn's obscenely stretched sex-lips as they absorbed and reabsorbed the thick length, then bent forward and licked her anus. This was enough to give Sammy-Lynn her third orgasm. She pumped her body wildly up and down and knocked Lisa away from her with her near-manic thrusts. Her muffled cry of delight was masked by the groan of the other man as he filled her sucking mouth with his seed. Lisa moved quickly and saw that she swallowed it all.

Sammy-Lynn fell forward on to her prone lover's body just as he came. His creamy fluid jetted from his throbbing cock and soaked her round little bottom as she rubbed her pussy against his hairy stomach. Once again, Lisa massaged the warm juice into her skin and thrilled to the touch of her firm buttocks.

At last the lovers fell apart and Lisa gazed down benignly at the exhausted student. 'And that, Sammy-Lynn,' she said, grandly, 'is the end of your first lesson.'

Madam Stone stood grim-faced in front of Lisa and Janet. She held a vicious-looking whip in her hand. 'The students Kelly and Serita must be punished for their impertinence. They must be whipped before the whole class, and I wish you both to administer the punishment.' Lisa looked at Janet nervously.

'But they are so young, madam,' she said. 'They may not –' Madam Stone interrupted her by lashing a nearby chair in fury.

'Know this, my young charges,' she barked angrily. 'After they have tasted the joys of sensual pain your pupils will be yours to command!' She handed the lash to Lisa, who smiled broadly. 'Now go. The class awaits you!'

Six

'I want this young man severely punished.'

Lisa was facing a stern-faced Madam Stone in the main hallway. She was gripping the naked youth's wrist tightly. Madam Stone eyed him contemptuously. 'What has he done?' she asked.

'He came before he had satisfied the needs of one of your pupils, madam,' replied Lisa.

The tall woman's dark features hardened, her eyes blazing. 'What?' she said, angrily. 'You did what?'

The young man was trembling visibly. 'I, I'm sorry, Madam, I couldn't stop myself. She was so lovely, so sexy.'

'That's no excuse!' snarled Madam Stone. 'You know the rules; the client's needs must always be paramount. Bring him to my room immediately!' She looked across at Lisa. 'You have done well to bring this to my attention,' she said, then turned and marched up the long staircase, taking two steps at a time. Lisa watched her go and savoured the undulating movement of her impressive bottom until she rounded a turn in the stairs. She then looked back at the young staff member and gripped his wrist even tighter.

'I think you're in for a whipping,' she said. He nodded. The expression on his face seemed to be one of fear, but the huge and firm erection that jutted from his bushy groin betrayed his true feelings. Lisa was glad that she'd dressed before dragging the hapless youth from Sammy-Lynn's bedroom. She was quite aware that the temptation to force the naked man to the floor and to get him to sink his long shaft into her willing pussy would have been too strong had she remained naked. Witnessing four young men sate their lust with Sammy-Lynn and not being able to indulge in the pleasures herself had left her feeling empty.

But, of course Madam Stone would be furious if she were kept waiting.

Lisa tugged the young man's arm and they began to ascend the staircase. As he moved, his stiff erection swung heavily from side to side. Lisa looked away. God, he was big. If there was one thing she loved above anything else it was a big cock. All this rubbish about size not mattering. What rot. She knew that there wasn't a girl alive who wouldn't prefer to be fucked by a guy with a nice, big prick.

And, after watching Sammy-Lynn's initiation, that was something that she knew she needed badly.

They reached Madam Stone's room and Lisa knocked loudly on the door. 'Enter!' commanded the voice from within. She looked down at the young man's cock. His erection was so fierce that his superb shaft was pressed firmly against his muscular stomach with the bulbous, damp head covering his navel. Lisa swallowed hard as she strove to ignore the sight and opened the door.

Madam Stone was standing in the centre of the room. She had removed all her clothing, save for a pair of high-heeled, PVC thigh-boots that stretched to barely an inch below her crotch. She was clutching a multi-stranded whip. The sight of her instructress in such an erotic pose made Lisa feel quite faint. She drank in the vision of the flawless, ebony sheen of her skin, her massive, heaving breasts and the visibly damp hair between her legs. For a moment she wished that it was she who was about to be punished. Then she looked again at the whip. Perhaps not, she thought. This was going to hurt.

She glanced back at the young man. His erection hadn't subsided in the slightest and his eyes were ablaze with lust. 'Take him to the bed,' ordered Madam Stone, 'force him to lie on his stomach and shackle him to the chains.' Lisa led the youth to the large bed. She regarded the chains that were fixed to the headboard with some amusement. They were clearly a permanent fixture.

'Lie down on your stomach,' she whispered. The man obeyed immediately and sprawled across the bed with his arms and legs outstretched. He had obviously found himself in this predicament before. Lisa fixed the shackles around his wrists and ankles and then stepped back. Madam Stone moved forward and stood close to the young man's face. She played the vicious strands of leather across the palm of her hand. His eyes widened in anticipation of the delights to come.

Lisa felt a familiar throbbing between her legs as she watched her instructress move to stand at the side of the bed with her back turned to her. She looked longingly at the perfect, sable buttocks and yearned to run her tongue between them. Automatically, her hand went between her own legs and she fingered herself through the thick material of her trousers. There was a long pause. The youth buried his face in one of the sumptuous pillows. Madam Stone raised the whip. It was clear that there was going to be no teasing nor any titillation on this occasion.

She brought the lash down on her victim's

backside, her buttocks rippling with the effort. Lisa bit her lip and tore her gaze away from Madam Stone's behind to look at the young man. Numerous, red stripes splayed across his bottom to form a leaf-like pattern. He had barely uttered a sound. The lash was brought down again, then again, and the marks were becoming angry and haphazard. Madam Stone administered a final, fierce stroke and, at last, he yelped with the pain.

'Untie him!' she commanded. Lisa rushed to free him from his bonds. He turned his body and lay partly on his back whilst he rubbed his bottom. His cock was as hard as ever, the end purple and weeping with lust. Madam Stone dropped the whip and knelt on the foot of the bed. She glared at the prone form before her. 'In future,' she said, 'you will control your feelings. Is that clear?'

'Yes, Madam,' whimpered the youth.

She looked at his hard erection. '*Now* you may come,' she commanded.

Lisa watched in astonishment as he stiffened the muscles of his lower body and his face broke into a grimace. Suddenly, he gasped loudly and the sperm jetted from his swollen cock to soak his chest and the pillows behind him. Lisa remembered how Mr Gee had forced Janet to orgasm without the slightest touch, and recalled how powerful she had said her release had been. From the expression on the young man's face, it was more than apparent that he was experiencing a similar sensation.

At last, he was done, and his breathing became easier as he lay his head back on the soaked pillow. 'Now go!' ordered Madam Stone. He leapt from the bed immediately and scurried from the room. 'He is very disobedient, that one. I am forever having to punish him. No doubt he will be back again tomorrow, for more.' She grinned broadly, and Lisa laughed out loud. Madam Stone slipped her arm around her shoulders. Lisa felt her hot breath on her cheek and turned to face her. They kissed. Lisa trembled as the thick, spongy lips engulfed her mouth and the long tongue probed inside. She wrapped her arms around the naked woman and stroked her large, firm bottom. She detected the faint, musky odour of her mentor's arousal and she took a deep breath in order to savour the delightful scent.

Madam Stone pressed her naked mound hard against Lisa's crotch and rubbed it from side to side. Lisa responded by pushing her hips forward. They gripped each other's buttocks and moved together in a sensual dance of delight. Their tongues circled and slithered against each other as their kiss became more and more urgent. Thoughts of big cocks vanished from Lisa's consciousness. Now all that she yearned for was the feel of Madam Stone's long tongue slipping inside her aching pussy and the exquisite taste of her mentor's sweet juices.

She released her grip of the big, pert bottom and wrenched her top off to release her otherwise unfettered breasts. Madam Stone smiled and cupped the huge mounds in both hands. 'You have beautiful breasts, Lisa,' she breathed. Lisa closed her eyes as her lover put her mouth to one of her long nipples and sucked the tender flesh, rasping her teeth gently against the hard bud. She felt Madam Stone unfasten her trousers and then peel them down to her ankles without once removing her mouth from her breast. Then she watched as she knelt down and tugged them from her feet, along with her trainers. Her face was inches from Lisa's soaked mound. 'Such a beautiful little thing,' her tutor breathed. 'It looks so small, so vulnerable, and yet we know that it has accommodated many, many thick, long cocks.' She moved her head forward and kissed Lisa's throbbing pussy gently. Lisa gritted her teeth as she waited for the silky touch of her wet tongue. There was another kiss, this time deeper and more passionate. Lisa felt the tip of Madam Stone's tongue trace the line between her sex-lips. Then it was pushed inside, a tongue as long as any cock, deep and probing, slithering and sliding within her whilst the thick lips of her lover's mouth sucked her aching cunt.

She gripped the hair on Madam Stone's head tightly and pressed her face against her groin. She was close, so very close. Soon her juices would flood from her body to soak the face of her beautiful instructress. The tongue began to move rapidly in and out of her, as if her lover sensed her impending release. Her sex-lips were sucked into Madam Stone's loving mouth as her tongue darted backwards and forwards. Lisa's knees began to tremble as the ache grew between her legs, building incessantly to her inevitable climax.

Suddenly, the sharp, stabbing sensations of sensual release tore at her groin and tremors of joyous electricity shot through her thighs. Lisa cried out loud and felt her juices flow. Madam Stone sucked Lisa's hot lips and lapped her long tongue feverishly around their pulsating shape. She drank from her like a woman who was dying of thirst and swallowed everything that Lisa could give. Finally, she pushed her tongue deep inside Lisa's cunt and kissed her with a passion normally shared by true lovers. It was a long, all-consuming kiss. The thickly pouting lips engulfed her throbbing sex completely and sucked her tenderly. Lisa felt Madam Stone's tongue snake along her open cleft and jumped as it touched her clitoris. She could take no more.

Her knees gave way and she collapsed to the floor. The two women sat facing each other, breathing heavily. Madam Stone's ebony features were soaked with Lisa's juices and shone with the reflected sunlight that streamed in from the window. She grinned broadly. 'I think you needed that,' she said, simply. She stood up and helped Lisa to her feet. 'Come, we must dress and return to the class.'

Janet sat quietly on the lounger and gazed at the shimmering surface of the pool. The lesson had been enjoyable, and the punishment of the two wayward pupils had been a joy to witness. Serita and Kelly were both very beautiful girls and, when they had been stripped naked for their punishment, Janet had found it difficult to control her desire to bury her face within the warmth of their young thighs.

The discussion had continued in much the same way as before, each student relating experiences from their diverse pasts. Janet had taken advantage of Madam Stone's brief absence to steer the conversation to her favourite subject, the pleasures and techniques of anal arousal. She had been delighted with the pupils' response, and congratulated herself on her apparent teaching abilities. She considered, with some pride, that perhaps she had found her true vocation.

The sight of the two girls' bottoms quivering as Lisa had administered the lash had thrilled her, and she had been more than happy when Madam Stone instructed her to smooth cool oil on to the naked buttocks. Slipping a finger into each tight little hole at the same time had made the girls groan with pleasure, and she knew that they too would soon become willing pupils.

She heard a sound coming from behind her. She

looked round and saw Mr Gee step out on to the patio. He didn't seem to see her as he stood looking out into the distance whilst he sipped on a long drink. Janet swallowed hard as she regarded the handsome figure of her host. There was something about him that intrigued her. He possessed an aura of power and of mystery and, whatever dark secrets he held, she knew that she wanted him.

'It's a lovely day, Mr Gee,' she said, weakly. He turned and looked at her. His dark eyes appeared cold as he clinically regarded her seated form. Apart from a tiny, black thong she was naked but his expression failed to register the fact. She lay back and smiled. She could feel her nipples hardening and knew that he would be able to sense her arousal as they lengthened visibly. To her dismay he looked away.

'Beautiful,' he said, presently. 'There is no place better than England on such a day.'

His words seemed like poetry to Janet's ears. She eased herself from the lounger and moved over to stand next to him. She gazed in the same direction and saw the same hills and the trees. But her mind was on other things. She searched her mind desperately for something profound to say. 'I would be happy to spend the rest of my life here,' she said, finally. He turned and looked at her, but there was no warmth showing in the handsome features of his face. He looked down at her near-nakedness, then turned his head and stared out at the landscape, as if unimpressed.

She was standing as close to him as possible without actually touching him. She reached up and gripped his arm gently. 'Have you lived here long?' she asked.

'Many, many years,' he replied. Janet moved her

body against him. Her naked breast touched his bare forearm lightly. Mr Gee moved away nonchalantly and sat on a nearby barstool. It was clear to Janet that she would have to make all the moves.

'Do you like me, Mr Gee?' she pouted.

'Of course, Janet, you are one of my guests.'

'But do you *like* me?' she repeated, walking towards him. He said nothing. He was looking at her through those fierce, cold eyes, and it made her want him badly. Without taking her gaze from his, she curled her thumbs under the thin sides of her thong and slipped it slowly down to her ankles, then stepped out of it. She stood erect with her legs slightly apart and her hands resting on her hips.

'I want you to make love to me, Mr Gee,' she whispered. 'I want you to fuck me.'

There was a long silence as he looked her up and down, as if considering an expensive purchase. Despite her arousal she began to feel distinctly uncomfortable. He turned his head and looked out at the horizon.

'Put it on, Janet,' he said.

'Don't you want me?' she breathed, walking towards him.

He rose from the stool and walked towards the house. 'I said, put it on, Janet.'

In anger and disbelief she watched him disappear through the patio doors. She had never been refused before, and she didn't like it. She felt stupid, standing there naked and alone. Furiously, she grabbed the thong and pulled it on, then covered her upper body with a flimsy T-shirt. She was just about to go into the house when she heard the patio door slide open. She looked up expectantly but, instead of the hoped-for return of Mr Gee, she saw the tall, dark form of Peter, one of Grantham Manor's older guests.

He must have noticed her look of disappointment. 'Why so glum, young lady?' he drawled.

'I'm sorry,' she fumbled. 'I, I think I've got a headache coming on.' He moved to her and stroked her head gently.

'Can I get you something?' he said, with genuine concern in his voice.

'No, no, it's all right. I'll be fine.' She looked into his deep, brown eyes and forced a smile. He put his hand under her chin.

'That's better,' he said. 'You have a beautiful smile.'

He was easily the best looking of the men at the manor. He was tall, slim but muscular and with skin that was as black as the night. He was wearing a small pair of white swimming trunks and a singlet top that showed off the perfection of his physique. Janet felt her anger melting away as she looked into his soft, brown eyes.

'Where's your wife?' she asked.

'She's being well looked after by a couple of the servants. She'll be fine.'

'Don't you mind?'

'Of course not. We wouldn't be here if either of us minded what the other got up to. We'll go to bed tonight, and she'll tell me everything that happened in the smallest detail and, by the time she's finished, we'll be fucking like animals.'

'Do you tell her what you do?'

'Yep.'

'I thought all the guests had a hang-up, you know, something wrong with their sex lives. You two don't seem to have any problems.'

'Jeannie is a diagnosed nymphomaniac.' Peter spoke quite nonchalantly, as though it was the most normal thing in the world to speak about a wife in this way. 'We fuck every day, but it's never enough for her, so we use places like this. It's better than having her wandering the streets, looking for guys.'

Janet grinned and sat back on the lounger. Peter took a seat next to her and slipped off his singlet. She gazed with admiration at his smoothly defined torso. 'D'you work out?' she asked.

'Yeh, I like to keep fit.'

'You've got a good body.' Janet reached over and ran a finger over his chest, tracing the line of his pectorals.

'Were you sunbathing?' he asked. Janet nodded. 'Well, don't let me stop you.' She smiled coyly and slowly pulled her T-shirt over her head, then lay back on the lounger. 'You've got a good body too,' he continued. He leant forward and moved the tip of his finger between her pert, firm breasts, then circled each in turn. She shivered, despite the heat. Slowly, Peter traced a line down, over her flat stomach to her navel. He pushed the tip of his finger into it, then moved down further until he was touching the edge of her thong.

'Won't you get a line if you sunbathe in this?'

'I suppose so.'

'Take it off, then.'

Janet shrugged and slipped the tiny garment down her legs and kicked it off. She lay back again with her legs drawn slightly apart. He smiled kindly and then looked directly at her hairy mound. Janet licked her lips. She was already wet thanks to her unsuccessful attempt at seducing Mr Gee, and she knew that he would soon see the tell-tale sheen of dampness on her pubic curls. She looked at his groin. His white trunks were bulging enormously. OK, she thought, he's not Mr Gee, but he certainly is gorgeous!

She opened her legs a little wider and felt a trickle

of warm juice slip between her buttocks. He must have seen that, she thought. He didn't move. He just stared at her bush.

'Are there any things your wife won't let you do?' she asked, more to break the silence than anything else.

'A couple of things, but it's no problem.'

'What kind of things?'

'It doesn't matter. Let's not talk about my wife.' He stood up and walked to the edge of the pool and looked out into the distance. For a moment, Janet thought that she'd lost another chance. She jumped up and joined him by the pool.

'D'you feel like a swim?' she asked.

'Yeh, why not?' He made to dive into the welcoming water.

'I think you should take your trunks off,' Janet purred, 'after all, I'm naked and it was your idea.'

'Fair enough.' Peter turned his back to her and slipped the white trunks down to his ankles and pulled them off. Janet savoured the sight of his firm, tight buttocks and wondered what they would taste like if she got the chance to run her tongue over them. He turned to face her and she gasped audibly. His cock was steel-erect. It was long and very thick, two-thirds of it as black as ebony whilst the top four inches or so was as pink as a baby's bottom. Janet felt her mouth go dry as she stared at the monster.

'Sorry about this,' Peter said sheepishly. 'Sometimes it seems to have a life of its own.'

Janet giggled girlishly and jumped into the pool. Surfacing, she trod water whilst she enjoyed the sight of the naked man and his huge erection. 'Come on,' she shouted. 'It's lovely!' Peter dived in and swam, eel-like to her side. She curled her arms around his neck and wrapped her legs around his waist, pulling him under the water. They kissed. Janet pressed herself to him so that he could feel the creamy-moistness of her pussy against his stomach. They rolled playfully around in the water like children, occasionally surfacing for air and fondling each other's bodies with frenzied passion. Lisa had told her of her session in the pool with the servant. Now it was her turn.

Peter pushed his hand between their bodies and his fingers found the open welcome of her sex-lips. He slipped them inside her and pressed the palm of his hand against her hard little bud. She kissed him harder and reached down until her fingers could circle his thick cock. They slipped under the water again and she wriggled herself around him until she could feel the tip of his erection touching her upper thighs. Peter pulled his fingers from her hot sheath as they surfaced once more and she purposefully aimed his prick towards her aching honey-pot and sank down on him.

She gasped as he entered her, and then slipped under the water until the full length was deep inside her. He was massive, not only in length but also in thickness, and it was just what she needed. She gripped his powerful shoulders and pulled herself up to break the surface, gulped in the air and then sank down hard again to absorb him completely. Peter thrust his hips forwards and she felt a slight, but entirely pleasurable pain as his cock-head hit her cervix. He gripped her thighs and rammed himself rapidly in and out of her, pummelling and stretching her into an oblivion of ecstasy.

Janet pulled herself up for air and his cock slipped from inside her. She took a deep breath and then duck-dived down again. In the gloom she could see him treading water, with his big dick waving menacingly in front of his superb body. She gripped his thighs and took the end of the monster into her mouth. She managed to move her body so that her legs were over his powerful shoulders and immediately sensed his tongue lapping the water and her juices from her cunt. She bobbed her head backwards and forwards and sucked him for as long as she could manage before, at last, she had reluctantly to pull herself from him and rise once again to the surface. They drifted apart in the warm water. Janet spluttered and coughed as she gulped in the air, then they both broke into a fit of laughter.

Without warning, Peter dived under the surface. Janet couldn't see him through the churning water and squirmed around to see where he had gone. Suddenly she felt a sharp bite on her bottom, and he rose to the surface behind her, laughing like a fool. She slapped the water in his face, and swam for the edge of the pool. She managed to crawl out just as he reached her.

'You've got a beautiful little ass,' he drawled as he stared blatantly at her pert behind. She struggled to her feet. Peter launched himself from the pool in one, lithe movement. He stood next to her and curled his arm around her shoulders. 'I've never fucked under water before,' he said, proudly. Janet merely smiled.

They walked over to the lawn, in full view of the house. Janet wanted Mr Gee to see that his rejection of her hadn't mattered in the least. She looked up at the windows but there was no sign of their enigmatic host. Shrugging her shoulders, she lay down on her back on the soft carpet of green and opened her legs wide. 'Come on, Peter,' she purred. 'Fuck me good.'

He knelt between her outstretched thighs and gazed at her welcoming pussy. His cock jutted forward angrily, the head purple with his lust. He moved forward until the tip touched her soft, wet lips. Janet raised her bottom slightly from the ground. He slipped the bulbous head inside her and at first she automatically stiffened her groin muscles to grip him inside her, then relaxed them as she realised that his thickness made it unnecessary. She closed her eyes blissfully and allowed him to slide inch after inch into her hot sheath. He fucked her slowly, using the full length with each thrust. Janet raised her legs high and gripped her feet with her fingers. Peter stiffened his body and supported himself on his hands and toes, then began to pound steadily in and out. Janet looked down and marvelled at the way she was able to accommodate such a monster. The sheen of her juices coated the plunging, ebony rod and her sex-lips seemed to be clinging to it each time he withdrew, as if desperate not to release him. He began to increase the speed of his movements and their groins slapped together loudly.

Suddenly, Janet wriggled from under him and turned on to her hands and knees. 'Do it from behind,' she mewed, 'then I can feel the whole length.'

Peter stroked her bottom lovingly. 'Are you sure?' he said, with genuine concern. 'That's one of the things my wife can't do. She says it hurts her too much.'

Janet looked over her shoulder and wiggled her bum provocatively. 'Do it,' she demanded.

Peter shrugged. 'OK,' he said as he positioned himself behind her. Janet bent her back so that her bottom was forced upwards obscenely. She felt him touch her hot little hole, and then he was inside, sliding deeper and deeper until his groin pressed against her buttocks.

'You OK?' he panted.

'It's beautiful,' Janet groaned. 'Now, give it to me hard. You won't hurt me, I promise.'

Peter needed no further encouragement. He took it steadily at first, clearly concerned that he might hurt her despite her assurances, then he began to thrust in and out of her at an alarming rate as his groin slapped against her backside. Janet looked up at the house. A number of people were watching, mainly students, but there was no sign of Mr Gee.

'Gee, you sure do have a lovely ass,' gasped Peter as he hammered into her like a man possessed.

'You can fuck it, if you like.'

Peter stopped short, as though he'd suddenly been frozen solid. 'Aw, no, I mean, I –'

'Is that the other thing your wife won't let you do?'

'Yeh, but hell, I could never get in there.'

Janet moved forward so that his cock slipped from inside her, and lay on her back, resting on her elbows. She looked at his fierce erection and grinned. He was big, but she'd had bigger. 'You can try,' she purred. 'Look, I've got some baby oil on the table over there that I use when I'm sunbathing. Go and get it and I'll show you what to do.'

Peter pulled himself to his feet with some difficulty and walked to the table. He found the correct bottle from amongst the various creams and lotions and brought it back. He crouched in front of her, his cock looking longer and thicker than ever. Janet turned back on her hands and knees and presented her bottom to him.

'Pour some between the cheeks and push a couple of fingers inside me. That'll loosen me up for you.' She heard Peter snap the top of the bottle open and then felt the warmth of the viscous fluid slip down her cleft. 'That's it. Now, your fingers. Soak them with oil and push them in.' After a few seconds she felt him move his fingertips between her buttocks, then felt him slide in. 'How many fingers have you got in me?' she asked.

'Two.'

'Try three. You're a big boy. You're gonna have to really open me up.'

She felt him ease his fingers from her, then sensed more oil being poured onto her anus. Then he was in her again, this time with three fingers. The tight sphincter relaxed quickly. She was ready.

'OK,' she breathed, 'now, put lots of oil on your dick and fuck me hard. I want to feel that lovely thing right up my arse!'

'Gee, I love the way you talk. You really are something,' he said as he eased his fingers from her. She heard him fumbling with the bottle, then felt the familiar prodding of a fat cock-head against her anus. He pushed forward and she jumped. 'You OK?' he said.

'Yes, I'm just getting used to you. Go on, fuck my bum now!'

She sensed him moving into her, slowly, cautiously until half of his superb length was inside her. She reached between her legs and gripped his bone-hard stalk. 'Put a bit more oil on it, then go all the way,' she demanded. There was more fumbling with the bottle, and then more trickling of warm fluid over her backside. Peter pushed forward. Janet felt his huge shaft slip effortlessly to the hilt. He held himself still with his full length trapped in her tight bottom. She could feel him throbbing inside her. He was going to come soon, that was for certain.

She found her pussy with her fingertips as he began to fuck her steadily. She rubbed her hard little bud rapidly. She was very close herself, and she wanted to come with him. He began to pound in and out of her, all his earlier concerns apparently dismissed from his mind. 'What an ass! What an ass!' he kept repeating in time with his rhythmic lunges. She rubbed herself harder. She was coming, and it was going to be good.

'Oh, baby, yeh!' he roared, and he rammed the full length of his cock up her bottom. He gripped her buttocks tightly and held himself deep inside her. She felt him throbbing, the heavy pounding of a fearsome ejaculation within her tight sheath. The thought of him filling her bottom with his sperm took her over the edge. She squealed loudly as she orgasmed and stiffened all the muscles of her lower body. The result was to grip Peter's gradually wilting rod with such an incredible tightness so that he yelped with pain. She couldn't have cared less. She circled her backside and forced herself back against his crotch, rubbing her buttocks against his hairy groin. The pulsating sensations within her pussy slowly abated and she moved herself forward, then relaxed as her moment passed and he eased himself from her and collapsed on to his back.

A cheer rang out from the house.

Lisa took the uniform from the wardrobe and laid it out on the bed. She examined it closely. It was identical to that worn by the students; a short, black mini-kilt, white blouse and light blue blazer. She searched the pockets of the blazer and found the striped tie which completed the outfit.

Compared to all the other wildly diverse and supremely erotic garments that had been provided for her and Janet to wear the uniform was quite staid, but Lisa had formed a picture in her mind of the students in the library, and how incredibly sexy they had looked. She pulled off her top and quickly wrenched off her jeans. Now naked, she held the pleated skirt against herself. It looked far too short. She threw it back on to the bed and donned the crisp, white shirt. She fastened the buttons with some difficulty. It was clearly too small for her. She decided that this must be Janet's uniform, and that perhaps there was another in her size. She searched through the rows of clothing in both wardrobes but found nothing. She shrugged and decided to continue to dress herself.

She pulled the little skirt over her long legs and tucked the blouse into the elasticated waistband. Searching through her drawer she found a pair of sheer, black stockings and a suspender-belt. Another cupboard provided a pair of black, flat-soled shoes that seemed ideal to complete the outfit. Finally, she donned the tie and pulled on the blazer and stood in front of the full-length mirror.

She gasped. Although in her late teens, she could have easily been taken for an innocent schoolgirl. As she had supposed, the skirt was very short, with the hem less than an inch below her crotch. The slightest swing of her hips and all would be revealed. The buttons of the blouse seemed destined to fail in their attempt to hold back the thrust of her huge breasts. Her large, erect nipples were clearly visible through the thin material. She tried to button the blazer, but the garment was too small to fit across her ample bosom.

Seeing herself dressed in this way, Lisa remembered the time when Janet had worn a school uniform to a fancy-dress party, and recalled the story that she had told of her numerous sexual encounters as a result. Now, as she gazed at her erotic reflection, she could well understand.

'Very sexy!'

Lisa swung round as Janet burst into the room. Her friend was wearing a small T-shirt and was carrying a tiny, black thong in her hand. She had clearly been busy.

'It's too small for me,' said Lisa as she turned back to look again in the mirror.

Janet stood next to her and grinned. 'You'll have to wear panties if you're going out like that,' she said.

'I've no intention of going out like this,' replied Lisa as she took off the blazer. 'I'd get arrested!'

'Oh, go on, it'll be a laugh. Look, there are no more lessons today, so why not?'

Lisa looked back at her reflection. Without the blazer, the full form and size of her magnificent breasts could be seen. She felt a familiar ache between her legs.

'Tell you what,' said Janet as she sat on the edge of the bed, 'I'll have a bet with you.'

'A bet?'

'Yes. I bet you can't go to town and walk through the high street, then come back here without getting laid.'

'Of course I could,' said Lisa.

'Go on, then, do it.' Janet's face was flushed with excitement.

Lisa looked at her friend, and then at herself in the mirror. 'OK,' she said after a moment, 'you've got a bet.' She reached for the phone to call a taxi.

'And no lying,' cautioned Janet, 'and, for God's sake, put some knickers on!'

Lisa walked to the front door of the manor, feeling positively apprehensive and regretting the fact that she'd taken on Janet's wager. Nevertheless, whatever happened, it would be fun.

Madam Stone appeared from the garden as Lisa

walked down the steps to the taxi. 'Where are you going, dressed like that?' There was a hint of amusement in the tall woman's voice.

'Oh, just to town,' replied Lisa as nonchalantly as she could.

'Let me look at you. We can't have the good people of the town getting the wrong impression about Grantham Manor, can we?'

Lisa tried her best not to breathe too deeply. The buttons of her uniform blouse were already straining to contain her voluptuous figure, with only the striped tie concealing her deep cleavage from her tutor's gaze. She tugged the hem of her short, pleated mini-kilt, but it barely reached the tops of her stockings.

'Have fun,' said Madam Stone. She turned and walked into the house, but Lisa could see that she was grinning broadly. She clambered nervously into the taxi, feeling glad that she had taken her friend's advice and donned a pair of tiny, white panties. The taxi driver glanced appreciatively between her legs as she settled next to him on the front passenger seat. She glared back at him and he looked away.

As they drove through the countryside he kept looking at her, occasionally smiling and making inane conversation. The nearer that they got to the town, the more terrified she became. Her outfit really was somewhat over the top. What if people laughed? She knew that she could cope with unwanted amorous attentions, but laughter would be too much. She mentally cursed Janet, and also herself for agreeing to this silly stunt. She began to perspire, despite the fact that the cab window was partly open. She took a couple of deep breaths. The middle button of her blouse finally surrendered, flew off and hit the windscreen with a loud ping. The driver didn't appear to notice, his eyes now firmly fixed on the increasing traffic ahead.

She adjusted her tie to preserve her modesty as the car drew up at the edge of the shopping precinct. 'I'm just going for a coffee, miss,' said the driver. 'D'you want to join me?'

'No, it's all right, thanks,' Lisa replied as she paid him the fare. 'I'm just going to do some shopping.'

'Come on, love,' he insisted. 'There's a little café just around the corner. You look like you could do with a drink.'

Lisa knew that he was right. Her hands were trembling and she could feel an uncomfortable tightness in the pit of her stomach. After all, she thought, what could possibly happen in a café? 'OK, just a quick coffee,' she said.

As they walked slowly down the side street, Lisa could already feel scores of eyes bearing down on her. Two old women stared directly at her breasts as she brushed past them on the narrow pavement and they tutted loudly. Strangely, she felt encouraged by their disapproval.

The driver took her arm and lead her into the café. The interior was dim and smoke filled, and there was an all-pervading aroma of fried food contained in the thick atmosphere. Lisa sat at a table near the window and the driver went to the counter to order the drinks. The room had fallen into silence. She looked round at the other customers and realised that she was the only female present. They all seemed to be workmen, dressed in scruffy clothes and with filthy hands gripping greasy sandwiches, and they all seemed to be looking at her. She began to wish that she hadn't taken up the cab driver's invitation.

He returned with two steaming mugs of coffee and

sat next to her. She picked up her drink and took a sip.

'How old are you, love?' said the driver.

'Nineteen,' she replied, truthfully.

'Nineteen? And still at school?'

She laughed nervously. 'Oh, no,' she said, 'this is fancy dress. I'm going to a party.'

'Going to a party? I thought you said you were going shopping.'

'I am. I'm going to the party later. Does it matter?' She wanted to leave, she wanted to get the walk over with and get back to the manor as quickly as possible. She looked around the café again. Most of the customers were still gazing at her. Some of them seemed quite attractive, despite their unkempt appearance. One of them in particular took her eye. He was a handsome man in his late twenties with long, dark hair and tanned features. He smiled when she looked at him, a broad, cheeky grin that she found most appealing. She half-smiled in response, and then looked down at her coffee.

'I'd better go,' she said. 'I need some fresh air.'

'It is a bit thick in here today,' replied the driver as he got up from his chair. 'Come on, then.'

He held her arm as she stood up, but she tugged it away from his grasp. 'I'll go on my own, thanks,' she said, firmly. 'You stay and have your coffee.'

He sat back glumly on his chair and Lisa struggled through the closely packed tables to the exit. As she reached the door she glanced back at the young man. He smiled again and she looked away.

Out in the street, Lisa took a deep breath and then headed in the direction of the main street. Time to get it over with. She fixed her eyes resolutely forward and strode determinedly along the precinct, carefully avoiding the gaze of any of the many passers-by. As she walked, her breasts bounced heavily and her little tie jiggled on its platform of firm flesh. Her tiny skirt billowed occasionally in the breeze, no doubt giving a lovely view to any lucky individual who might be looking in the right direction.

She reached the end of the precinct quickly, turned round and stopped. All she had to do now was walk back, find another taxi and return to Grantham Manor. She was feeling much more confident now, and chided herself for being so foolish. She strode quickly forward. About halfway down she stopped and looked at her reflection in the darkened window of one of the shops. She looked good. She looked sexy, and she looked beautiful. She had nothing to be nervous about. She took off her blazer and swung it over her shoulder then carried on walking, her head held high and her hips swaying provocatively. This was easy.

A couple of workmen whistled as she past them, but she merely grinned and ignored them. Another couple of men who were seated on one of the many benches that littered the precinct stared at her as she walked towards them, with their eyes firmly fixed on her bobbing breasts. She nodded in greeting to them and smiled warmly, then walked on.

There was only one taxi at the rank when she reached it. She happily realised that it wasn't the same one that had brought her to town. She clambered into the back and sat down heavily on the seat. She breathed a long sigh of relief.

'Hello again, miss.' The driver turned round to greet her. It was the young man from the café, the one with the cheeky grin. She smiled weakly and pulled her blazer so that it lay protectively across her lap.

'Grantham Manor, please,' she said.

'Grantham Manor? Are you one of the students?'

'No, I'm a teacher. This is just fancy dress. I'm going to a party.'

'Whatever you say, miss,' chuckled the driver as he drove off. Lisa looked out of the window and watched the town disappear quickly into the distance. 'Is it true what they say about Grantham Manor?' continued the driver.

'And what do they say?'

'That it's a school for sex.' He looked round and grinned.

'Do you mind watching the road,' she said, haughtily.

'Well? What d'you teach then?'

Lisa thought quickly. 'Applied mathematics,' she said.

'Oh, right.' It seemed to do the trick. The journey continued in silence. Lisa watched the trees drifting by and thought about her short adventure. In a way, she felt a trifle disappointed that nothing had happened. Janet wouldn't be very impressed.

The car gave a sudden jolt. 'Shit!' exclaimed the driver. 'What's that?'

Lisa's first thought was that it was some sort of ploy, now that they were deep in the countryside, and she wasn't having any of that. Before she could say anything, however, she heard the distinct sound of a wheel scraping on the tarmac. The driver pulled the vehicle to a stop. 'Bloody flat tyre,' he said as he opened his door. 'Sorry about this.'

Lisa climbed out of the car and sat on a grassy mound by the side of the road. The driver retrieved some tools from the boot and began to work on the puncture. She watched him appreciatively as he laboured. As he bent over to unfasten the wheelnuts she was treated to the sight of the most perfect, trim behind she had ever seen on a man. His jeans were tight, and he didn't appear to be wearing any underwear. She licked her lips hungrily.

He seemed to be having trouble with one of the wheelnuts. She could see his muscles stiffening as he strained with the effort but the thing didn't seem to want to budge. He looked up at her. 'Can you give me a hand, miss?' She walked over and took hold of the wheelbrace where he indicated. 'Now, on three. One, two, three!' The nut gave way easily, perhaps too easily, and Lisa fell backwards with the driver sprawling across her. He laughed out loud but made no effort to move from her. Their eyes met, and his grin disappeared.

'Sorry about that, miss,' he said as he struggled to his feet. He took hold of both of her hands and helped her up, then brushed the dust from her back and bottom. 'Don't want you messing up your outfit,' he said. He seemed to be concentrating rather too much on her backside, and the brushing of his hand across her buttocks was having a profound effect on Lisa. She glanced down at his groin and saw that it was having a not inconsiderable effect on him as well. She moved away from him and resumed her seat on the grass.

'That's a hell of an outfit,' he said as he sat next to her. 'I bet you win first prize.'

'First prize?'

'At the party.'

'Oh, yes, the party. D'you think so?'

'Definitely. I'd certainly give you top marks.'

'Aren't you going to fix the tyre?'

He looked into her eyes. His were deep brown and full of emotion. 'There's no hurry, is there?' Lisa tore her gaze from his and looked down. She could see the outline of a firmly erect and quite substantial cock encased in the thick denim of his jeans. She swallowed hard. He put his fingers under her chin and turned her face to his. 'You're not in a rush, are you?'

Lisa shook her head gently. The driver moved his face closer. She closed her eyes and parted her lips slightly. She felt the roughness of the stubble on his chin as they kissed, and it excited her. She wrapped her arms around his neck and pressed her mouth hard against him. Their tongues met and circled each other wetly. He ran his hand down her back then up again to her shoulder. She shifted her position and his hand slipped round to cup her breast. Lisa sighed deeply to indicate her pleasure.

'God, you've got beautiful tits,' he breathed as he kneaded the firm flesh. He moved slightly and cupped both of her breasts in his hands as if weighing them. 'Fabulous,' he murmured. They kissed again, deeply and passionately and Lisa lay back. The driver moved her tie to one side and unfastened the remaining buttons of her blouse. He pushed the thin cotton to either side of her heaving mounds then lay the tie between them. He gazed at them in abject appreciation. 'Wow,' he breathed. He bent his head and kissed each nipple in turn and then sucked gently on one. She felt it harden between his rasping teeth. He transferred his attention to the other nipple and she felt his hand stray to her thigh. She could sense her pussy-lips opening in anticipation of his touch as his fingers trailed slowly up her leg. She gasped as he touched the V of her panties.

'God, your knickers are soaked,' he said.

'I know.' He moved his face back to hers and they kissed again. His finger slid deftly under the damp cotton and slipped between her sex-lips. She began to move her hips in response.

'You really want it, don't you?' he whispered. She nodded. He moved to kneel in front of her and reached under her mini-kilt with both hands. She raised her bottom from the ground as he pulled down her panties and then automatically smoothed her hands over her stockings. She lay back with her legs spread wide apart. The driver gazed at her pussy in admiration. 'That's beautiful,' he murmured. 'I've never fucked a shaven one before.'

'Well, you're going to now.'

She watched as he unzipped his jeans and eased his rampant erection into view. She wanted to suck it, and she wanted him to lick her, but it was clear that he had other things on his mind. He moved between her legs, gripping his stiff stalk at the root with one hand and aimed the head at her succulent prize. She felt it touch her tender flesh and she gasped. Now all she wanted was to feel him inside her, to have him fill her with his thick stalk and fuck her like crazy. She raised her bottom from the grass but he teased her by moving the tip of his cock up and down along her soaked lips. He rubbed his glans against her clitoris and she shuddered.

'Oh, God, fuck me! Fuck me!' she pleaded.

He grinned, that cheeky, stupid grin and moved forward. She felt him slide into her, filling and stretching her until their groins met. Lisa rammed her mouth against his and dug her fingernails into his backside. He rubbed his pubic mound hard against hers whilst keeping his full length deep inside her. She was coming already. She tugged at the denim of his jeans and bucked her hips wildly, all the time stiffening the muscles of her thighs and groin to grip his throbbing cock tightly within her.

He raised himself and she looked down between their bodies. She watched in delight as he began to move his thick cock in and out of her oozing lips and she shuddered into a terrifying climax. Suddenly he pulled from her and knelt across her stomach whilst rubbing himself furiously. He groaned and the sperm jetted from him to soak her breasts, her tie and her blouse. Lisa reached up and grabbed hold of his pumping shaft and put the end to her mouth, then licked and sucked it and swallowed his delicious cream.

He fell from her, fully sated. It had been quick, too quick. Lisa needed more. She had to get back to the manor. Paul, Mike, anybody; she had to find someone.

The driver zipped himself up. 'I'd better change that wheel,' he said. Lisa cleaned herself up with the sodden pair of panties and then threw them over a hedge. He finished the work quickly and then held the door of the taxi open for her, grinning as ever. He was clearly very pleased with himself, but Lisa was shaking with the need for more sex.

And she'd lost her bet.

Lisa awoke with a start. The room was in almost total darkness and there was an eerie silence. Normally, the house would have been filled with the sounds of laughter and love-making. She glanced at the electronic clock by the bedside. 4.15. Even the most ardent of the guests would have collapsed from exhaustion by now.

Janet's side of the bed was empty. Her friend was no doubt still with the gorgeous American, Peter, and possibly his lovely wife, continuing where she'd left off at the pool-side. Lisa felt a pang of envy, tinged with mounting frustration. This had been one of the few nights that she'd spent alone for some considerable time, and she didn't like it.

She pictured Janet taking Peter's huge, black cock into her saucy little bum, and wondered what his wife thought. Would Janet have persuaded her to do the same? No doubt her friend would tell her all about it on her return.

The moon must have appeared from behind the clouds and the bedroom was suddenly filled with a silvery, white light. Lisa stared at the ceiling and allowed her fingers to slip between her legs. She began to caress her clitoris, feeling the bud harden quickly to her touch. She ran her other hand over her breasts and pinched her nipples to erection, then reached over and opened one of the drawers in the bedside cabinet. She quickly found what she was looking for. A long, slim vibrator which gleamed provocatively in the moonlight. She put the end to her mouth and licked the smooth surface, coating it liberally with her saliva, then moved it down between her legs. She turned the control knob at the base of the implement and it buzzed into life. The moment the vibrating sleeve touched her wet sex-lips she shuddered with delight and pushed it hard against herself.

Suddenly, she threw the pleaser on to the floor and sat up angrily. She was furious with herself. She was staying in a house of sex, and she was masturbating alone! She swung her legs from the bed and grabbed her robe, then made for the door.

Out in the dimly lit passageway, she stopped and listened. There was no sound coming from any of the bedrooms that led from the long corridor. She moved to the head of the stairs and looked down. Silence. Her throat felt dry. She sensed that she could still taste Janet's juices on her lips. At least her friend had done that for her – a wonderful hour of mutual oral enjoyment which had helped to ease her sexual tension on her return from town. But it hadn't been enough. Janet's tongue had worked its usual wonders and given her four, or possibly five orgasms but it had only served to increase her desire for a good, hard fucking.

A drink. That's what she needed. A cup of coffee, perhaps. She moved quickly down the long staircase and headed for the kitchen at the rear of the house. She was about to open the door when she heard voices. One she recognised as that of Mr Gee; the other she didn't know, although its tone seemed strangely familiar to her. She drew her robe around her nakedness and listened, barely daring to breathe.

'Believe me, my friend,' said the stranger's voice, 'with this power the most important and influential people in the world will be under our control.'

'But the amulets, are they dangerous? Can they harm the wearer?' Mr Gee appeared to be genuinely concerned.

'Not at all. They give only pleasure. Trust me, my friend. Come, I will show you.'

Lisa heard sudden movements from the other side of the door and ducked behind a large sofa. The door opened and she sensed the men walk past her refuge, then heard the sound of another door opening. She waited for a moment, then cautiously peered over the top of the sofa. The door to the basement was slightly ajar. Summoning up her courage, she decided to follow.

She padded over to the door and opened it just enough to allow her to slip through. Slowly, she descended the steep stairway, stepping as lightly as she could. She was trembling with fear, but she knew that she had to find out what was going on.

At the foot of the stairs she stopped and listened. The voices were muffled, coming from behind another door. She moved cautiously towards it and tried to discern what was being said. Suddenly there was a loud click as the catch was turned. Lisa shrank quickly back into the shadows as the door opened and the two men exited. She held her breath as they ascended the stairs. The light was turned off and the upper door was closed. She stood in pitch blackness, her heart thumping. Feeling her way by sliding her hand across the surface of the wall, she found the other door and pushed it open. The small room was illuminated by a strange, green light that emanated from a large, open chest on a table. She walked over to the table and looked inside. It contained dozens of amulets, dark green in colour, each fitted with a thick, gold chain and each glowing incandescently. She put her fingers to one of the jewels. It felt warm to her touch. Suddenly, she shivered, but it was not a feeling of fear that made her tremble, but an incongruous desire for sexual release that surged through her body. She drew back her hand and the desire waned as suddenly as it had appeared. She touched the amulet again. The effect was instantaneous. A feeling like a mild electric shock shot through her arm and seemed to fill her entire body with an all-consuming need. She gasped as she felt the juices flow from between her legs to soak her inner thighs. She was going to come! She gripped the amulet tightly and the ache in her pussy grew to a shattering climax in moments. She fell back, still clutching the jewel. She panted heavily. She'd wanted sexual relief, but hadn't expected this.

She began to feel strange. Normally, after an orgasm her clitoris would be tender to the touch, but not this time. Her fingers found the hard bud and she rubbed herself furiously, desperate to come again. The amulet seemed to be glowing much more brightly, and it felt hot against the skin of her hand. Suddenly, she threw it back into the chest and crouched on the floor. She thrust all four fingers of one hand inside her throbbing cunt and rubbed her clitoris wildly with the other. But the need seemed to be fading. Gradually she slowed her movements until she stopped and eased her wet fingers from inside herself.

It was the amulet that had done it. Her mind raced. She had to tell Janet, and they had to find a way of discovering how the stones would be used.

Seven

'You mean that you had an orgasm by just holding one of those things in your hand?' Janet's eyes were staring in disbelief as her friend recounted the story of the previous night's adventure. Paul and Mike sat impassively on the sofa.

'Yes,' replied Lisa, 'in the space of a few moments. I didn't even need to touch myself. It was incredible.'

'Oh, come on, Lisa,' continued Janet, 'you must have been dreaming.'

Lisa looked for support from the two young men. 'You believe me, don't you? I wasn't dreaming.'

'Of course you were,' said Janet, impatiently. She turned to face Paul and Mike. 'We both have very realistic dreams. We have since, since –' She stopped short.

'Since you first met the old man?' said Paul, suddenly.

Lisa gasped. 'What do you know about the old man?' she said, her voice trembling.

Mike got to his feet and walked over to her, resting his hand on her shoulder. 'I think it's about time we told you about ourselves,' he said slowly. 'Paul and I are investigators. We work for a special branch of the government, looking into paranormal activities.'

'Paranormal?' Lisa sank to a chair.

Mike sat on the edge of the bed next to Janet.

'Seemingly unexplainable events. We usually discover very real and ordinary reasons behind them but sometimes even we can't explain what we find.'

'Go on,' said Janet, quietly.

'We learnt about the old man some time ago. Who, or what he is we don't know, but what we do know is that he is very dangerous. We also know that you two were involved with him some time ago, and that you thwarted his attempt to take over power of governments throughout the world. We've been watching you for some time.'

'Why?' said Lisa, crossly. 'We aren't in league with him or anything!'

Mike stroked her hair gently. 'We know that,' he said, softly, 'but we also felt certain that you were the key to finding out his next move.'

'What do you mean?' said Janet.

Paul stood up and faced her. 'Men of his kind don't take defeat lightly. We knew that he would return to find you.'

'For revenge, you mean?' Lisa's eyes widened as she realised the implications of his words. 'Are we in danger?'

'Very possibly,' said Paul as he sat next to the girls on the bed. 'We knew about Mr Gee's involvement, which is why we came to Grantham Manor. It was no surprise to us that you two turned up. You both have very special powers, as you know. We believe that the old man intends to use those powers to gain his evil ends.'

'But how?' asked Janet.

'That much we don't know,' continued Mike, 'but what Lisa has discovered gives us a clue. The old man is intent on world domination, and he uses sex as his weapon. Those amulets are the link. They clearly possess unearthly powers and somehow they are going to be used as part of his plan. What we all have to discover is how.'

Lisa had a sudden thought. 'Maybe if one of us could get to Mr Gee,' she said. 'You know, if one of us could –'

'Seduce him?' Janet interrupted, 'I've already tried that and got nowhere. I think he might be gay.'

Lisa laughed out loud at her words. 'Just because a guy doesn't fancy you,' she smirked, 'it doesn't automatically mean that he's gay!'

Janet shrugged. She clearly believed what she had said. 'I've never had a man turn me down before,' she pouted, 'and I didn't like it one little bit. It was a really weird feeling.'

'I wouldn't know,' bragged Lisa, smiling with mock sympathy at her friend. Janet looked positively glum. 'Look, maybe he prefers other types of girls,' Lisa added in an attempt to make amends for her teasing.

'You know the strength of our powers,' retorted Janet. 'We can bend the will of any man or woman that we choose. If I couldn't fuck him, nobody can.'

'No, maybe Lisa's got a point,' said Mike. 'It could be that he simply prefers blondes.' He grinned at Lisa. 'How about it, Lisa?'

Lisa shrugged nervously. 'I don't mind. In fact, I think he's rather gorgeous. I still haven't got over the story that Janet told me, about the way that he made her come, just by looking at her.'

'It's worth a try,' said Paul, standing up and walking towards the door. 'We have to know what he intends to do with those amulets. But, for now, we've all got work to do.'

'Oh God, yes,' exclaimed Janet with sudden realisation, 'the students. I'd quite forgotten about them.'

'I looked at the rota on the hall noticeboard before

we came up. Lisa's down for oral techniques and Janet, well, you're down for something that's quite the reverse!'

Janet laughed out loud. 'I've a pretty shrewd idea what that is,' she chuckled. 'Come on, let's get breakfast. We'll talk more in the lunch break.'

There was only a handful of students in the dining room, together with a couple of the older guests. Janet and Lisa sat at a small table opposite Serita, the olive-skinned girl who had refused to make love in front of the class, and another girl, whom they'd not seen before. She was of small build and had very dark skin with huge, shining eyes and a remarkably full mouth. Lisa felt that she and Madam Stone could be sisters, so alike were their features.

Serita smiled weakly as they sat down.

'You look exhausted,' said Lisa.

'I got fucked by six guys last night. I hardly slept a wink.' Serita spoke matter of factly as she nonchalantly dug her spoon into a grapefruit half. The other girl gasped and her big eyes widened even more in her astonishment. 'It was Madam Stone's orders,' Serita continued. 'She made me go to the staff restroom and take off my clothes in front of everybody there. It was to punish me for not performing in front of the class like you did, Lisa.'

'But you were given a good beating.'

'I know, but apparently I enjoyed it too much.'

'And didn't you enjoy getting fucked by six guys?'

'I'll say. It was weird at first. I mean, walking into a room full of strange men and pulling off my clothes without saying a word. They just sat and looked at me for what seemed like an age as I stood there stark naked, then one of them came over to me and stroked my bottom and then kissed me. He sat on a dining chair and took out his cock. It was as stiff as anything. He made me turn my back to him and sit on his lap. I was so wet that I hardly felt a thing as it slid right up me. I began to move up and down and looked at the others. They were all staring at my pussy, watching me getting fucked. Suddenly I was so turned on I thought that I'd scream. Madam Stone was right; it is great doing it in front of an audience.'

'You mean you did it with all of them?' It was the newcomer who spoke in a quiet, nervous voice and thick, African accent.

Serita nodded.

'I don't think we've met you,' said Janet.

'I only arrived about an hour ago,' said the young girl. 'There were problems at the airport in Nigeria. My name is Zenga.'

'This is Lisa and I'm Janet. We are teachers here.'

'Oh.'

There was a long pause. Suddenly, Lisa seemed to think of something. 'Tell me,' she said to the young girl, 'is your father very important in Nigeria?'

'He is the deputy prime minister. Why?'

'Oh, nothing,' replied Lisa as she cast a knowing look towards Janet. 'I just wondered.'

'I could really do with another fuck,' said Serita wistfully. Zenga shot her a surprised glare.

'Do you always talk like that?' she said.

Serita grinned. 'It's this place. You'll be talking like it soon.'

Zenga shook her head vigorously. 'I don't think so,' she said.

Serita's grin broadened. 'We'll see,' she said as she took a sip of her orange juice.

'This morning we are going to look at the techniques and pleasures of oral sex.' Lisa looked around at her small group of students as they sat in the large conservatory. Kelly, the chubby American was there, as were Sammy-Lynn, Serita and the new girl, Zenga. All the pupils seemed to be excited at the prospect of the lesson; all but Serita. She was gazing out through the glass into the garden, and looked positively bored.

'Is there something wrong, Serita?' asked Lisa.

'No, Miss,' pouted the girl, sullenly. 'You go ahead.'

'You won't learn anything if you don't listen,' Lisa said, crossly.

Serita turned to look at her. 'Look, Miss,' she said, 'I'm sure you know what you are talking about, but so do I. I've sucked more dicks than I care to remember.'

Lisa walked over to her and rested her hand on her slim shoulder. 'Serita,' she said, quietly, 'with sex you can never stop learning.'

'What's to learn? You put a cock in your mouth and suck it. That's it.'

Lisa shook her head benignly. 'Oh, Serita,' she whispered, 'trust me. There's a lot more to oral sex than merely sucking a cock.' She turned to face the others. 'Now,' she said in a loud voice, 'we have a guest who will help us. My colleague, Janet, recommended him as ideal for this class.' She clapped her hands and the door opened. Peter, Janet's pool-side lover walked in wearing a short towelling robe. He stood next to Lisa with a broad smile on his handsome face. Lisa reached out and pushed her hand under his robe and stroked the smooth skin of his firm chest. 'Janet tells me that you are eminently qualified,' she breathed.

'That's real kind of her,' he replied. She ran her other hand over his taut buttocks and noticed the front of his robe begin to bulge out noticeably.

'He's gorgeous,' breathed Sammy-Lynn, resting her chin on her hands and gazing at him with adoring eyes. Lisa untied the belt of his robe and it fell open. His semi-erect cock hung heavily. The students gasped in admiration.

'Now that's what I call a cock,' sighed Kelly. Lisa pulled the garment from Peter's shoulders and let it fall to the floor, then stood behind him and gently caressed his bottom with both her hands. The girls watched, wide eyed, as his penis stiffened rapidly until it jutted forward as hard as steel.

'Look at the size of it!' drooled Sammy-Lynn. 'I don't think I could get it into my mouth! What do you think, Zenga?'

The young girl said nothing, but merely stared at the proffered monster.

'Now, Serita,' said Lisa, 'as our most experienced student, perhaps you would care to demonstrate your abilities.'

Serita shrugged and rose from her seat. She walked calmly over to stand in front of Peter and looked him directly in the face. Lisa moved over to sit with the other students and the couple turned sideways so that all could see clearly what was about to happen. Serita allowed her haughty expression to soften a little and ran her tongue suggestively across her lips, then knelt down in front of the naked man. She gripped his thick stem and opened her mouth. Lisa saw Peter stiffen his buttocks as Serita closed her lips over his ebony rod and she took about four inches into her mouth. She gripped the remainder with both of her hands and moved her head slightly to and fro, then pulled back to let the gleaming flesh fall from her lips. She stood up and turned to face the class with a proud smile on her face.

There was a short pause, then Lisa rose to her feet.

'Is that it?' she said, in mock surprise. 'Is that all you do?'

Serita looked hurt. 'What else is there?' she protested. 'I sucked his dick. That's what you told me to do.'

Lisa walked over to her. 'Yes, Serita, you sucked his dick, but we are here to learn about oral sex and all its pleasures. Anyone can put a cock into her mouth. There's a lot more to it than that. Go to your seat.' The girl did as ordered and sat heavily on her chair. She folded her arms and sighed audibly like a spoilt child. Lisa stood with her hands on her hips and looked at the students for a moment. 'Now, ladies,' she said, presently, 'watch, listen and learn.' She turned to face Peter and smiled sweetly. 'Try not to come too quickly,' she breathed so that only he could hear. She pulled off her skimpy top to reveal her naked breasts.

'I'll try, Lisa,' said Peter hoarsely as he stared at her heaving mounds, 'but it won't be easy.'

Lisa looked down at his erection. He was ragingly hard, and the thick shaft was gnarled and bloated with his lust. The huge, plum-sized end was still wet with Serita's saliva and a small blob of white fluid had seeped from the angry slit. Lisa put her finger to it and smoothed the cream over the tip of his penis then put her finger to her mouth and licked and swallowed his cream whilst staring into his deep, brown eyes. She saw him gulp. She turned to face the class once more.

'Firstly, ladies, you must remember that there is more to Peter than just his huge cock. You must use your mouth on his entire body, until he is screaming for you to suck him.' She pushed her face towards Peter's and they kissed. She felt him slip his tongue into her mouth and she circled it slowly with her own whilst pressing her lips hard against him. Then she drew her head back a little and sucked his tongue in and out of her mouth like a small prick. She licked around his full lips and then moved her face downwards to let her tongue trail across to his chest. Tracing the shape of his firm pectorals she eventually found one of his nipples and drew it between her teeth. She bit it gently and he groaned. She rasped her teeth against the hard bud and lapped around it then sucked harder in the way that she loved her own nipples to be sucked.

Peter held her tightly about the waist as she turned her attention to his other nipple. She felt his hard cock resting between her pendulous breasts and stiffened her arms so that it was trapped in the cushion of her warmth. The thick shaft throbbed and she felt the wetness on her neck. She drew back and straightened up, more in order to give him the chance to cool his ardour than for any other reason. 'Some men like their nipples to be suckled and bitten and some are quite indifferent to it,' she said, resuming her role of tutor, 'but now I am going to do something which no man can resist.'

With that, Lisa moved behind Peter and began to gently lick his broad back. She moved slowly down, soaking his ebony skin with her saliva until she reached the top of the dark cleft between his buttocks. Gradually, she drew her tongue downwards, tickling the small hairs and soaking them until they glistened. She heard him suck the air through clenched teeth as the tip of her tongue touched the tight sphincter of his anus. She licked wetly against the little hole, and then probed inside with the tip of her tongue.

'I *will* come if you don't stop,' he moaned. Lisa kissed his bottom and then crawled round until her face was level with his crotch. She wanted to engulf the huge, black stalk inside her mouth, but knew that he must wait if the students were to benefit from the lesson. She turned her back to him and sat on the floor. Bending backwards, she gripped his strong thighs and moved her head between them. She traced the shape of his balls with the tip of her tongue, then drew one, and then both into her wet mouth. Reaching up, she gripped his long shaft with one hand and rubbed it gently. 'Oh, God, be careful,' he sighed.

Lisa moved from him again to assume a kneeling position facing him. She turned to the class. 'Peter is going to come very soon,' she said. 'Watch closely. A man can experience no more fierce an orgasm than inside a hot, wet mouth.' She leant forward and gripped his cock. She licked the end and ran the tip of her tongue around the bulbous head. He tasted deliciously salty. She moved her head down and ran her tongue along the full length of the underside of his rod from the root to the tip, then greedily enveloped his achingly hard stalk within her mouth. Peter gripped her head tightly and began to thrust in and out of her sucking lips. Lisa drew in her cheeks and lapped her tongue round and round his shaft. Arching her neck, she swallowed as much of his length as she could, at the same time finding his anus with the tip of her finger. She pushed it inside the tight hole and moved her head further forward until she was barely able to breathe.

'God, oh yes! That's it!' he cried and she felt his thickness throbbing between her lips. She swallowed voraciously in the full knowledge that her undulating throat muscles would be teasing his spurting length unmercifully. She felt him dig his fingernails into her head as he surrendered himself to the delights of a violent come. She swallowed hard, the tightness of her throat gripping his pulsing flesh like a vice. 'Jesus, I can't stop coming!' he groaned. Lisa drew her head back until just the tip of his cock was pressed against her lips then moved back further and knelt with her mouth wide open whilst gripping his stalk with her free hand. As each streak of hot sperm jetted across her lovely features she felt her pussy becoming more and more soaked with her own juices. Still he came, the monster throbbing heavily within her firm grip. Yet more of his creamy fluids jetted into her mouth in full view of the students. Lisa rubbed him rapidly as he soaked her face with his release, and then she licked the sperm that trickled down his shaft until he could take no more.

She heard somebody applaud as she finally released the slowly wilting monster from her grip and eased her finger from his bottom. She turned to look at the girls grinning, fully aware that her face was splattered with his come. 'And that is how to give good oral sex,' she said, triumphantly.

Lisa and Janet were sitting with Paul and Mike at their customary place by the pool. They watched as the students frolicked playfully in the cool water. Each was naked, of course. It was a sea of lithe, young bodies cavorting in the sunshine. Lisa sipped her drink.

'That new girl seems very shy,' said Janet.

'Zenga?' replied Lisa, looking in the young girl's direction. Madam Stone had instructed that all the students were to remain naked for the remainder of the day and Zenga had complied, but she didn't appear ready to join in with her fellow students. She was sitting on one of the sun-loungers, her hands resting in her lap as though she was trying to conceal her most precious attribute from view. She was watching her colleagues avidly, nevertheless. Her expression was that of a small child who had been excluded from a playground game.

'She is very quiet and ever so nervous,' continued Lisa. 'When I gave the class a demonstration of oral sex this morning I thought she was going to pass out.'

'She'll be OK when she's been introduced to a few more of the delights of Grantham Manor,' said Janet as she slipped her T-shirt over her head, dropped it lazily on to the ground and relaxed back on her lounger.

'I'd love to be the one to do it.' It was Paul who spoke. Lisa looked over at him. His eyes were fixed directly on the lovely newcomer. She saw him lick his lips. He turned to look at Lisa with an embarrassed expression on his face.

Lisa grinned. 'She is gorgeous,' she said. 'Why don't you go over to her?'

'I tried to talk to her at lunch. She just seemed to clam up and made it clear that she didn't want to know. It didn't do much for my ego, I can tell you.'

'That's no bad thing,' laughed Janet, clearly referring to her own lack of success with Mr Gee. Paul took her words as a jibe and chose to ignore them. He looked wistfully back across the pool to where Zenga was sitting.

'She reminds me of a girl I used to know,' he said, quietly.

'Tell us about her,' said Lisa in a gentle, understanding tone of voice.

'There isn't much to tell. I met her some years ago, when I was at college. I saw her on an underground train in London, of all places. It was quite late and I was travelling back from seeing some friends. I was sitting on one side of the carriage, not really thinking about anything in particular and the train pulled into a station. There were only a couple of other people in the carriage and they both got off at that stop. The doors were just closing when this girl dashed on and fell into the seat almost opposite me. She'd obviously been running, as she was panting quite heavily. I glanced at her and caught her eye. I looked away immediately, but I'd seen enough.

'I'd always had this thing about black girls but I'd never been out with one until then. There's something special about them; not only the colour of their skin, which is beautiful, but their bone structure, their eyes, the way they walk –'

'I think we get the general idea,' Mike laughed.

Paul grinned. 'Sorry,' he said, 'I was getting carried away. Anyway, this girl was beautiful. With that fleeting glance I had already worked that much out. I looked at her again and she smiled, the sweetest smile I had ever seen. Her eyes were huge and deep brown and her skin was almost golden and completely flawless. She had a very full mouth with thick, pouting lips and gleaming, white teeth.

'I smiled back at her and looked away again. I pretended to be reading the advertisements on the carriage wall whilst I desperately tried to think of something to say that would not sound too pathetic. I was still pretty inexperienced in those days. I forced myself to look back at her again. Her head was turned away this time, so I was able to take a longer look. She was wearing a pair of tight, bright orange trousers that looked like they were made out of satin or something, and a white T-shirt. Her breasts weren't big, but they were a nice, rounded shape, and she was obviously not wearing a bra. They were bobbing gently with the rhythm of the train, and I could see the size and shape of her nipples. I think I was beginning to sweat.

'She suddenly turned her face towards me and looked straight into my eyes. She smiled again and I thought I would burst. I decided to go for it. She wouldn't have been able to hear what I said from where I was sitting because of the racket the train was making, so I made a sign with my arm as if to ask her if I could move over to her. She nodded, and I was there in a flash. I asked her for her name, and she told me it was Candy. I resisted the obvious joke about it being a sweet name and told her mine. We started to chat and quickly we were talking as though we'd known each other for years. She was a student like me and was staying with friends in London for the weekend.

'Anyway, to cut a long story short, she invited me to go back with her and meet her friends. I jumped at the chance. I was besotted. I'd never seen such a beautiful and warm girl in my life before. We arrived at her stop and got off the train, then I followed her like a pet dog up the escalator. All the way up I just stared at her bottom. It was perfect; really round and sticking out just a little too much which I found most appealing. And from the way her trousers hugged her bum it was obvious that she wasn't wearing any panties. She'd either got a thong on or, better still, nothing at all. It took a lot of willpower for me to resist reaching out and stroking it, I can tell you.

'When we reached the house where she was staying we found that her friends were still out. I was overjoyed. My mind was racing. I kept thinking to myself, would she, could she? She was so beautiful, though, so devastatingly gorgeous. I just couldn't imagine a girl who looked as good as her being interested in me.

'She made me the obligatory cup of coffee and we sat together on the sofa. We chatted for ages. I can't remember anything that we talked about. As she spoke, I found myself staring at her mouth and imagining what it would be like to have those thick, wet lips around my cock. I was totally spellbound and had developed an incredible erection which I was having difficulty in concealing.

'After a while, I excused myself to go to the toilet. I was so nervous and so hard that I could hardly manage to pee. I managed it eventually then washed my hands and walked back into the lounge. I couldn't believe my eyes at what I saw. Candy was sitting with her back to me, looking over her shoulder with the most sultry expression on her face, and she was completely naked. I stood stock still, rooted to the spot. I could feel my knees trembling violently and my throat felt so dry it seemed to be closing up. She patted the side of the couch next to her and smiled sweetly. I managed to walk over to her without collapsing and sat down. Now, I could see her entire body, and it was even more perfect than I'd imagined. Her breasts seemed larger and her nipples jutted out firmly. Her waist was narrow and her legs were long and shapely with the cutest little bush of black hair between them. But it was her skin which captivated me the most. It seemed to shine, a flawless golden-brown that looked like it would taste delicious.

'I stared at her groin and she opened her legs slightly, as if in invitation. I sat there like a dummy. She must have realised that she was going to have to make all the moves because she took hold of my hand and tugged it towards her so that I put my arm around her shoulder. She snuggled up close to me and I could smell her scent. My cock was as stiff as it could be and I was worried that I might come before I could get inside her. She put her face to mine and we kissed. Her lips were so soft and so incredibly warm. Her mouth seemed to want to engulf mine. Our tongues met and circled each other as we kissed. I put my free arm around her tiny waist and pulled her body towards mine, at the same time slipping back along the length of the sofa. She moved across me until, by the time I was lying down, she was on top of me with her legs spread on either side of mine. I could feel her pubic bone pressing hard against my erection and she began to move her hips against me, rubbing her cunt against my dick.

'I ran my hands down her smooth back and cupped her fabulous bottom. She pressed herself even harder against me as I fondled her buttocks. I traced their pertness, then ran my fingertips along the cleft between them. She groaned, still kissing me passionately. Then she was tearing my shirt open and licking my chest. She took one of my nipples in her mouth and nibbled it whilst she finished undoing the buttons and then she wrenched my shirt from my trousers. I helped her by pulling my arms from the sleeves. As she threw the shirt across the room I pushed myself to sit up and tore off my shoes and socks in almost blind panic.

'She sat back and watched as I unfastened my belt and pulled down the zip of my trousers. Then, all I was wearing was my boxer-shorts, with the front jutting out ludicrously. I don't think I'd ever been so hard.

'Candy knelt in front of me and looked up into my eyes. The expression on her face was a mixture of promise and lust. I couldn't take my eyes off her mouth. Those lips, those thick, hot lips were going to suck my cock! I was actually going to get it inside that fabulous, sweet mouth! I prayed to every God known to mankind to help me stop shooting my load down her throat the minute that she touched me. She reached up and tugged the waistband of my shorts, pulling them quickly down to my ankles. My cock was sticking out like a flagpole. She looked at it and then put her finger to the end. It was wet. She worked the juice over the head with her fingertip, then circled my shaft with her warm hand. She moved her head forward, and looked up at me again as if asking permission.

'She opened her mouth slowly, agonisingly slowly. She pushed her tongue forward, flat against her lower lip and took the wet end of my cock inside her mouth. As her luscious lips enveloped my raging stalk I felt it throb and bit my lip so hard that I tasted blood. She took the whole length into her mouth. No girl had ever done that to me before. I could feel her tongue circling my hard flesh as her lips sucked me. She had clearly done this many times before.

'She drew her head back until just the head of my cock was inside her mouth. She licked rapidly around it and rubbed the stem slowly whilst cupping my balls with her free hand. I knew that, with much more of this treatment I was definitely going to come, but I desperately wanted to fuck her. I pulled her head back reluctantly and lifted her up to her feet by her arms. We gazed into each other's eyes like true lovers. I kissed her gently on the mouth. She smiled suggestively, turned her back to me and knelt on the carpet, then bent forward and rested on her forearms so that her perfect bottom was presented to me in the most blatant but appealing fashion.

'I kicked my shorts from my feet and knelt behind her. I couldn't believe it. All my dreams, all my fantasies about making love to a girl like Candy, and now it was going to happen! I stroked those wonderful globes lovingly then bent forwards and kissed her at the top of her deep cleft. I caught the scent of her pussy, and knew that she was as aroused as I was. I ran my tongue around her buttocks and then between them until I was able to dip the end into her hot, little cunt. It tasted as delicious as it looked. I sucked her wet lips, drawing them into my mouth and nibbling them gently between my teeth. From the sound of her moans, she was obviously enjoying what I was doing, even though my experience of such things was somewhat limited.

'I couldn't hold back any longer. It had hardly been masterly foreplay, but I needed to fuck her badly. I moved my face from her bottom and took hold of my stalk by the root. I inched forward on my knees and pressed the head against her soaking sex-lips. They seemed to open for me automatically and I sank deep into her in one, long movement until my groin was pressed against her sumptuous bum. I held myself still, somehow managing to resist the temptation to pound in and out of her unmercifully, and looked in adoration at her lithe, shapely body. Then I began to move, slowly at first, gradually sliding my full length from her then back, until she engulfed it completely within her hot, wet flesh.

'I reached under her and found her clitoris with my fingertips. I rubbed her hard bud gently as I increased the pace of my fucking and she began to move with me. Gradually we moved faster and faster until my groin was slapping noisily against her bottom. Candy started to groan loudly as she thrust against me. I rubbed her faster and harder. I was determined to make her come with me.

'Suddenly, she raised herself up on to her hands and knees and held herself still with her head thrown back. I carried on pounding into her and rubbing her clitoris as hard and as fast as I could. I knew she was coming. She gave a long, low moan which got progressively louder until she squealed and gasped. I could feel the muscles of her cunt tightening and drawing my cock as deep as it would go into her. She suddenly rammed her backside hard against me and moaned again, then started panting like an animal. My cock felt like it was stretching inside her and swelling up to enormous proportions. I knew I was going to come with her. Nothing could stop me, and I didn't want it to. The sensation was almost unbearable, tearing at my balls and my cock, right down to the root. I took my hand from her pussy and gripped her bottom tightly and came with an incredible surge of release. My cock throbbed violently as I sent jet after jet of sperm deep into her lovely, hot sheath. Candy wriggled her body and squirmed her backside against me and I felt her stiffen her thigh muscles to grip me hard within her. My orgasm seemed to last for ages as I pounded in and out of her, so hard that she fell forward on to her arms again.

'It was at that precise moment that her friends decided to come back.'

Lisa stood in front of the full-length mirror and carefully checked her appearance. She smiled proudly. Mr Gee would surely not be able to resist her tonight. She smoothed her hands over the tight, rubber basque that moulded itself around her sumptuous form. If anything, her breasts looked even bigger, encased as they were in their black cocoon of sensuous, clinging material. Even her long nipples were clearly defined. The basque ended at her waist and hugged her closely, like the arms of a strong lover. Her freshly depilated pussy was bare and already the lips were pouting and wet. The shapely forms of her legs, made to appear even longer by the remarkably high heels of her shoes, were accentuated by shiny, rubber stockings which stretched almost to her groin. She touched herself between the legs and felt a charge of excitement course through her body. Yes, tonight she would have Mr Gee, and discover the truth about Grantham Manor.

She slipped on a small, black mini-dress and the outfit was complete. She ran her fingers through her long, blonde hair and stood sideways to the mirror. She breathed in deeply and held her stomach muscle taut. Her breasts jutted forward like ripe melons. She ran her fingertips over her nipples which made them even harder and more prominent under the silky dress. She checked her watch. He would be in his room, unaware of the delights that awaited him.

Lisa left her room and walked nervously along the corridor to the rear of the house. She couldn't understand why she felt so terrified; he was just a man, after all. But there was something about him, something strange and powerful, and he exuded sensuality. She thought again about the time that he had made Janet come just by looking at her and she began to feel a surge of excitement within her trembling body. If he could do that to a girl with just his eyes, what on earth could he do to one with his body? She reached his door and stood still for a moment, barely daring to breath. She knocked lightly. There was no answer. She knocked again, louder this time. She could hear movement from the other side of the door. She ran her tongue over her lips and took a deep breath. The door opened.

'Yes?' Mr Gee stood in the doorway. He was dressed as always in a dark, formal suit. Somehow, he seemed taller, and more menacing. Lisa looked him directly in the eyes. For a second she felt her willpower fading away and was grabbed with the desire to turn and run. 'What do you want, Lisa?' he asked. His tone was officious and cold.

'I wondered if I might see you,' she replied, weakly. 'I need to talk.'

Mr Gee stepped back and Lisa walked into the room. He motioned for her to sit down and she perched nervously on the edge of a chair. Mr Gee closed the door and sat opposite her. He regarded her curiously. She smiled slightly and glanced around the room, seeing nothing.

'You've got a nice room,' she said, angrily finding that her voice shook noticeably.

'What do you want, Lisa?' He was getting impatient. This wasn't working.

'I, I –' She stopped short as she caught his gaze. He was working his magic on her. She felt a tremor of desire between her legs. It was now or never. She rose to her feet and unclasped the back of her dress. The flimsy garment slipped to the floor and she stepped out of it. She stood before him brazenly and saw him look directly at her pussy. She could actually feel the lips opening in invitation. He stood up to face her, then bent down and picked up her dress.

'Put the dress on, Lisa,' he said as he handed it to her.

She shook her head. 'No. I want you, Mr Gee. I want you to fuck me, I want you to fuck me right now!' He reached out towards her with his free hand. She trembled. He was going to touch her! He was going to give her what she so desperately wanted! She looked into his face. His expression was not one of lust, but more one of anger. He caught hold of her arm roughly and forced the dress into her hand.

'Put the dress on,' he repeated sternly, 'and come with me.' Lisa obeyed immediately, her excitement quickly overtaking her initial fears. Perhaps he was taking her to another room, possibly a chamber with shackles and other implements of delight, where he would chain her up and take her in whatever way he wanted. She followed him out of the room like a willing slave. He strode purposefully down the corridor and quickly descended the stairs. Lisa hurried to keep up with him as her anticipation grew with every step.

They came to the cellar door and he opened it. Lisa swallowed hard as she remembered his earlier conversation with the old man. Was he down there, waiting for her? 'Where are you taking me?' she asked, nervously.

'You'll see,' he replied. 'Come on – it's what you want, isn't it?'

Despite her misgivings, Lisa knew that she had to obey. Her good sense had left her. Her mind was being controlled by this enigmatic man, and by the uncontrollable surge of desire that emanated from between her legs. And she had to find out his plans. She had to discover just what was going on behind the scenes at Grantham Manor.

She followed him through the small door and down the steep flight of steps. He lead her, not to the room she had visited before but to another, through a heavy, iron door which she hadn't noticed before. The room inside was in total darkness and had a dank, putrid atmosphere. Lisa jumped as Mr Gee flicked on the light switch. She looked around in astonishment. She had fantasised about being shackled and chained by her handsome host, but the scene before her was beyond even her wildest dreams. The room resembled some kind of medieval torture chamber, with racks and frames of every possible design. One wall was lined with an array of whips. Some were small and looked relatively harmless, but others appeared positively vicious. She looked up at Mr Gee's face. His expression remained cold.

'You will have some fun here, my dear,' he breathed.

She looked down at the front of his suit trousers. There was no sign of an erection. 'What are you going to do to me?' she trembled.

'Don't worry, Lisa, you won't be harmed. Think of this as another lesson, the ultimate training.' He took her by the arm and led her to one of the frames which leant back slightly against one of the walls. 'Take off the dress,' he ordered. She did so quickly and stood before him in her rubber basque, stockings and high-heeled shoes. He reached out with both hands and cupped her breasts. She smiled gratefully and took a deep breath. 'Remarkable,' he said, simply. He tugged down the front of the basque and exposed her large, firm globes then cupped them again and pinched the nipples to hardness. Lisa sighed.

Turning her, Mr Gee shackled first one wrist and then the other to the wooden frame. He repeated the action with her ankles, which caused her legs to be spread wide apart. Standing, he smoothed the palm of his hand over her bottom. She could feel his warm breath on the back of her neck.

Then he was gone. The door crashed shut behind him and she was alone. The sudden silence was unnerving. Lisa tugged at the leather straps that bound her wrists to the shackles but they were securely fixed. All she could do was wait.

After what seemed to her like an eternity the door opened again. Lisa looked over her shoulder excitedly, expecting to see her host dressed in attire more suitable for the occasion. Instead, she was confronted by the tall, menacing figure of Madam Stone. She was naked, save for a thick, leather belt tightly strapped around her waist and a pair of thigh-high, high-heeled boots. She walked quickly over to Lisa. Her face made it clear that she was most displeased.

'You have been very impertinent, Lisa,' she snarled, 'and the master has ordered that you must be punished severely.'

'But I only –' began Lisa in a shaking voice.

'Silence! You dared to imagine that the master would succumb to your seductive powers? A man as powerful as he? How arrogant you are!'

'Please, Mistress,' begged Lisa as she started to sob, 'I didn't mean any harm!'

'Quiet! You already know something of the pleasures of pain. Now you will learn more.'

Lisa turned her face away and pressed her forehead against the hard wood of the frame. She heard Madam Stone cross the room. Moments later, her tormentor was back, carrying a small bottle. Lisa watched as she poured some of the contents into the cupped palm of her hand. She moved forward and spread the cool liquid over Lisa's buttocks. Some of it trickled between her legs. Madam Stone massaged the oil gently, adding more until Lisa's bottom was soaked. Then she eased a well-lubricated finger into Lisa's anus and relaxed the muscle of her sphincter by expertly turning it and probing ever deeper. Lisa closed her eyes to savour the delightful sensation.

After a moment the finger was removed to be replaced by something larger and more bulbous. It hurt slightly but, once it was inside, the feeling was entirely pleasurable. Lisa began to relax as she started to find the thought of even a severe whipping quite an exciting prospect. The combination of the sensuous oil and the wonderful fullness caused by the plug had caused the nerve-endings in her bottom to tingle and she found that she was longing for pain. Madam Stone smoothed her hands over Lisa's buttocks again which caused her to press her mound against the rough, splintered wood of the frame. Her pussy was soaked, and her juices slipped from her to dampen her inner thighs. She closed her eyes again and heard the click of the other woman's heels as she walked across the room. Lisa looked round and saw her take a small, multi-tongued whip from the wall. She turned her face back to the frame and waited eagerly.

Madam Stone stood behind her and Lisa clenched her buttocks automatically. She felt the leather strands of the whip trail over her oiled behind. Lisa shivered. The bitch was teasing her, and she wanted it now! She yearned to feel the first kiss of the whip across her bottom, and she wanted the pain to be sharp.

Suddenly she got her wish. She yelped as the leather stung her flesh and she dug her fingernails into the palms of her hands. She looked over her shoulder and saw Madam Stone raising her arm to administer a second stroke. Lisa watched as the lash was brought down with considerable force and gritted her teeth as the pain shot through her loins and seemed to merge with the throbbing sensations deep within her pussy. Over and over, Madam Stone whipped her hot bottom until she felt the sudden surge of orgasm building up inside her. She came with a cry as the lash stung her for the last time and shook so violently with the force of her pleasure that the frame rattled.

Madam Stone laughed cruelly and returned the whip to its place on the wall. 'The oil will ensure that the marks disappear quickly,' she said as she untied Lisa's bonds and freed her. Lisa moved stiffly from the frame and rubbed her tingling bottom. The slippery oil soothed her skin as she massaged herself and it felt good. She looked at Madam Stone and smiled. The dark woman ignored her and walked towards the door and opened it. She indicated brusquely that Lisa should follow her and walked out. Compliantly, Lisa picked up her little dress and followed.

They arrived back at Madam Stone's bedroom. The bedclothes were ruffled and the pillows had been tossed on to the floor, clear evidence that there had been some frenetic activity there recently. Lisa heard noises coming from the bathroom as the toilet was flushed and taps were turned. 'The master interrupted a very pleasant moment,' said Madam Stone, angrily. 'Now you must help me make amends.'

The bathroom door opened and the lovely new student, Zenga appeared, naked and fresh faced. She stopped in her tracks and smiled guiltily when she saw Lisa standing there. Lisa wasn't shocked that her tutor's bed-partner was female, but just that it was the seemingly innocent Zenga. Her surprise must have shown on her face. 'Zenga came to me tonight and confessed that her desires are for those of her own sex,' Madam Stone explained as she circled the young girl's waist with her strong arm, 'and I was only too pleased to help her discover some of the delights of love with another woman. I had just slipped my tongue into her sweet honey-pot when I was ordered downstairs to deal with you, Lisa. Now you must help me recapture the moment.'

Lisa looked at the pretty student and savoured the sight of her small, firm breasts, her tiny waist and broad hips. Her skin colour was much lighter than that of Madam Stone. It shone with a golden hue which seemed to shimmer in the soft light. Zenga looked back at her with wide eyes and her face broke into a broad smile. Lisa felt her pussy tingle and knew that she didn't mind at all. She walked over to the young girl and slipped her arms around her neck and drew her face towards hers. They kissed, a long, passionate embrace. She felt Zenga's button-hard nipples brushing against the sensitive flesh of her own breasts. She stepped back and peeled the rubber basque from her body, then stepped out of her shoes and rolled off the tight stockings. Madam Stone, too, stripped herself completely naked. It seemed right, somehow. There was no need for any visual stimuli.

Madam Stone took Zenga by the hand and led her to the bed. Lisa watched as she lay on her back and coaxed the young girl to squat over her face. Her long tongue slipped and slithered around Zenga's tiny pussy. The student groaned and rotated her hips in response. The tongue worked ever faster and began to move in and out of her moist opening, which caused Zenga to gasp with delight. She fell forward slowly and buried her face in Madam Stone's lap. The older woman raised her legs and bent them back as far as she could. She circled Zenga's body with them and gripped her tightly.

Lisa watched the two women licking each other voraciously for a few moments, then crawled on to the bed and knelt behind Zenga. She could see Madam Stone's tongue lapping rapidly against the swollen bud of her clitoris. She leant forward and kissed Zenga's little bottom then ran her tongue down between the cleft to her tiny, puckered sphincter. The young girl gave a muffled cry of joy as her two holes were licked and probed simultaneously by two expert tongues. Lisa gripped her buttocks and pushed her face against her bottom. She moved the tip of her tongue in and out of her tight anus whilst Madam Stone continued to lap hungrily against her pussy-lips.

Suddenly, Zenga squealed and her small body shuddered with the force of her orgasm. Her juices seemed to flow from her and were soaking Madam Stone's beautiful face. She squealed again and drove her crotch hard down on the mistress's sucking mouth. Lisa lapped wetly against her bottom until the trembling girl finally collapsed on to the soft cushion of Madam Stone's body.

The three lovers lay entwined for a few minutes whilst Zenga recovered from her powerful release. Her smooth, golden skin was soaked with sweat and her eyes were shining with pleasure. Lisa lazily caressed herself between the legs as she waited for the next move.

At last, Madam Stone slipped from the bed and walked over to a small cabinet. Opening it, she took out a long, thick phallus of the deepest black, fitted with an array of straps and buckles. She moved back to the bed and handed the implement to Lisa. 'She is ready, Lisa,' she said, commandingly. 'Make love to her, but be careful – this is her first time.' Lisa examined the dildo closely. It resembled Peter's stiff, ebony erection and was perfect in every detail, from the long, ribbed shaft to the broad, bulbous head. With help from her mistress she strapped the device on and stood next to the bed, smiling at the beaming face of her willing victim.

Zenga looked directly at the monster protruding from Lisa's voluptuous body and her smile broadened. There was no fear or trepidation in her expression. She knew exactly what she wanted and she knew that she was going to get it. She turned over and lay on her arms and knees with her lovely, little bottom presented to the other two women. Madam Stone took up a bottle of oil and poured some of the liquid into her hand. She smoothed the oil along the full length of the phallus until it gleamed in the bright light. Then she stepped back and nodded to Lisa.

Lisa looked down at the almost comical sight of the huge cock which was jutting from her groin. It seemed far too big for its purpose, but the student hadn't voiced any concern. She moved forward and knelt on the bed behind Zenga. The girl bent her back and moved her legs further apart, offering a perfect view of her soaking wet sex. The lips were open and glistening with excitement. Lisa inched forward and pressed the head of the phallus against them. It sank in immediately with no effort from her. Zenga's sex-lips closed around the thick stem and seemed to be drawing the shaft within her. Madam Stone's words of caution had been unnecessary; the girl had clearly enjoyed such an intrusion before many times, albeit by her own hand.

Lisa began to move the hard, rubber dildo in and out of Zenga's wet flesh. As she thrust her hips, the base of the implement pressed firmly against her own pussy, and sent tremors of delight throughout her lower body. She fucked harder and gripped Zenga's narrow waist tightly. Madam Stone moved to sit in front of the panting student with her legs spread on either side of her body. Zenga immediately began to lap the offered prize of her pussy. Lisa could see the look of desire on her mistress's face and saw that she was staring at her breasts and watching them bounce heavily with the rhythm of her labours. She moved faster, driving the rod deeper into Zenga's receptive sheath.

She was coming. She could feel the waves of release building up inside her groin as the hard base rubbed her erect bud. She closed her eyes and hammered backwards and forwards even faster, stimulating herself with each thrust. Zenga mewed contentedly within the wet cushion of Madam Stone's pussy as Lisa went over the edge. Lisa threw back her head and groaned loudly. Her juices flowed down the length of the pumping shaft. Zenga squealed again, and Lisa knew that her young lover had joined her in the sheer rapture of ultimate release. Madam Stone suddenly gripped the student's head and rammed her face against her crotch. Her expression was like a grimace of agony, but it was not pain that she was experiencing. Lisa could see Zenga's head bobbing up and down and could hear the wet sounds as she licked the older woman into an oblivion of pleasure. The sight was too much for Lisa. She came again. The spasms tore at her very soul, sending sharp jolts of electricity coursing through the muscles of her thighs. She forced herself forward so that the dildo sank completely into Zenga's cunt and the feelings slowly subsided as she leant over the young girl's trembling body.

Madam Stone leant forward and kissed her lightly on the mouth. 'You have done well,' she breathed. 'Stay here with us tonight. I have many more delights to teach our young charge.'

Lisa smiled in happy acquiescence. Somehow, she knew that she was about to learn much herself.

Eight

Lisa woke suddenly. She opened her eyes and took in the familiar surroundings of Madam Stone's bedroom. She was alone. The ornate clock on the bedside cabinet told her that it was past eleven o'clock. The sun streaming in from the large window reminded her that it was eleven o'clock in the morning. It had been a long and eventful night.

She sat up on the bed slowly as she coaxed herself into full consciousness. She felt strange, as though drunk, and she ached between the legs. As she slipped more into reality the ache became stronger and more demanding. She touched herself. Her pussy was soaked. She lay back and began to finger herself whilst she recalled the delights of the previous few hours. Quickly, she found that she was able to slip all four fingers inside her silky sheath with ease. She was often aroused when she woke in the morning, but such feelings were not normally as intense as this. The more that she toyed with her fleshy lips the more the ache increased. She began to breath in short, sharp gasps as she rubbed her hard clitoris with the palm of her hand whilst her fingers turned and probed inside her. She was coming. Almost without warning her orgasm hit her like a thunderbolt, causing her to cry out loudly. She bucked her hips and rubbed herself furiously as the tremors of delight took control of her body. Her juices flowed and soaked the sheet beneath her.

Gradually, she eased her self-caress and moved her hand from her throbbing pussy. She lay her head back and breathed deeply. But the ache was still there, stronger than ever. Normally, after a come she would be able to relax for a while, but not this time. Her mind was overwhelmed with a burning need for sex. She found her hand trailing, almost automatically, back to her crotch. Resisting the temptation, she rubbed the sleep from her eyes and moved swiftly from the bed. She suddenly felt dizzy and sat down again. Her head was swimming, and the light that was streaming in through the open window hurt her eyes.

After a moment she rose gingerly to her feet and padded into the bathroom. She squatted over the toilet and began to pee. At first, the flow excited her but gradually the ache decreased and she felt better. She moved to turn on the shower. The handle felt like a small, cold penis. Lisa caressed it lovingly as she set the temperature of the water. The ache returned, even more powerful than before. She knew that she had to get someone to fuck her, and quickly.

Stepping under the hot stream, she soaped herself liberally, using her hands sensuously all over her body. Even the bar of soap seemed to resemble a nice, slippery little cock. She moved the bar against her sex-lips and her orgasm began to build up inside her groin once more. She gripped the shower handle for support and worked the soap in and out of herself. The water gushed and bubbled over her, feeling for all the world like the fingers and tongues of a thousand lovers. She moved the soap rapidly and came again just as suddenly and with as much ferocity as before.

The soap slipped from her fingers and fell to the floor. Lisa's entire body was trembling, and the need for sex was still tearing at her. She turned off the shower and staggered out. She looked into a mirror and gasped. There, tied securely around her neck was one of the mysterious amulets she had seen in the cellar. No wonder that she felt so incredibly randy. She moved her hand to tear the thing from her throat but something seemed to stop her. She tried again, but it was as though an unseen hand was clutching her arm and forcing her to leave the amulet where it was.

She began to feel a little more relaxed. Having two violent orgasms in such a very short time appeared to have a soothing effect on her. She looked again at her reflection in the mirror. The amulet seemed to glow faintly against her damp skin. She tore her gaze away from the thing and towelled herself quickly. She knew what she had to do. She would go back to her room and dress and then go downstairs. She would be sure to find one or more of the guests to satisfy her needs. After all, that was what they had come to Grantham Manor for, to fuck and be fucked, and she was more than ready to do whatever they desired.

Lisa wrapped the towel around herself and hurried out of the bedroom. Reaching her own room, she paused. She heard familiar sounds coming from the other side of the door – the rhythmic panting of her friend Janet accompanied by heavy, male breathing. Lisa opened the door slowly and grinned. Janet was squatting across the prone form of a young man with her back to him and his hard cock firmly embedded in her pussy. Janet smiled in greeting as Lisa entered the room and closed the door behind her.

'Where'd you get to last night?' asked her friend as she eased herself from her delightful impalement. The young man's cock flopped heavily on to his stomach and he looked up at Lisa with a bemused expression.

'It's a long story,' replied Lisa. 'Who's this?'

'This is Tom. He's one of the garden staff. The guests have all gone to a health centre in town and the students are up in London for the day, so there's nothing much happening.'

'Thanks a lot,' grumbled the young man as he made to clamber out of the bed.

'I didn't mean that,' laughed Janet. She slapped his bare bottom playfully, but it was clear that she had hurt his feelings. Tom started to pull on his jeans.

'Oh, look,' said Lisa, 'don't let me stop you.'

Janet pulled Tom's hands away from his waistband and tried to wrench his pants down again. 'Yes, come on, Tom, don't mind Lisa,' she giggled. He gave up the effort and she tugged his jeans from his ankles and threw them across the room. He sat back on the bed and Janet knelt beside him. She gripped his flaccid tool and expertly coaxed him back to full erection as Lisa let her towel slip to the floor. Tom's eyes widened as he gazed upon her nakedness.

'Lisa!' exclaimed Janet, 'you're wearing one of those things!'

'I know. It was round my neck when I woke up. I can't seem to take it off.'

Janet released her grip of Tom's stiffness and walked over to her. She reached up to grasp the chain. 'Let me,' she said. Lisa pushed her hands away.

'No, no, it's all right. I'm getting used to it. It makes me feel really horny.'

'More so than usual?' laughed Janet as she returned to the bed.

'Much more.' Lisa moved to the bed and knelt on the other side of the young man's reclining body. She reached out and gripped his thick cock. It felt good within her grasp. It was hot and stiff and coated with Janet's juices. She bent forward and took it into her mouth. She tasted Janet's sweet scent on his hard flesh and she found it intoxicating. She sucked him gently and circled the bulbous head with her tongue. Tom groaned.

'Don't make him come,' pleaded Janet in the full knowledge that her friend could work magic with her mouth. Lisa ignored her for a moment and sucked the stiff rod with all her expertise. She felt him throb heavily against her tongue and tasted his saltiness. Anxious for him to do more than merely satisfy her craving for the flavours of his come, she pulled her mouth from him. His cock slapped firmly against his stomach. It was ragingly hard. The head was purple with lust and glistening with the mixture of Lisa's saliva, Janet's juices and Tom's own creamy fluids. Lisa clambered across him and squatted over his groin. She reached down and gripped his stiffness and aimed it at her soaking pussy, then lowered herself slowly. Inch by inch, she absorbed the thick stalk inside her luscious body. Her cunt burned fiercely with the heat of unsated lust. She stiffened the muscles of her inner thighs to grip him tighter and pressed down hard so that her swollen clitoris was crushed against his hard pubic bone. Circling her hips, she rubbed herself rapidly against him. Her orgasm was immediate. She gasped as the tremors tore through her and she began to grind her pussy even harder against her supine lover as the sweet sensations coursed through her trembling body.

He felt good inside her. He was thick and immensely hard, but she wanted more. She didn't know what, but she knew that this wasn't enough. She felt the familiar, wet tickle of Janet's tongue running along the cleft of her bottom. That was good, but it still wasn't enough. She raised her body until just the head of his cock was clasped inside her tight sheath. Using the muscles of her pussy she gripped him under the ridge and squeezed hard. Janet's tongue found her anus and Lisa held herself still whilst her friend began to probe wetly inside her. She closed her eyes to savour the joy of the moment, but the ache was returning, with even more power.

Suddenly, she rammed her body down. Tom gasped for breath as she forced him to sink the full length of his cock into her. Janet fell backwards from the bed with the force of Lisa's movement. Lisa didn't care. Her second come was already building up within her oozing sex-flesh. She began to thrust up and down, slowly at first but with a demanding and tireless force. Tom simply lay there, seemingly content to let her fuck herself on his rigid pole. She moved faster. Tom's strong, young body shuddered each time she hammered her groin down on his and her huge breasts bounced heavily.

'Hey, save some for me,' said Janet jokingly. 'I need another come!' Lisa ignored her friend and pounded ever faster. She came, a shattering, gut-wrenching orgasm but it still didn't satisfy her needs. She moved even more quickly and her backside slapped noisily against Tom's thighs. He gripped her buttocks and dug his fingernails into her soft flesh in an effort to take control. He tried desperately to slow her movements but she was filled with a strength that he couldn't deal with. His face broke into a grimace.

'Jesus, I'm gonna come!' he bellowed through clenched teeth. 'I can't hold back!'

'No!' cried Lisa as she hammered herself with incredible force on the hapless young man.

'I can't, I –' She could feel his stiff prick throbbing

inside her aching flesh. Furiously she pounded her body up and down as hard as she could.

'No!' she repeated. 'Fuck me! Fuck me!'

Janet reached out and touched her friend's back. 'Lisa, you bitch!' she said, angrily. 'I told you I wanted some!'

Lisa turned her head without slowing her frenzied movements one iota. She glared at her friend and lashed out with her arm. She caught Janet a glancing blow to the face. 'Leave me alone! I've got to have it!' she yelled.

Janet fell back on to the floor and sat there, totally shocked. Lisa felt Tom's wilting cock slip from inside her but she continued to grind her hot cunt against his limp flesh. 'Fuck me, you bastard!' she cursed. 'Get hard and fuck me!' Tears streamed from her eyes as she vainly attempted to force the exhausted young man to erection. She came again, but the searing desire only increased within her groin. 'Please,' she sobbed. 'Fuck me, please fuck me!'

'I can't, I can't,' pleaded Tom as he gasped for air. 'Let me rest for a while.'

'No! I want it now!' She looked across at the dazed form of her friend who was staring in disbelief. 'Janet, get a vibrator or something! Now!'

A look of realisation appeared on Janet's face and she jumped to her feet. 'The amulet!' she cried. 'It's that bloody amulet! Get it off!'

'No! I need it!'

'No you don't! It's driving you insane!' Janet made to grab the chain around Lisa's neck but was knocked away by another fierce blow. She fell back on to the floor with a thump. Lisa snatched at Tom's tiny penis and forced the soft flesh into her soaking cunt. She pumped wildly against him, but his cock slipped from her again. Suddenly, Janet grabbed her around the waist from behind and hauled her from the bed. They fell in a heap of writhing nakedness on to the carpet. Tom leapt from the bed and grasped her tightly by the shoulders, pinning her down. Janet gripped the chain and wrenched it from her friend's neck. She flung the amulet across the room as though it were some evil, viperous creature. Lisa stopped struggling immediately. She lay her head back and stared vacantly at the ceiling. Sweat trickled from her body and she suddenly felt cold. She shivered and blinked her eyes and then looked at Janet She swallowed hard and took a long, deep breath. Janet leant forward and kissed her lightly on the forehead. 'You'll be all right now,' she whispered.

'What the hell's up with her?' asked Tom.

'Never mind,' replied Janet as she stroked her friend's head gently. 'Leave us alone please, Tom'

The young man got to his feet and quickly dressed. 'Can I help in some way?' he asked.

'No, it's OK.'

Tom looked down quizzically at the exhausted form of Lisa, then shrugged and left the room.

Janet kissed the sweat-soaked cheeks of her friend's flushed face in turn. 'Are you all right?' she asked. Lisa nodded and tried to sit up. She clearly found the effort too much and fell back again.

'God, that was horrible,' she said after a moment. 'I kept coming, but it didn't stop the terrible ache. A hundred men could've fucked me and it wouldn't have made any difference!'

There was a knock on the bedroom door. 'That'll be Tom, come back to look for his dick.' Lisa laughed at her friend's joke and Janet smiled gratefully. Janet then pulled herself to her feet and walked to the door. Opening it, she found Paul and Mike standing in the hallway, looking very concerned.

'Is Lisa OK?' asked Paul as they rushed into the room. 'One of the gardeners said she'd gone mental!' He looked at her, lying prostrate on the floor. Lisa attempted a smile. The two men knelt by her and helped her to her feet. She sat back on the edge of the bed.

'What the hell happened?' asked Mike as he brushed Lisa's tousled hair from her face.

'Somebody fixed one of the amulets around her neck,' said Janet. 'Its powers are deadly!'

'Then we've got real trouble,' said Mike, gravely.

'What do you mean?'

'The girls, the students. They've been sent home.'

'But I thought they were in London?' queried Lisa, her voice still trembling.

'So did we,' continued Mike. 'Mr Gee must be on to us. He must have realised that we know something's going on and panicked. One of the other guests told us that the girls were each given one or two of the amulets and that they were instructed to fasten them to their parents' necks as soon as they got home. Apparently, Mr Gee told them that it was a custom, a gesture of esteem and friendliness and that if they didn't do it they would not be allowed to return to the manor. We've given the girls a damn good time. They won't refuse.'

'It's just like last time!' exclaimed Janet, suddenly.

'What d'you mean?' Mike looked at her seriously, for once ignoring her nakedness. She sat on the edge of a chair, facing the others.

'All the girls are the children of politicians or powerful business people. We even had a couple of princesses here! The old man tried it once before. He wants power; he wants to control the world!'

'But how will the amulets do that?'

'I'm not sure, but we now know that they can completely control your mind. All you want is sex, and more sex. Anything could happen!'

Paul leapt to his feet. 'We've got to stop them! If we drive across country we should beat the train to the airport. Janet, you come with me. Lisa, you and Mike find Mr Gee. He's got to be stopped. There are more students due here next week!'

'How are we going to stop him?' asked Mike.

'I don't know,' said Paul as he waited impatiently for Janet to dress herself. 'You'll have to think of something. Call the police.'

'And say what? That some maniac is bent on world domination through some magical sex-rays?'

Paul didn't answer. He grasped Janet by the wrist as she made a grab for her trainers and almost dragged her from the room. 'Do something,' he called as they hurried into the hallway.

Lisa and Mike sat in silence for a few minutes. Eventually, he slipped his strong arm around her shoulders and hugged her lovingly. 'Are you OK now?' he asked, kindly. Lisa nodded.

'Once the amulet was taken from me I was fine,' she breathed. 'What are we going to do?'

Mike scratched his brow. 'I don't know,' he said, 'but we've got to do something.'

'What about your people, you know, the ones you work with? Can't you tell them, get help from them?'

'Paul and I work on our own. We're tolerated by the department. Most of them think we're a couple of weirdos. We could try the minister himself, but I don't think that would be much use.'

'Why? Surely he'd believe you.'

'He might, but the problem is his daughter was here last week. He hasn't been seen for days. God knows what he's getting up to.'

'Then it's started.' Lisa felt the blood drain from her face. She shivered and cuddled closer to Mike.

'Yes,' he said, 'it's started. Last week was the first

intake, so there are about six men out there who could cause an awful lot of problems if their minds aren't completely on their jobs. There's nothing we can do about them, but just six politicians screwing around won't be anything unusual, just more public. If Paul and Janet manage to beat the train to the airport, and if we can find Mr Gee and stop him somehow, and if we can destroy the amulets –'

'That's a lot of ifs.'

Mike shrugged and rose to his feet. 'We've got to try. First, we've got to find him. Get dressed.'

Lisa rushed to retrieve some clothing from a drawer and hurriedly dressed. Her fingers trembled as she zipped up her jeans. She searched for a T-shirt and found one quickly. Mike looked at her as she stood, bare breasted in front of him. 'You've got beautiful tits,' he said, wistfully. Lisa glared at him and pulled the T-shirt over her head and smoothed it over her sensuous form.

'Later,' she pouted, 'let's go.'

Lisa and Mike headed directly for the cellar. The amulets had to be destroyed first, and then they would search for Mr Gee. What they would do when they found him neither of them knew but, with the amulets gone, at least the old man's plans would be thwarted temporarily. They found the door to the cellar slightly ajar. Cautiously, they moved down the steep staircase. The lights were on but at first they could hear no sound. They reached the bottom of the stairs and listened intently. Both doors to the cellar rooms were shut. Lisa pressed her ear to each in turn, then shook her head. 'Nothing,' she whispered.

'Why would the lights be on?' hissed Mike.

'I don't know.' She tried one of the doors. It opened. 'The amulets were in here,' she said. They entered slowly and Mike flicked on the light switch. The chest was still there. Lisa stopped short. 'I don't think I can go any nearer,' she trembled. 'You'll have to get them.' Mike moved forward, then stood stock still.

'I can feel it,' he breathed. 'God, there's an incredible power here.'

They paused for a few moments, both of them summoning up the courage to continue. There was a sudden roar as the boiler fired up behind them. 'Oh, my God!' jumped Lisa. 'I wonder what that was!'

'Only the boiler. It must heat the pool.' Mike opened the furnace door. The heat seared into the room. 'This is it,' he suddenly said excitedly. 'We'll chuck them in here!'

Lisa shook her head. 'I don't know if I can touch them,' she moaned.

'I'll do it. You listen for the stairs.' Mike wrenched open the lid of the chest. The glow filled the room with a greenish tinge which competed with the weak light above them. 'Christ, it's getting to me!'

'Do it! Do it quickly!'

He took a deep breath and plunged his arms into the chest. Grabbing fistfuls of amulets, he rushed over to the open furnace and flung them into the flames. The fire roared complainingly and crackled loudly. Mike rushed back and scooped up more of the devilish brooches and hurled them into the fire, then staggered back for more. Lisa could see that he was weakening and his large erection was clearly visible through the material of his jeans. Taking a deep breath, she almost ran to the chest and, closing her eyes in terror and disgust, grasped as many of the amulets as she could. The electricity surged through her body. She felt her pussy-lips open and her juices begin to flow. Gritting her teeth, she rushed to the furnace and disposed of the load, then returned for more. Mike was on his knees by now. He'd unzipped his jeans and his hand was pumping furiously on his erect cock.

'Keep going,' he gasped. 'I can't do it!'

Lisa grasped the remaining amulets. One of them fell to the floor in front of Mike. He turned his head away but the power was too strong. He reached out and gripped the stone, then pressed it to his chest. His ejaculation jetted from his swollen knob and streaked across the stone floor.

'Let go of it!' ordered Lisa. He dropped it as if it were red hot. His erection wilted rapidly. 'You'll be all right. Just don't touch that thing.'

Mike staggered to his feet as Lisa stooped to retrieve the remaining amulet. There was a sudden sound, like the crack of a spark. It wasn't the furnace; the sound was coming from elsewhere in the cellar. 'What's that?' whispered Lisa.

'Sshh,' Mike hissed. 'Let's go and see.' They crept out of the room and moved to the other door. They listened intently. Another crack echoed against the cold walls that surrounded them, followed by a man's low groan.

'It's him, it's Mr Gee!' said Lisa under her breath.

'How do you know?'

'It must be!'

Mike pressed his ear to the door. There were more cracking sounds, and more groans of pleasure. He tried the handle. The door opened slightly. He peered through the gap, then closed the door again quickly and silently. 'It is him,' he whispered, 'and Madam Stone. He's tied to a bench and she's whipping him.'

Lisa suppressed a desire to giggle. 'What are we going to do?' she asked.

Mike thought for a moment. 'Wait here,' he said.

He hurried into the other room and reappeared carrying the last amulet. Lisa could see that he was sweating profusely. 'Mike, for God's sake be careful!' she pleaded.

He held the token in front of him. 'Can you stand to hold it, just for a while?'

She gritted her teeth. 'I don't know; I'll try.'

Mike handed it to her. Her palm seemed to burn as it dropped into her hand and she felt a trickle of warm fluid slip down the inside of her leg. She gripped the amulet by the chain and this seemed to ease the pressure. Mike's cock was jutting firmly from his jeans again. Lisa wanted to forget Mr Gee and Madam Stone and dive to his feet to force his lovely rod into her mouth. She looked away from the tempting sight.

'I'll take care of Madam Stone,' Mike whispered. 'You put the amulet around Mr Gee's neck. He can't harm you. She's got him trussed up like a chicken in there.' Lisa nodded. Mike took a deep breath and suddenly crashed the door open and rushed in. Taking advantage of the element of surprise he grabbed Madam Stone from behind and threw her backwards to the floor. She struggled violently but he was too strong for her. Deftly, he wrapped the long whip that she'd been using to torment her master around her arms, then quickly completed the job using some of the many ropes that were strewn about the floor. Mr Gee struggled vainly on the bench.

'Get the fuck out of here!' he roared. Lisa walked over to where he lay and regarded him contemptuously. He was naked, his cock hanging limply and his body scored with red stripes from the lash. She held the amulet in front of his face. His eyes widened in terror. 'What are you going to do?' he barked. Lisa said nothing. Half smiling, she bent forward and slipped the chain around her host's neck and secured the clasp tightly. She stood back and watched with a feeling of utmost satisfaction as his cock thickened and rose to a huge erection. 'Take it off! Take it off!' he pleaded.

'You fools!' spat Madam Stone from her position on the floor. 'You'll ruin everything!'

They ignored her, and stood by the bench, looking down at the prone form of Mr Gee. His face and body was covered in sweat and he was trembling markedly. 'Please,' he begged. 'I'll do anything! Help me!' Lisa reached out and gripped his thick shaft. She raised his cock vertically and gripped it tightly. Mr Gee groaned and his cream fountained from the purple end to soak his chest. She let his erection fall to his stomach. As she'd expected, it remained as stiff as before. She knew exactly what he was going through. She looked down at Mike's hard stalk and had an idea. She reached out and caressed it gently.

'Let's give our host a little show,' she pouted. Mike grinned. She removed her T-shirt and jeans quickly. Mike stripped and the two, naked lovers hugged each other tightly. To Lisa, it seemed a just punishment for the torment that she had gone through earlier. She just wished that she'd saved another amulet to fix around the neck of Madam Stone.

Turning her back to Mike, she bent over until her hands rested on the cold, stone floor with her legs straight and slightly apart. From this position she knew that Mr Gee would be able to see everything. Mike moved behind her. 'No!' roared the voice from the bench, 'for pity's sake!' They ignored the desperate entreaties of their shackled host.

'Fuck me,' said Lisa pointedly. 'Fuck my cunt with your big, hard cock.' She knew the effect that her crude words would have on Mr Gee. She glanced over her shoulder, just in time to see him ejaculate again. She smiled smugly, then turned to look at Madam Stone. The big woman's dark eyes blazed with fury.

'You'll regret this, my girl,' she growled. Lisa looked away and felt the wonderful touch of Mike's knob on her open pussy-lips. He entered her fully in one long, easy movement. Mr Gee moaned in abject misery.

'Fuck me!' she ordered. 'Fuck me hard! Ram that massive prick in and out of my tight, wet cunt!' Mike was in no mood to refuse. He gripped her bottom and began to slide his stiff erection in and out of her. He allowed her to savour the full length with each measured thrust. Lisa quickly forgot their audience and surrendered herself to the pleasure of Mike's deep, expert penetration of her hot sheath. She knew that he wouldn't last long; he had held the amulet for too long. But so had she, and she was coming already. Mike seemed to sense it, and he started to pound rapidly into her. The loud, slapping noise of his groin smacking against her bottom echoed around the room. Mr Gee groaned pitifully. Lisa knew that he had orgasmed yet again, and that the pain of desire would be unbearable by now.

'Harder, Mike, harder,' she pleaded. 'Come with me.' Mike dug his fingernails into her sumptuous buttocks and thrust in and out of her wildly. Suddenly he groaned and rammed his full length deep into her. She felt the thumping of his thick shaft and came with him, as powerful an orgasm as she'd ever had in her life. Mike pulled from her and sent the remains of his cream streaking across her back. Lisa smiled to herself as she felt the warmth of the fluid on her skin. Mike's display was clearly for the benefit of their hapless captive.

Lisa stood erect and reached behind her back to scoop Mike's semen from her skin. She looked directly into Mr Gee's eyes and put her creamy fingers to her lips. She licked the warm juice from her fingertips. He came again, and began to sob uncontrollably. His chest and stomach were soaked with his juices. Lisa gripped Mike's hand and retrieved her clothing. 'Come on,' she said, 'let's leave them to it.'

'You can't leave me like this!' moaned Mr Gee. She glanced at him once more then turned her back and walked through the door. She didn't turn her head again as she walked up the steps, even when she heard the bolts sliding into place as Mike secured their captives in their cellar prison.

Lisa sat on the lounger at the pool's edge and lazily watched as Peter and his lovely wife, Jeannie, enjoyed the inviting water. Peter was moving languorously on his back, more floating than swimming. He was wearing small, white trunks that contrasted sharply with his sable complexion. They were rendered almost transparent by the water, and she could clearly make out the shape of his long, limp penis. She thought about how large it grew when hard, and how sweet it tasted. She imagined him sliding it into Janet's tight little bottom and wondered at her friend's capability to absorb such a monster in that way with such apparent ease. That was Janet's thing, of course. As she often put it so delicately, there was nothing she liked better than a good, hard arse-fuck.

She began to think about their captives in the cellar. Even if they had managed to free themselves of their bonds they would be unable to break down the heavy door of their prison. All she had to do was wait and hope that Paul and Janet had retrieved the amulets from the students and somehow convinced the police. It wouldn't be an easy thing to do but, if anyone could, it would be Paul.

Mike joined her and offered her a cold drink. 'Where are the other guests?' she asked as he sat next to her.

'Kenrick and Page are coming down in a minute. The others are still in town, shopping or something.' He stretched out on the sun-lounger and sipped his drink. Lisa began to think about Kenrick and realised that he was the only one of the male guests, as far as she could remember, that she hadn't had sex with. She thought about his haunting, dark eyes and his handsome features. The young American couple had been noticeable by their absence throughout the week. Perhaps they were newly married, and preferred their own company. But, if so, why come to a place like this?

Her thoughts were interrupted by the sound of the patio door sliding open. Lisa turned round expectantly. Her face fell when the large figure of the brash salesman, Harman, appeared, closely followed by his tiny wife, Emily. 'Hello, everyone,' said Harman as he sat on one of the bar stools and poured himself a shot of vodka. Lisa nodded in greeting. Emily stood at her husband's side as if waiting for him to offer her a drink. He didn't. His wife finally gave up and walked to the edge of the pool to watch Peter and Jeannie cavorting in the water. She was wearing a short, white dress which clung to her slender form tightly. The sunlight shone through the material and outlined her lithe little body perfectly. Lisa could see the attraction that Janet had felt for her. She looked back at Harman. He was staring blankly into the distance and was totally oblivious to his wife's tender beauty. He belched loudly. What an arrogant, unpleasant pig, thought Lisa. She remembered Janet telling her of her session with them, and of the way Emily had abused and tortured her husband with words and deeds, and she smiled to herself with a feeling of perverse satisfaction. She had known men like Harman in the past, men who charmed unwitting females into their beds with slick words and promises, then revealed their debauched and faithless selves when it was too late.

And yet Emily and he had ended up in each other's arms. Perhaps, thanks to her treatment of him he had learnt his lesson, although Lisa very much doubted it.

The patio door slid open again and this time it was Kenrick and his wife who appeared. Kenrick was wearing a pair of white shorts and a matching T-shirt, whilst Page was dressed in a skimpy, black bikini which seemed to be two sizes too small. Her body was plump but voluptuous and not at all unattractive. She bounced over to Lisa and crouched by her side.

'Another lovely day,' she drawled thickly. 'England is a beautiful place in the summer.'

'Yes, it is,' replied Lisa as she found herself looking directly at Page's large breasts. They seemed to be threatening to burst from their inadequate covering at any moment. 'We haven't seen much of you,' she continued. Kenrick gave his wife a drink and perched himself on the edge of Lisa's lounger.

'It's our honeymoon,' he said with a grin. 'We've been busy.'

'Your honeymoon?' said Lisa in surprise, 'but why come here?'

'We met here last year,' replied Page. 'We fell in love, right here, by this pool.'

'Fell in lust, more like,' laughed her husband.

'So you're only interested in each other, I suppose,' said Lisa, her voice tinged with disappointment.

'Oh, no, not at all.' Page stood up and stretched herself. 'We have a very open relationship. There's nothing I like more than to watch Kennie fucking a pretty, young girl. I get a real buzz from it.'

'And what about you, Kenrick, er, Kennie?'

'I feel the same. I get my pleasure from Page's pleasure.'

'That's nice,' said Lisa.

'Are you going to let Kennie fuck you?' asked Page. Before Lisa could answer, they heard the sound of a car speeding up the drive. She jumped to her feet and hurried to the front of the house, closely followed by Mike. To her delight, she saw that it was Paul and Janet. She ran over to the car as Paul stepped out. She searched his face for an expression of triumph or disappointment.

'Well?' she said, anxiously. He reached into the back of the car and pulled out a large, airport bag. 'The amulets?' Lisa panted. Paul nodded and grinned. She closed her eyes. 'Thank God,' she breathed.

'It wasn't easy,' said Paul. 'The girls really didn't want to let them go. They've got an incredible power.'

'We told the students that they were stolen,' said Janet. 'We said that the police would be after them, and that it wouldn't look good for their parents if their little daughters were found to be smuggling stolen goods.'

'I'll take them down to the cellar and throw them into the furnace,' said Mike as he took the bag from Paul and held it at arm's length.

'But they're jewels,' said Paul. 'They won't burn.'

'They seem to. They're not ordinary gemstones. Anyway, we couldn't think of anything else at the time.' Mike was beginning to tremble. The amulets were having a profound effect on him, despite being held in the bag.

'Let me take them,' said Paul as he retrieved the bag. 'I'll watch them closely to see if they do burn.'

'Be careful,' said Lisa, suddenly. 'Mr Gee and Madam Stone are locked down there. Did you tell the police?'

'A waste of time. They've not committed any crime. You'll have to let them go.'

'But we can't –'

'We've no choice. They know we're on to them. We'll try to burn the amulets and at least that'll stop them for now.'

Lisa shrugged. 'OK, but not yet,' she said. She took hold of the bag and immediately felt a surge of electricity course through her body. She threw the bag back on the car seat and took Paul and Janet by the hand. 'Let's have a bit of fun, to celebrate,' she pouted.

As they rounded the house and arrived back at the pool-side, Lisa marvelled at the power of the amulets. Just a momentary grasp of the bag had filled her with the need for sex. She glanced at Paul. From the expectant look on his face she knew that he felt the same way. She looked down. His long, thick erection was clearly defined in his tight jeans. She reached out and squeezed it, then turned to face the others. 'Let's have an orgy,' she said.

'You'll get no argument from us,' said Kenrick as he leapt to his feet and quickly tugged his T-shirt over his head. Page yelped with delight and almost tore off her bikini top to completely reveal her huge breasts. Lisa eyed the delicious mounds hungrily. It was the first time in her young life that she'd seen a girl with breasts larger than her own.

Page yanked down her pants and threw them into the pool, then clawed at her husband's shorts and wrenched them to his ankles. His cock sprang up before him and she immediately took it into her mouth and began to suck him voraciously. Lisa casually removed her own T-shirt and bikini bottom and moved to kneel next to her. She watched for a moment as Page bobbed her head backwards and forwards rapidly. She licked her lips and Page took her mouth from her husband's penis and offered the hard stalk to her. Lisa closed her lips around the stiff flesh and rolled her tongue wetly around it whilst drawing in her cheeks and moving her head slowly forwards until the full length slid down her throat. She swallowed repeatedly, driving him to distraction. He stiffened even more, almost choking her.

'Oh, God, not already!' he groaned. Lisa gripped his buttocks tightly and pressed her lips firmly against his pubic bone as she felt his thick rod throbbing heavily inside her mouth. She sucked hard on the pumping stalk and drained him. She felt the heat of his cream as it slipped down her throat and she came. She bit into the base of his cock as the force of the orgasm overwhelmed her and he cried out. Lisa let him slip from her mouth and stood up.

'Sorry,' she said as she wiped her mouth with the back of her hand. 'I got a bit carried away.' Kenrick just stood there, his eyes glazed and his body trembling. She looked at the others. Janet was already naked and kneeling on the ground, once more preparing to accommodate Peter's huge cock inside her tight little bum. Mike was lying on one of the loungers with Page firmly impaled on his groin and Peter's wife, Jeannie, was happily paying oral homage to Paul. Emily had slipped out of her dress and was merely watching the proceedings as she playfully toyed with the thick curls between her legs. Only Harman remained fully dressed, although he had his small, erect cock gripped in his hand. He looked at Lisa and leered suggestively. She responded with a glance of disdain and walked over to Emily.

The slim woman smiled as Lisa slipped her hands around her waist and then cupped her small bottom. Their lips met and their bodies crushed together. Lisa rubbed her pussy against Emily's and felt the warm wetness as their juices intermingled. They slipped down to lie on the grass. Emily moved to lie on top of her and writhed her body against her. She mewed happily as she moved her mouth down to suck Lisa's nipple. She nipped the hard bud between her teeth and sucked it like a baby, then moved herself to kneel at Lisa's side without taking her mouth from her breast for a second. Lisa closed her eyes and felt Emily slip her fingers between her saturated sex-lips. She opened her legs as wide as she could. Emily bunched her fingers and pushed them all inside. Lisa looked down and watched through glazed eyes as Emily's hand disappeared within her soft flesh. She gripped the plunging wrist with her wet sex-lips and felt Emily clench her fist inside her. Emily twisted and turned her hand and gradually began to pump in and out of her. The feeling of such total fullness was rapidly bringing Lisa to the point of no return. She thrust her hips, gasping as the hard bone of Emily's arm rubbed against her clitoris. Emily must have sensed her pleasure and she increased the pressure and rubbed harder until Lisa came with a squeal of delight. She raised her bottom from the ground and took most of Emily's forearm inside her throbbing sheath as her lover moved to squat over her face.

Lisa pushed out her tongue and lapped hungrily against Emily's cunt as her orgasm subsided. Emily returned the compliment, taking care to avoid her tender bud with her fluttering tongue as she eased her hand from inside Lisa's wetness. The two women sucked each other for what seemed like ages. Emily's taste was sweet, and her juices flowed copiously.

Lisa felt a familiar prodding between her legs. With Emily's delicious bottom pressed against her face, she couldn't see who it was, but the size of the blissful intrusion made her realise thankfully that it wasn't Harman. The cock filled her ravaged pussy in one, deep thrust causing her to moan happily as she lapped her tongue over Emily's soft sex-lips. Somebody else knelt by the side of her face. She recognised the stiff erection as that of Mike, glistening in the bright sunlight with Page's wetness. She reached out and circled it with her fingers, then guided it to Emily's open pussy. She licked the full length as it slipped into her, then concentrated the flicking of her tongue against Emily's hard little bud. Emily did the same to her, whilst whoever was fucking her began to pound in and out of her soaking hole faster and faster. She eased Mike's cock from inside the other woman by gripping it by the root. She put it to her mouth and swallowed the full length until she was able to lick his balls with the tip of her tongue. At the same time, she soaked two of her fingers with Emily's juices and then eased one, and then both into the other woman's anus.

She heard Emily groan with pleasure as she pushed her fingers deep into her bottom. She twisted and turned them until she felt the muscles of the tight sphincter relax, then eased her fingers out and took Mike's hard stalk from inside her mouth and guided him to its target. As he moved the thick, gnarled rod into Emily's backside Lisa returned her fluttering tongue to the sweet pussy. She engulfed the soft flesh with her mouth and sucked hard whilst slipping her tongue deep into the hot sheath. She felt Emily slip her finger into her own bottom and knew what was going to happen. After a few moments gentle coaxing Emily removed her finger from Lisa's anus and she felt the hard cock withdraw from her cunt. Within seconds, the spongy tip touched her tight little hole. She relaxed her muscles and he entered her slowly. He eased each inch gently into her bottom until she held the full length inside her vice-like grip. Emily lapped furiously at her pussy whilst Lisa tilted her head slightly and watched in awe as Mike's fine erection plundered the other woman's arsehole.

The two men seemed to be working in tandem as they thrust in and out of them rhythmically. The cock that Lisa was accommodating seemed to be huge; it had to be Peter's. The thought of that big, ebony pole plunging in and out of her most precious sheath filled her mind and made her head swim as she drank from the chalice of Emily's hot cunt.

It was Emily who came first. With a muffled groan she ground her crotch against Lisa's face. The fluids seemed to gush from her, filling her mouth and running up her nose. Lisa drank gratefully and swallowed the sweet honey-juice as her own release became more and more imminent. Peter began to pump wildly in and out of her bottom until, suddenly, he rammed the full length deep into her and gripped her thighs tightly. She heard him moan and felt his thickness throbbing inside her tight hole. She came with a sudden violence that tore through her lower body like a knife. Emily realised what was happening and bit her pussy-lips hard, which only served to increase the power of her release. Mike suddenly pulled his cock from inside Emily's bottom and sent jets of his cream to soak Lisa's face and breasts. She reached up and rubbed his pumping stalk until he had no more to give.

Slowly, the four lovers fell apart and lay back on the grass, exhausted. Lisa felt her heart thumping as she watched the white, cotton-wool clouds drift across the blue sky above her. She heard the sounds of water splashing and the giggles and laughter of Jeannie and Paul and knew that they were fucking in the pool. She raised her head and looked across at the bar. Harman was still perched on his stool. His small cock lay limp and flaccid and his shorts were soaked with his cream. Lisa smiled to herself. What a sad sales manager he was.

Lisa and Janet stood nervously with their backs to the wall as Paul prepared to turn the handle on the door to the cellar room. Mike stood squarely behind him, having already slipped the bolts. He was gingerly holding the bag of amulets in his outstretched hand. They were both strong, young men; they would be able to deal with Mr Gee and Madam Stone if they tried anything. Paul opened the door slowly. Lisa was immediately hit by a strong aroma of sweat and sex. She moved forward cautiously as Paul and Mike entered the room. Paul peered into the gloom and then turned to her and grinned. 'I don't think they'll cause us any trouble,' he said. He stepped to one side and Janet and Lisa moved into the room. Lisa gasped and Janet sniggered under her breath. Their two captives had somehow managed to free themselves of their bonds. Now, it was Madam Stone who lay shackled to the bench, completely naked and with her legs splayed wide apart. Virtually all of her shining, sable skin was streaked with the cream of a hundred ejaculations. Her pussy-lips were red and engorged and glistened in the dim light.

Mr Gee was lying on the floor on his back, fast asleep. His erection was as fierce as ever, a huge pole of demanding, plundering flesh. Madam Stone raised her head wearily and looked into Lisa's eyes. 'Please take the amulet from him,' she pleaded in a hoarse, weak voice, 'I can't take it any more. I've never been fucked so hard and so long in my life. It's killing both of us.'

Lisa looked at Paul. 'What d'you think?' she asked.

Paul said nothing, but knelt down beside the prone figure of Mr Gee and broke the clasp of the chain around his neck. Madam Stone let her head fall back and breathed a sigh of relief. Mike walked quickly out towards the other room and they heard the clank of the furnace door opening, followed by the roar of the flames as the bag of amulets was consumed by the intense heat. Paul took hold of the last stone and stood up. He held the amulet in his hand and regarded it curiously. 'Christ,' he exclaimed. 'I've got a hard-on already!'

'Throw it in the fire!' ordered Janet.

Paul hesitated, and his hand slipped to the front of his shorts. 'I don't know,' he said. 'If there was some way of controlling it –' Lisa snatched the amulet from his grasp and rushed to the other room to fling it quickly into the furnace before its energy could stop her. The flames crackled and seethed as they engulfed the power held within the strange stones. Mike slammed the furnace door shut and they returned to the other room. Janet moved to the bench and untied Madam Stone. Their erstwhile mistress struggled to her feet, then fell back to sit on the edge of the hard, wooden support.

'I never want to see another dick as long as I live,' she said as she rubbed her tortured wrists.

'We're going upstairs to pack, Madam Stone,' said Lisa, giving voice to the thoughts of the others. 'We're leaving on the next train.'

The woman nodded in reluctant acquiescence. Lisa looked down at the still sleeping man on the floor. His erection had wilted and, somehow, he appeared far less intimidating than before. Paul slipped his arm around her shoulders. 'Come on,' he said, softly, 'let's go.'

As the train pulled slowly from the tiny country halt, Lisa looked out of the window in the direction of Grantham Manor. She felt strangely sorry to leave; it could have been so good, were it not for the old man. She wondered what would happen to Mr Gee and Madam Stone, especially Madam Stone. She'd learnt a lot from her, and was positive that there was much more she could have been taught, given the chance.

The train slowed almost to a halt as it rounded a sharp bend. Suddenly, in the distance she saw him. The bent, aged figure that she'd come to fear and loathe was standing there in the middle of a field, and he was watching them go. She turned swiftly to the others. Janet was lying with her head in Paul's lap and gently sucking his thick cock. Lisa made to speak, but thought better of it. She looked back out of the carriage window. There was a scarecrow in the field; a scarecrow, nothing more. She breathed a long, deep sigh and turned to face Mike. She unzipped his trousers and bent her head. But as she absorbed Mike's long, hard rod in her soft mouth she knew that they would meet the old man again.

The elderly tramp sifted wearily through the endless piles of rubbish on the town dump. Pickings had been bad today, and he was beginning to feel that it was time to give up. Suddenly, he noticed something glinting in the ashes. Excitedly, he reached into the still-warm putrescence and retrieved the object. A jewel! It was a jewel, and it looked real! There was another, and another! The old man scrambled over the heap, retrieving the stones from the mire. They were caked with what appeared to be molten gold, but they were most definitely valuable.

He sat back and clutched the jewels to his breast. His luck had changed at last. He had never felt so happy.

And it had been an awfully long time since he'd had such a stiff erection.

NEW BOOKS

Coming up from Nexus and Black Lace

There are three Nexus titles published in January

Emma's Secret Domination by Hilary James
January 1988   Price £4.99   ISBN: 0 352 33226 3
In this, the final instalment of the *Emma* series, Emma returns to London only to fall back into the clutches of her cruel former mistress Ursula. Realising that she has missed the bittersweet delights of lesbian domination, she begins finally to enjoy Ursula's attentions – but this only serves to anger and humiliate the prince, who is still her master. How will he administer the discipline she deserves?

'S' – A Story of Submission by Philippa Masters
January 1998   Price £4.99   ISBN: 0 352 33229 8
When S answers an advert which seems to promise an escape from her dull life, little does she realise that her fantasies of total submission are soon to be fulfilled. Entering into a secret world of domination, subservience and humiliation, she explores the bounds of her sexuality, finally realising the depravity of her darkest desires.

The Governess at St Agatha's by Yolanda Celbridge
January 1998   Price £4.99   ISBN: 0 352 32986 6
Miss Constance de Comynge's unusual education and correctional techniques are always in demand – by the residents of her village, the staff and pupils of the young ladies' acadamy she founds, and a number of other gentlemen of the locale. Nexus are reprinting some of their best-selling titles throughout 1998. This is the second book in the popular *Governess* series.

A Degree of Discipline by Zoe Templeton
February 1998   Price £4.99   ISBN: 0 352 33233 6
A new disciplinary law for young offenders has come into force and affects two naughty but naive young ladies, Juliette and Lucy, in quite different ways. They soon find themselves at a leading corrective establishment, Carstairs, and realise that their interest in discipline and humiliation is more than just academic, developing a taste for administering as well as receiving punishment.

Private Memoirs of a Kentish Headmistress
by Yolanda Celbridge
February 1998 Price £4.99 ISBN: 0 352 33232 8
Having learnt the delights of discipline, Miss Abigail Swift is keen to share that knowledge with others. She sets up an exclusive training academy for naughty young ladies at Orpingham Hall, with an intricate system of rules, ranks, and corporal punishment and restraints – all designed to teach her pupils the rudiments of correction.

Unhallowed Rites by Martine Marquand
January 1998 Price £5.99 ISBN: 0 352 332 220
Twenty-year-old Allegra di Vitale is bored with life in her guardian's Venetian palazzo – until temptation draws her to look at the bizarre pictures he keeps in his private chamber. Her lust awakened, she tries to deny her powerful cravings by submitting to life as a nun. But the strange order of the Convent of Santa Clerisa provides new temptations, forcing her to perform ritual acts with the depraved men and women of the convent.

Lake of Lost Love by Mercedes Kelly
December 1997 Price £5.99 ISBN: 0 352 33220 4
Princess Angeline lives on a paradise island in the South Seas. Married to Prince Hari and accepted into the native culture and customs, she has a life of ease and debauched sensual delights. When Prince Hari's young manservant is kidnapped and used as a sex slave by the cruel and depraved female ruler of nearby Monkey Island, Angeline sets about planning his rescue.

The Succubus by Zoe le Verdier
February 1998 Price £5.99 ISBN: 0 352 33230 1
When Adele, a young and innocent ballet dancer, learns that her dance company is in danger of losing its funding, she is only too happy to put on private performances for a wealthy patron of the arts. In order to save the company, she must dance the role of the sex-crazed Succubus, and learns to relish the role as it awakens a voracious appetite for new experiences in her which must be satisfied.

Ménage by Emma Holly
February 1998 Price £5.99 ISBN: 0 352 33231 X
When Kate finds her two flatmates in bed together, she is surprised by the strength of her arousal. When one of them asks her to join in, she leaps at the chance, little realising the extent of the experimental and perverse games they will soon come to play. The pleasure she experiences is beyond anything she had ever dreamt of, but will the implications of the kinky ménage à trois become too much?

NEXUS BACKLIST

All books are priced £4.99 unless another price is given. If a date is supplied, the book in question will not be available until that month in 1997.

CONTEMPORARY EROTICA

THE ACADEMY	Arabella Knight	
AGONY AUNT	G. C. Scott	
ALLISON'S AWAKENING	Lauren King	
BOUND TO SERVE	Amanda Ware	
BOUND TO SUBMIT	Amanda Ware	
CANDIDA'S SECRET MISSION	Virginia LaSalle	
CANDIDA IN PARIS	Virginia LaSalle	
CANDY IN CAPTIVITY	Arabella Knight	
CHALICE OF DELIGHTS	Katrina Young	
A CHAMBER OF DELIGHTS	Katrina Young	
THE CHASTE LEGACY	Susanna Hughes	
CHRISTINA WISHED	Gene Craven	
DARK DESIRES	Maria del Rey	
A DEGREE OF DISCIPLINE	Zoe Templeton	Feb
THE DOMINO TATTOO	Cyrian Amberlake	
THE DOMINO ENIGMA	Cyrian Amberlake	
THE DOMINO QUEEN	Cyrian Amberlake	
EDEN UNVEILED	Maria del Rey	
EDUCATING ELLA	Stephen Ferris	
ELAINE	Stephen Ferris	
EMMA'S SECRET WORLD	Hilary James	
EMMA'S SECRET DIARIES	Hilary James	
EMMA'S SUBMISSION	Hilary James	
EMMA'S HUMILIATION	Hilary James	
EMMA'S SECRET DOMINATION	Hilary James	Jan

FALLEN ANGELS	Kendal Grahame	
THE TRAINING OF FALLEN ANGELS	Kendal Grahame	
THE FANTASIES OF JOSEPHINE SCOTT	Josephine Scott	
THE FINISHING SCHOOL	Stephen Ferris	
HEART OF DESIRE	Maria del Rey	
HIS MISTRESS'S VOICE	G. C. Scott	
HOUSE OF INTRIGUE	Yvonne Strickland	
HOUSE OF TEMPTATIONS	Yvonne Strickland	
THE HOUSE OF MALDONA	Yolanda Celbridge	
THE ISLAND OF MALDONA	Yolanda Celbridge	
THE CASTLE OF MALDONA	Yolanda Celbridge	
THE ICE QUEEN	Stephen Ferris	
THE IMAGE AND OTHER STORIES	Jean de Berg	
THE INSTITUTE	Maria del Rey	
SISTERHOOD OF THE INSTITUTE	Maria del Rey	
JENNIFER'S INSTRUCTION	Cyrian Amberlake	
JOURNEY FROM INNOCENCE	Jean-Philippe Aubourg	
JULIE AT THE REFORMATORY	Angela Elgar	Feb
A MATTER OF POSSESSION	G. C. Scott	
MELINDA AND THE MASTER	Susanna Hughes	
MELINDA AND THE COUNTESS	Susanna Hughes	
MELINDA AND SOPHIA	Susanna Hughes	
MELINDA AND ESMERELDA	Susanna Hughes	
THE NEW STORY OF O	Anonymous	
ONE WEEK IN THE PRIVATE HOUSE	Esme Ombreux	
AMANDA IN THE PRIVATE HOUSE	Esme Ombreux	
PARADISE BAY	Maria del Rey	
THE PASSIVE VOICE	G. C. Scott	
PRIVATE MEMOIRS OF A KENTISH HEADMISTRESS	Yolanda Celbridge	Feb
RUE MARQUIS DE SADE	Morgana Baron	
'S' A STORY OF SUBMISSION	Philippa Masters	Jan
THE SCHOOLING OF STELLA	Yolanda Celbridge	
SECRETS OF THE WHIPCORD	Michaela Wallace	

SERVING TIME	Sarah Veitch	☐
SHERRIE	Evelyn Culber	☐
SHERRIE AND THE INITIATION OF PENNY	Evelyn Culber	☐
THE SPANISH SENSUALIST	Josephine Arno	☐
STEPHANIE'S CASTLE	Susanna Hughes	☐
STEPHANIE'S REVENGE	Susanna Hughes	☐
STEPHANIE'S DOMAIN	Susanna Hughes	☐
STEPHANIE'S TRIAL	Susanna Hughes	☐
STEPHANIE'S PLEASURE	Susanna Hughes	☐
SUSIE IN SERVITUDE	Arabella Knight	☐
THE TEACHING OF FAITH	Elizabeth Bruce	☐
FAITH IN THE STABLES	Elizabeth Bruce	☐
THE REWARD OF FAITH	Elizabeth Bruce	☐
THE TRAINING GROUNDS	Sarah Veitch	☐
VIRGINIA'S QUEST	Katrina Young	☐
WEB OF DOMINATION	Yvonne Strickland	☐

EROTIC SCIENCE FICTION

RETURN TO THE PLEASUREZONE	Delaney Silver	☐

ANCIENT & FANTASY SETTINGS

CAPTIVES OF ARGAN	Stephen Ferris	☐
CITADEL OF SERVITUDE	Aran Ashe	☐
THE CLOAK OF APHRODITE	Kendal Grahame	☐
DEMONIA	Kendal Grahame	☐
NYMPHS OF DIONYSUS	Susan Tinoff	☐
PLEASURE ISLAND	Aran Ashe	☐
PYRAMID OF DELIGHTS	Kendal Grahame	☐
THE SLAVE OF LIDIR	Aran Ashe	☐
THE DUNGEONS OF LIDIR	Aran Ashe	☐
THE FOREST OF BONDAGE	Aran Ashe	☐
WARRIOR WOMEN	Stephen Ferris	☐
WITCH QUEEN OF VIXANIA	Morgana Baron	☐
SLAVE-MISTRESS OF VIXANIA	Morgana Baron	☐

EDWARDIAN, VICTORIAN & OLDER EROTICA

ANNIE	Evelyn Culber
ANNIE AND THE SOCIETY	Evelyn Culber
ANNIE'S FURTHER EDUCATION	Evelyn Culber
BEATRICE	Anonymous
CHOOSING LOVERS FOR JUSTINE	Aran Ashe
DEAR FANNY	Michelle Clare
LYDIA IN THE BORDELLO	Philippa Masters
MADAM LYDIA	Philippa Masters
LURE OF THE MANOR	Barbra Baron
MAN WITH A MAID 3	Anonymous
MEMOIRS OF A CORNISH GOVERNESS	Yolanda Celbridge
THE GOVERNESS AT ST AGATHA'S	Yolanda Celbridge
THE GOVERNESS ABROAD	Yolanda Celbridge
PLEASING THEM	William Doughty

SAMPLERS & COLLECTIONS

EROTICON 1	
EROTICON 2	
EROTICON 3	
THE FIESTA LETTERS	ed. Chris Lloyd
MOLTEN SILVER	Delaney Silver
NEW EROTICA 2	ed. Esme Ombreaux

NON-FICTION

HOW TO DRIVE YOUR WOMAN WILD IN BED	Graham Masterton
HOW TO DRIVE YOUR MAN WILD IN BED	Graham Masterton
LETTERS TO LINZI	Linzi Drew

- -

Please send me the books I have ticked above.

Name ....

Address ....

....

....

.... Post code ....

Send to: **Cash Sales, Nexus Books, 332 Ladbroke Grove, London W10 5AH**

Please enclose a cheque or postal order, made payable to Virgin Publishing, to the value of the books you have ordered plus postage and packing costs as follows:

UK and BFPO – £1.00 for the first book, 50p for each subsequent book.

Overseas (including Republic of Ireland) – £2.00 for the first book, £1.00 for each subsequent book.

If you would prefer to pay by VISA or ACCESS/MASTER-CARD, please write your card number and expiry date here:

....

Please allow up to 28 days for delivery.

Signature ....

- -